THE '1492' CONSPIRACY

Disclaimer

All situations in this book are fictional and any similarity to existing situations, institutions or persons is wholly coincidental. Any evocation of living or dead public figures in this work of fiction is made for the historical time frame of the novel and satirical purposes only, and does not constitute judgment on their personal or moral qualities.

THE '1492' CONSPIRACY

A Machiavellian Plot to Seize the Holy Land and Keep the White House

*****

FICTION

*****

ASSEM AKRAM

*****

2006

THREE-HORNED LION, INC.

ISBN-10: 0971078114
ISBN-13: 978-0-9710781-1-6

Three-Horned Lion, Inc.

Printed in the United States of America
May 2006

Cover: Three-Horned Lion, Inc.
Design and Layout: Three-Horned Lion, Inc.

Three-Horned Lion, Inc.

www.threehornedlion.com

Acknowledgement

I could have never completed this book without the loving support and the infinite patience of my wife Maryam and my two sons, Zahiruddin-Abqa and Temur.

I would like to thank the following people who so willingly read the manuscript in its various stages and greatly helped me improve it: Dennis Latham, David Weidner, Farahnaz Yaqubi, Fariba Hogge, Homa Abedi.

Finally, I would like to extend a particular acknowledgement to Roya Abedi for her priceless assistance in all aspects of this project.

THE '1492' CONSPIRACY

FICTION

ASSEM AKRAM

THREE-HORNED LION, INC.

Chapters

The Invitation 15

The Two Hassans 27

Balthazar Residence 39

FourteenNinetyTwo@Hotmail.Com 51

May the Spirit of Ferdinand and Isabel Guide You 71

Point of No Return... 85

Anthrax and Red Wine 99

The Nuncio 111

The Fourth Rome... 123

Cabin Pressure 133

Sea Turtle Enchilada... 149

The Red Door 161

These Baklavas Will Kill You................................... 177

The Senator's Wife 185

Passed Damocles... 197

Madame Secretary 207

Georgetown Twist... 225

Dr. Zhivago 239

Conversions... 259

Lifting The Veil 275

Paloma Picasso Vs The Japanese Emperor.............................. 289

THE '1492' CONSPIRACY

Assem Akram

The Invitation

The doorbell rang late one afternoon. I opened the door and found a white envelope a messenger had placed on the floor mat. It was an invitation for dinner that evening. In classic Bristol, the card gave the address and the time without further indication. I looked at the back to see if there was any mention of the host, a phone number, an RSVP… Nada!

After a shower and a fresh shave, I jumped into a tailored black suit; sprayed some of my favorite cologne; checked whether my tie matched the rest; dropped some visit cards inside my pocket and I was ready for what I had concluded would be an adventure. I had decided that I would be elegantly fashionable, but not too much: just enough to be ready to tackle any social situation.

I hadn't even entered the building cited on the invitation when a lady abruptly opened the door.

"Mr. Haftemizan?"
"Yes, that's me."
"Follow me, please. Where is your car?" she asked.
"Right around the corner," I replied.
"Let's take it."

I had an old British convertible that I had bought for a good price in an auction and that I would only take out on occasions. I saw a quick smile briefly break her serious mask when she saw the vehicle.

"I like these older cars," I added in an attempt to break the ice. "You really feel the road and experience sensations that you can no longer have when you drive today's high tech cocoon cars."

"Sure," she responded without any interest.

"May I know where we are going?"

"I can't tell you, but be patient and in a few moments you'll know all about it."

"How about giving me a clue?"

"I wish I could, but I can't. Please, be patient."

This time, her voice was slightly supplicating. It may be cliché, but I can't resist an imploring pretty woman. So, I stopped short of grilling her and accepted my fate.

I may have never told this to any one before, but a great advantage to driving a low convertible sports car – even an antique like mine – is not just the sensations you're getting from driving - when the weather is amicable - but it's also that the compression of space in the cabin, the low seats, and the stick shift just inches away from your passenger are all factors that could play to your advantage, if you're riding with a lady you are courting. By letting your hand slide "inadvertently" to the side of the stick shift - or miss it as you are twisting your body to negotiate a narrow turn, you initiate physical contact and test her reaction. If you have - as I have - acquired some expertise in this field through the years, you can get a pretty good feel of where you stand on her "likeability" scale based on how she reacts...

I didn't feel like using any of what I just revealed. I didn't know where she was taking me, and whether it's one of those Russian mafia deals where they use pretty girls to hook up some naïve guys and then blackmail them for the rest of their lives with compromising pictures. But I am not married, so nobody cares with whom I hook up.

My guide avoided looking at me and directed me from street to street, from light to light, without giving me any further insight as to the target location. After just a few minutes of blindfolded ride, we arrived at our destination.

"Here we are; that's the building Seventy-seven forty-four," she indicated. "Go up to the third floor."
"Left or right?" I asked.
"There is only a red door."
"All right; thank you, Miss…. I am sorry; I did not get your name…"
"You have a good evening… and, by the way, nice car!"

That was unexpected. I knew she would not give me her name, but her admission that she liked my car came as a surprise. I think she liked me. Or, maybe I am being naive and self-indulgent.

The door was Japanese red. A brunette with striking good looks opened the door. What's with these babes? I wondered. Is this a modeling agency or some kind of preview staged for some 'happy few' *fashionistas* to which I am invited by mistake?

The space was empty: no furniture and nothing on the walls. Only the floor, with its nice mosaic tiles of Greco-Roman theme, created some liveliness in an otherwise gloomy environment. My guide was not exactly beaming from excessive joy either, but I had gotten used to that already and I didn't mind.

A "welcome" cheered me as I entered a large room where two gentlemen sat on the bare floor. This was the first greeting with some real warmth in it that I had heard since the beginning of this evening, while I was bounced from one robotic guide to another cold hostess. The gentleman was possibly in his sixties, a bit obese, wearing a three-piece dark suit…unexpectedly covered by a *Jelabah*. The other person was younger and definitely slimmer, but dressed almost similarly - with the Jelabah. What kind of eccentric fellows am I dealing with? I wasn't really afraid but I wasn't sure where I had landed. The two men look pretty harmless.

"So, what's this invitation about: a romantic Bedouin dinner on the deserted office floor?" I asked. Forgive me, but I could not resist. Both laughed politely.

"Allow me to introduce myself: I am Hector Elias Shumington III. And here is my good friend: the respectable Dr. Benvenisto Necromonti."

We shook hands and I sat on the bare floor.

When I dressed classic chic 'to suit any social occasion,' I hadn't exactly in mind this kind of indoor picnic. But then again, as the saying goes, 'when in Casablanca, do as the...' or maybe was it something slightly different? I can't remember.

"You may be wondering," started Shumington, "why we have brought you in here. But before that, I would like to apologize for the mystery that has had to envelop your visit. All I can tell you is that we didn't have any choice; they were simple security measures for your own safety."

"Yes, I am still clueless," I said, faking self-confidence. "But I am here and I am listening."

"How can I phrase this?" Shumington's face expressed intense cogitation while Dr. Necromonti either stared at the floor or at Shumington, obviously boiling with impatience, "...we need your help."

This being said, what did they need my help for? What do I know or what do I do that can help them? I do 'consultant on international affairs' for a living. I sell my pseudo-expertise to big businesses and political organizations alike. I also write a book and some articles from time to time, just to stay in sight. I know: these guys have just discovered the Jelabah and want to launch the trend in the US, but don't know how to approach the Moroccan Government to get export licenses and need my help to teach them how to court Rabat with cultural sensitivity in mind...

"How can I help you?" I said.

"This is where it becomes a bit complicated," Shumington said.

Necromonti took over. "We are here on a mission to convince you to help us save the planet from a potentially deadly danger."

"Come on; give me a break!" These guys, with their three-piece suits and their Jelabahs, sitting on the floor of an empty office, couldn't expect me to buy into these cheesy lines.

"I know; please, *perdone* our methods," Necromonti said. "But the truth is that you are the person we need to conduct this mission."

"What mission?" I asked with some irritation.

"Be patient, *per favore*," Necromonti said. "We work for an international agency that fights unconventional crime and terrorist activities. We believe we are onto something very important, which, if not prevented, could have catastrophic consequences. In your books, you have addressed the subject long before anybody else. Our analysts have meticulously studied both your professional and private lives - to an extent you can hardly imagine - and, out of several potential candidates, they have concluded that you are best qualified for this task."

"I am flattered, but is this a joke? Is this a prank? Come on, gentlemen, wherever you are hiding, come on out. I got it. It was wonderfully planned. Now, come on out and let's celebrate your revenge. Dinner is on me." I scanned the room looking for a door to open and see my friends jump out laughing. "You too, gentlemen, you were great. I don't know which talent agency they've hired you from, but give me your cards because I may need your services one of these days: I am an inveterate prankster myself."

"Sir, this is serious business. Many lives are at stake," Necromonti said with his marked Italian accent, a bit offended by my reaction.

Shumington was not laughing. Necromonti was consternated. Looking at their faces, I realized that either I was wrong or these guys were very good. So, I decided to go along with their story and let it unfold.

"Okay, my apologies. Continue, *per favore, dottore*."

"*Grazie*; what was I saying?" Necromonti was trying to recover from a moment of confusion. "Oh, yes… that we picked you to help us track and neutralize a looming danger. We have received indications that a group of individuals somewhere, somehow, are preparing to hit. But we don't know where, when and how."

"You sound like George W. Bush and the Iraqi WMDs."

"We have some trails to follow God knows where - actually, allow me to correct: 'Hell knows where' would be more appropriate. It would take someone like you to figure it out."

"I am no James Bond. This is a job for the CIA, the FSB, the MI5, the Mossad, the Mukhaberat, or even La Piscine, and definitely not for me. The only thing that I see in my profile, that may have caught your attention, is the word 'international'; other than that, I am just a cerebral - a pathetic intellectual. I analyze others' actions and minds and theorize and gloze about them and sell the result to make a living. Besides, I make it a point of ethics not to get involved with any of the subjects of my studies."

"We have done our homework," Shumington said, "and we know a lot about you - probably more than you would want us to know. But, since you asked, the one thing that qualifies you more than the other competitors is your sense of instinct, your aura. You guess and subodorate things like no other can."

"Thank you." I was indeed flattered by the compliment.

"I am not flattering you," Shumington said. "You had guessed years ago that some dangerous minds could use the collapse of the Soviet-Union to acquire bio-weapons to harm people..."

"I recall how my publisher laughed at me and the media dismissed it as 'unimaginably fantasist,' preferring to put the emphasis on the collection and destruction of nuclear warheads only."

"Well, Sir, I think that what we are on right now is exactly that or something similar. But we are not sure, and this is why we need you."

"All I had done was to mention the eventuality. Perhaps it was a chapter in the book..."

"Let us not diminish the value of your premonition," Necromonti said, as if my expression of realistic modesty was going to cost him some disappointment.

"Dr. Necromonti is absolutely right; do not sell yourself short. You had the sense of it before anybody else: it was the work of a genius."

"Well, if you put it that way… then, I guess maybe I had an intuition that probably was ahead of its time," I said, playing it falsely modest. I haven't had these kinds of compliments in years. "Forgive my insistence, but I still don't understand how in practice I can help you. You know, I have a job to do, I have clients who count on my analysis, I have deliverables, and *tutti quanti…*"

"We know all that," Shumington said, almost offended that I was underestimating their professionalism. "As I told you, we did our homework before we finally decided to bring you here."

"And…?"

"You are going to announce that you're taking a sabbatical to research your new book. Besides, this is a terrific idea for your cover."

"And what about my clients: they really depend on me… I can't just close the doors and let them down like this…I would lose them forever. It took me years to earn their trust."

"We know that and we know there is no easy solution. This is why we thought that while you would have to reschedule the type of commitments that require your presence, for the rest - i.e. reports and other written analyses - your staff of assistants will take care of it in your absence."

"I don't have a 'staff of assistants.' The only assistant I have is wired, has buttons and is sitting on my desk, pitifully motionless."

"We know that, Mr. Haftemizan. This is something we'll be taking care of. And as for the analysts, I can guarantee you that they are the best the market can offer. If you help us, we won't spare any effort to help you keep your activities up and running in your absence. I have the authority to give you absolute assurance in this regard."

These Jelabah-wearing gentlemen were committed to hire me at all cost and had foreseen all possible scenarios. There was not much more that I could do to slip away from their grip. But before I made any commitment, I needed some assurance that this was not some type of phony scam.

"Well, gentlemen, you got me. I am in, but I need you to show me something more than your serious faces to convince me of the authenticity of your... whatever it is you are doing."

Shumington smiled. He had obviously foreseen this one, too. He retrieved a laptop from the bag next to him and turned it on.

"Here, Sir; this is Interpol's highly secure website... and here is the link to Erebus. As you can see, I've been able to access it, which, I would hope, is giving you confidence that we are in serious business here."

"So, you work for Interpol?"

"I've been working there for many years, but Dr. Necromonti is new. He jumped on board - a little bit like you - not so long ago."

"You mentioned 'Airbus'... Is that a code name for something?"

"It's EREBUS," corrected Necromonti, as if I should have known better.

"Erebus is the name of our project. It's a small project in terms of the number of people involved – as you well know, only quality matters – but it's of vital importance. Only a very select number of people know of its existence. Our mission is to fight 'unconventional terrorism.' The UN has tasked Interpol and Interpol has tasked us and…"

"That's a pretty heavy burden," I commented.

"Yes, especially if you consider that now we count on you."

"Yes, sure…"

"I am not joking, Mr. Haftemizan," Shumington said. "If you don't help us on this case, we are toast and probably half of the planet as well."

"Are you fucking kidding me? You pick me out of nowhere and seat me on the floor with your, your…Jelabahs and tell me that if I don't help out, half of Humanity will perish? There is no way I am going to take this kind of responsibility. *Ciao, dottore* Necromonti and *a riverderci*, Mr. Shumington. I wish you good luck!"

"I understand your ire," Shumington said. "We're all irritated by the enormity of the task, but think about its nobility. Think about the lives that we are helping to save. And besides, we are a team; you are not alone."

"Think of the Musketeers," Necromonti said, lifting his hands to the sky. "We are the world's new Musketeers."

Necromonti's literary image struck a cord within me. This comparison gave me a more concrete image of what I was asked to do. I would be chasing the Cardinal's bad guys, while ending up in bed with some gorgeous ladies dressed in superb gowns with more laces than I would have the patience to untie… Yes; now, we are talking… I was ready to serve Humanity.

"All right, I'm in. I apologize for my outburst. You have to admit that this is not a normal situation for me. I am usually much more guarded than that in my reaction."

"We understand," Shumington said. "And, believe it or not, when our big boss personally assigned me to this task, I had the same kind of reaction or probably worse."

Judging from his round face and jovial expression, despite the seriousness of the situation, one wouldn't expect Hector Elias Shumington III – what a tediously long name - to explode into a violent outburst. But then again, you can never know. There is a saying, somewhere in the world - I can't remember where - that warns us to 'beware of the sleepy water.' To the contrary, one could expect this kind of irritability from Necromonti. His lean, long and somewhat marked face gave him an appearance of worried seriousness. Necromonti's facial features were so expressive that he did not need to raise his voice to express his discontent; a slight convergent movement of his eyebrows and everyone would get the message. He had 'tragedy' written all over his face.

Assem Akram

The Two Hassans

We had dinner after all. We walked to a nearby restaurant named 'The Two Hassans.' As we walked in, loud Arabic music was playing. On a small stage, a belly dancer twisted like a snake, and on a larger dancing area some customers – male and female – tried to mimic her moves. A large sign hanging above the scene read 'Arabian Nights Party; costumed clients get free drinks.'

Now, I understand why Necromonti and Shumington were sporting Jelebahs. These two bastards – I am sorry, these two gentlemen - had already planned their dinner out after grilling me and giving me 'the world is in danger, you have to save it' speech, making me lose my appetite - and probably my sleep, too - for the rest of my life, let alone thinking about getting free drinks and enjoying a theme night with belly-dancers on the deck.

"You may think that coming here is… inappropriate, isn't it?" Shumington said. "And you're probably right, somehow. But you've got to understand that we need to release the pressure that becomes rapidly overwhelming if we let it simmer. Too much pressure translates into over-stress, which is not good because it freezes your mind and handicaps your judgment." He pointed this out while knocking on his forehead.

"Besides," added Necromonti, "we're just back from a short trip to Morocco. I think I can speak for both of us when I say that it's a beautiful country... and the food..."

"Were you vacationing over there?" I asked.

"No, no, we were on a mission to collect information," Shumington said.

"Because you were sounding like you were describing to me your vacation..." - and, frankly, I couldn't care less about it.

"Dear Mr. Haftemizan, you're once again underestimating us," Shumington said. "We'll tell you more about it later; it's not appropriate here."

"I understand."

"Do you like Moroccan food, Mr. Haftemizan?" Necromonti asked.

"Yes, I do... but do me a favor: just call me Haftemizan."

"As for me," Shumington said, "I can't get enough of their couscous: I just love it."

Our conversation went on, talking about countries we had visited and the ones we would like to see. Passed the first minutes of guardedness on my part, the Moroccan spicy cuisine, the *harissa*, and the ambiance surrounding us started to take their effect. I loosened up. After a while, I realized that they were asking me questions in subtle ways to collect data on my preferences and on my family and friends while they were fending off any reciprocal questions I had. I was being naïve and clearly I was not used to being 'debriefed,' so I went along with their 'questionnaire' without realizing what was happening. I should learn to be more careful than that...

They did that for a reason. If I ever decided to drop the ball, they would know how to pressure me or even how to find me through friends and relatives. That was a sizable mistake on my part. But I learn quickly and I can guarantee you that they won't be able to get me so easily the next time around.

I had left Necromonti and Shumington late in the night and returned home. At the end of that night, I knew a lot more about Moroccan food, belly dancing and the diverse types of pasta and anti-pasta, described in detail by Necromonti, than I knew about Erebus.

One thing had intrigued me: throughout dinner, Dr. Necromonti would mutter something like "not tonight" to himself with a strained air on his face, giving the impression that he was trying to control some type of addiction perhaps, or maybe some kind of mania? Several times, I felt like asking him if he was doing all right, then I thought that it would embarrass him more than anything else. After all, we are all fighting with our inner demons.

The Next Day

I was told that I would be receiving some documents in the morning and that I'd most likely meet with the "duet" in the evening, some place away from inquisitive eyes and ears to provide answers to my questions, if I had any.

It was a beautiful, bright sunny day. I turned the TV on. The news announced that President Bush had appointed yet another commission - the eighth or the eighty-eighth one, no one knows anymore - to scourge Iraq in search of the missing WMDs.

Then they showed footage of George W. Bush upset and pestering: *«They've got to be somewhere... I can assure the American public that we'll find them. »*

«Now we are back 'live' with our correspondent Elizabeth Mulberry at the White House, who is following for us the press appearance of the President in the Rose Garden. I think the President is speaking right now...»

«Good morning, Ladies and Gentlemen. As you know, today, I welcome in the White House the Prime minister of a friendly country. My fellow citizens, let me tell you that we may have lost Spain and some other allies, but we are fortunate to have great nations such as the Lish... 'the Leash and the Stein' [sic] and 'Equitable Ghana' [sic] - I mean 'Equa-tutorial Guinema' - who have joined our coalition in the fight against terror in Iraq and around the globe. »

He can't be serious! I screamed. I couldn't help.

«My friend Omar Hustler[1] [sic] is present here on my side today to show his determination... our resolve. Omar [sic] is a steadfast leader, a great leader and...I am humbled by his friendship. Mr. Prime Minister, America is grateful... And, now, a few questions from the Press... »

«You heard it, Mike and Jenny; the Liechtenstein and Equatorial Guinea are joining the coalition in the fight against terror. Will it make up for the defections witnessed recently? We'll keep you updated on this issue in the coming days and weeks. I am Elizabeth Mulberry, live from the White House; back to you. »

---

[1] I.e. Otmar Hasler.

Where have we fallen? I was bothered by what I had just heard. I am an international affairs specialist, and, frankly, I'd be ready to give this president, entrenched up on Penn avenue, free lessons any time.

I decided to turn the TV off to stop the carnage and put on some music that would compliment the nice weather and the beautiful seasonal colors. I thought that some Baroque music would do perfectly. It would get rid of my anxiety. I didn't know what to expect from the 'Interpol/Erebus' guys… I really didn't think I had what it takes to fight conventional terrorism, let alone 'unconventional terrorism.' Yes, the sound of clavecin: that's what I need to instill confidence and optimism in me.

As I was attempting to choose between Lulli and Bach to pump up my spirit, the doorbell rang repeatedly. That's it. It's the delivery. "Coming… just a minute…" I wrapped a robe around myself and opened the door.

"What a surprise! I was expecting the courier to be…"
"Yes?"
"…Somewhat different."

It turned out that the courier was my first guide. The girl who said she liked my car. Maybe she volunteered to bring me the documents? She looked a bit different this time. I could sense that she was not completely closed to any type of communication with me.

"Come on in, please."
"I am afraid I can't; my role is only to deliver these documents to you in person."

"You've got to come in. I have some hot cyanide coffee with some belladonna marmalade for you."

She smiled. "Don't kill the messenger."

"As far as I am concerned, you're guilty. You're the one who took me there, whereas you could have warned me that I would be...meeting two lunatics in Jelabahs picnicking on the bare floor of an empty office."

"Very funny: you are true to your reputation."

"What reputation?"

"That of being sarcastic..."

"I get it. So, everyone knows everything about me and I remain ignorant of everything about everyone I've met so far: isn't there something fundamentally unfair with this picture?"

"Perhaps, but I think it's the nature of this type of activity that makes everyone very cautious."

"What about me? Nobody told me that I should be cautious and not open my door to mysterious strangers. And not a damn person warned me not to accept some 'mystery' invitation where I would be assigned to a 'mystery' mission."

"You're perfectly right; someone should have warned you, had they known something about it, but now it's too late. You're on board and here is the material you need to start your mission. Perhaps some of the 'mysteries' you are wondering about will be partially resolved."

I looked her straight in the eyes. "I'll see about that once I've reviewed these files, but there is a big unresolved mystery standing right before me."

"Am I a mystery to you, Mr. Haftemizan?" she asked with a smile.

"Well, yes. You seem to know everything about me and I don't even know your name."

"Let us say, for the sake of giving you a sense of confidence, that my name is Ava."

"All right; now, I can formally introduce myself: hello, my name is Haftemizan. It's a real pleasure to make your acquaintance."

"Hi, I am Ava; nice to meet you, too, Mr. Haftemizan."

"Everyone calls me Haftemizan; no formality needed, please."

I was happy to be able to put a name to her face, at last. After all, she's the person I have seen the most – two times in less than twenty-four hours - in this unusual journey I have embarked on. Ava is indeed a beautiful girl. She may be in her mid to late twenties, brunette, not extraordinarily tall, but with a slim, slick profile and the right curves at the right places. It's as if someone had read my mind or explored my fantasy and then sculpted this creature just to tease me. I had to keep my emotions under control. No matter how attractive and irresistible she may seem – *mama mia* - I will not let my pheromones lead me.

During our first encounter, on our way to the alleged dinner, as I was observing her hands - to casually check if she had nice ones - I had noticed an unusual ring on one of her fingers that had a flat red stone bearing an engraved insignia.

"Ava - I hope you don't mind me calling you Ava - I couldn't help but notice that you are wearing a very unusual piece of jewelry on your left hand. May I ask you if it is some type of family emblem or just an antique piece?"

"Oh, it's not much; I got it from my father. It has sentimental value."

Obviously, she was reluctant to reveal personal information. She is just being consistent. How foolish of me to ask, since she did not even want to give me her name, let alone talk about a ring that may or may not have a story behind it. I am

33

not even sure if Ava is her real name or just an alias. I'll probably find that out some day.

All right, I have made my last attempt trying to be friendly and engage in somewhat of a conversation with agent 'ice cube.' She's right; she's just a courier. She could have been a 'Joe Moustache' and I couldn't care less.

"Thank you, Ava; now, if you'll excuse me, I'd like to review these documents and get going."

"Sure," she said, a bit surprised by my sudden change in demeanor.

"I'll probably see you again… until then, take care."

"Before I leave, could you kindly sign this, right here?"

"What is it?"

"It's an acknowledgment that you received these documents in person."

"Certainly; here you go…"

"And here is another piece. Keep this one with you. It lists all the documents included in this package that need to be destroyed – by that, they mean 'burned' – once you're done reading them."

"Are you suggesting that I should keep some of them? That's a good idea," I joked, implying that I could misuse them in some espionage scheme.

"Yes, you'll see for yourself."

For some reason, as she closed the door behind her, I got this impression of déjà vu, as if I had been thrown in an old episode of 'Mission Impossible.' I hated that predictable *papier mâché* series when I was a kid and, unlike some other old ones that have aged well, this one is still unwatchable.

As I went through the files, I understood that this was no Hollywood - and even less Bollywood - material. Someone had tipped off Interpol that impersonators - presenting themselves as World Health Organization representatives working for a program destined at fighting against the proliferation of biological material that could be used as weapons (bio-weapons) - had spent large sums of money to acquire significant quantities of bio-weapon material from two former Soviet labs. They had made the transaction appear as 'compensation' paid in exchange for 'removing' hazardous material. So far, to Interpol's knowledge, only two labs had become victim of the malicious deception.

Intelligence reports say that what had been acquired from one lab were canisters containing the Congo-Crimean Hemorrhagic Virus, and from the other, Anthrax. Interpol analysts are certain that the impersonators were the same in both cases and it is very possible that the terrorist group behind it is making efforts to acquire more.

The World Health Organization had never employed nor assigned those con artists in question; but the only interesting piece of information they found was that the men who posed as such were described as 'American' based on their accents. It was more than likely a sophisticated multi-level operation with many intermediaries in order to preserve the terrorist organization from being tracked.

"Very smart," I commented to myself. At the lower end, they used some American thugs, probably in it for the money, pretending to work for a big international agency, to remove all suspicion about any misuse of the highly lethal bio-weapons…

In the anarchy following the collapse of the Soviet-Union, where money was scarce and delinquent, and legitimate organizations were competing for it, it was difficult to blame those labs of intentional wrongdoing.

It was now my assignment, under the cover of conducting research for a book, to inquire about this affair and figure out who had conspired to organize these transfers, what other labs were being targeted, and figure out with certitude the intention and immediacy of the perpetrators' plans: not exactly a cakewalk.

Time was of the essence. Interpol had already prepared a list of all the labs in the former Soviet-Union and even Eastern Europe that could possibly be targeted by these terrorists to acquire more bio-weapons. But the task was difficult since it could be any of the couple of dozens of labs listed.

These guys are not serious. If they think that I am going to go and check one by one each and every one of the facilities noted on the list, they are seriously mistaken!

I decided that I would give it all up. This was turning out to be a Police job that, if done by a single individual, would take probably a couple of years. By then the terrorist group would have already accomplished whatever malicious design it had in mind. I was furious. I inserted all the documents back into the big envelope and decided to wait to see Shumington and Necromonti at dinner to tell them what I thought of their silly plan and lack of realism.

I spent the rest of the day running errands and taking a stab at some work. I also attempted to find some information on Shumington and Dr. Necromonti on the Internet, but didn't get a single hit. It is understandable. After all, these two gentlemen are no celebrities and I figured that with the kind of job they are doing, it is not very likely that they've posted a family home page on the net... Although this may be true for Shumington, who has worked for Interpol for a very long time, but what about Benvenisto Necromonti? If he joined Interpol and Project Erebus only a year or so ago, he should have left some tracks in cyberspace: research papers, publications, even a graduation list or a home owners' association board members' list - anything in appearance anodyne but useful to the inquisitive eye.

Unlike some of my friends, I don't put all my faith in the Goddess of the Cyberspace - i.e. the Internet. It's not because Shumington and Necromonti are not mentioned on some Internet sites that they do not exist - at least I presume so. Do you remember that, not so long ago, people used to make all kinds of odd, exuberant and sometimes insane statements; and if you questioned the basis of their statements, they would respond: "it's in the books," as if anything, even the most fallacious ideas or erroneous information, once in print, became universal and unquestionable truths? These days, the Internet has replaced books. The new consecrated expression is: "It's on the Internet!" And when someone backs his or her words with that kind of definite assertion, it would be heresy to question their act of faith...

While I was out during the afternoon, a woman had left a message on my voice-mail, informing me that I would be meeting 'my friends' at the same place and at the same hour as the previous night. The date with Shumington and Necromonti was set.

Although the papers I had reviewed specifically warned me against confiding in any one about Erebus and my mission, I thought that perhaps I should let someone - a very close friend or a family member - know that I was drawn into something a little bit out of the ordinary, and give them a 'to do' list, should something happen to me. I quickly gathered back-up CDs of everything I had written for the last decade, or so, a few family souvenirs, and I deposited them in a safety deposit box at my bank.

On my way home, I mailed one key to my attorney and another one to an old pal of mine I had known since childhood. To both I had given the same 'to do' list, which could be considered a 'last will.' I felt confident that, if something went wrong, I had somehow readied a 'backup' of my life that I or someone else could recover. In retrospect, this was clearly a tragic manifestation of human grandiloquence on my part.

Balthazar Residence

"It doesn't look good," I told myself as I saw the area around 'The Two Hassans' cordoned off by the Police. Ambulances, police cars and fire-trucks blocked the access. I parked my car further away and walked quickly towards the entrance. I had a feeling that whatever may have happened inside was related to what I had become involved in. Onlookers lined up on the opposite sidewalk, feeding their voyeuristic curiosity, while neighbors were hanging out on their balconies despite the rain that had started to pour.

"Sir, where do you think you're going," a police officer yelled, as I attempted to get near the entrance.

"Inside, Officer. I am meeting with some friends for dinner."

"Nobody's going inside; this is a crime scene now."

"What happened?"

"I can't tell you. But if you have questions, ask that officer, over there, with the blue and white umbrella."

"All right; thank you, Officer."

As I was gearing to head toward another officer, somebody seized my arm from behind and pulled me sideways.

"Where do you think you're going?" This time, it was Ava asking me the same question.

"What are you doing here?" I asked, obviously startled. "In fact, I shouldn't be surprised…"

"I told you that we'd meet again," she whispered.

"What's happening here?"

"Let's go to your car," she replied as she kept pushing me forward, holding my arm. "I am wet from head to toe from the rain."

"Did you do something?"

"Don't be ridiculous," she said, obviously irritated by my question.

My car was parked just around the corner. We hopped in.

"Shumington is dead and Dr. Necromonti has been seriously wounded and is on his way to the hospital."

"What happened? Why?" My incomprehension was total.

"Somebody sitting at the table next to them pulled a gun and shot them before escaping."

"Wow…" I exclaimed, not knowing what to say.

"He shot Shumington first, in the head, killing him instantly. But Necromonti, whose back was facing the shooter, ducked: the bullet went to his back instead of his head."

"Though I am no expert, it appears to me that this is a rather professional job."

"No doubt about it. Just two bullets fired and the assassin disappears."

"Do you think that what happened is related to the present case or is it linked to some old ones Shumington was involved with?"

"I don't know. My guess is that we will never know, unless we are able to catch the perpetrator. Even then, we may not be able to find out who sponsored the hit."

"You're right."

"As for you, you can thank your patron saint, whoever he may be."

"Why?"

"Well, had you been a few minutes early or even on time, you'd probably be dead or, at best, be on your way to the hospital fighting for your life like Necromonti."

She was right. I was running fifteen minutes late – I am usually late for this kind of occasion, I should admit – and that's what saved my life. Who said that being late was a bad habit?

"Let's go to the hospital," I suggested. "We have to see how our friend Necromonti is doing."

"I am afraid we can't," Ava said. "Not right now."

"But this colleague of yours is probably battling death as we speak and you're saying that we cannot get to the hospital to offer some support and show that we care?"

"Negative. I am sorry." Ava was firm. No room for negotiation. "We'll go later; tomorrow. If we go right now, there are risks."

"What kind of risks?"

"If the assassins are looking for you, they'll be able to easily track you to the hospital. Second, if we reveal that we are in any way connected to the victims, the Police might want to question us, too. Believe me; we have absolutely no time for that. So, tomorrow, if we can, we'll visit Dr. Necromonti - if he is not already dead."

Judging by the way she talked about it, without apparent emotion, it was easy to tell that, despite her young age, Ava had been hardened by years of experience.

"What do we do now?" I asked.

"Chill," she replied.

"How about going to my place?" I offered.

"I don't think it would be safe. I have a better plan," Ava said.

We left the crime scene for a safe location. Going to Ava's apartment would have been equally risky. So, we went to a hotel, not far away from the hospital where Necromonti was supposed to have been transported. Naturally, I offered to pay, but she laughed and pulled a credit card from her pocket instead:

"This one is untraceable."

The hotel was decorated with some questionable semi-Art Deco gusto. The lady at the reception desk didn't even look at us. She stared at the TV screen, unwilling to miss a single second of some sappy soap opera. The hotel was not a luxury establishment, but it looked clean and functional. The quality of the rooms and the hotel rating were the last things on my mind.

The idea that I could have been shot in that restaurant half an hour earlier had started to freeze my flesh and slow my heartbeat. I was trying to imagine what I would have done in that situation. Would I have had the type of reflex Necromonti had? Had I been sitting on the same bench as the poor Shumington, the killer would have lodged a bullet right between my eyes before I could have moved. "Tssshuuk... and you're dead!" I am glad I did what I did this afternoon. I had a premonition that something could go wrong, fast...

On the way to the room, I was shivering and weak. Damn it! If I don't reinvigorate myself, I am going to faint and become the laugh of Interpol and Erebus. "No, no; it's not going to

42

happen. I am strong. Breathe deeply... Yes, yes; breathe again and relax... Everything is fine... Breathe again," I kept repeating to myself, as if I were chanting a mantra at a Yoga class. As odd as it may sound, it worked. I was able to recover my senses a little; otherwise I would have lost consciousness in the middle of the hallway.

"Are you all right?" Ava asked.

"Oh, yes. Thank you."

"You look so pale..." There was no mocking in her voice. She was genuinely concerned. "Don't you worry, I've been through that. I know exactly how it feels like when you have this kind of near-death experience for the first time."

"Oh, really...?" I said as I dropped on the bed.

I could hear her but it was as if we were on a plane and the pressurization hampered my audition. She gave me some water to drink and advised me to lie down and close my eyes for a minute or two.

"How are you feeling now?" she asked.

"Much better, thanks. I closed my eyes for two minutes and I guess I dozed off."

"Yes, you did. You slept for two hours; you needed it."

"I am feeling much better now."

"I ordered some Chinese. It should be here any minute."

Ava was sitting on the other bed, drawing something on a piece of paper and scribbling some notes.

"What's that?"

"Nothing; I was just killing time," she replied before carefully folding the paper and putting it in her pocket. I was able to see that it was in fact something like a map or a plan. "While you were asleep, I communicated with our office to tell them what had happened."

"And what did they say," I asked.

"That they'll pursue through the proper channels to figure out what happened this evening and that, for the rest, we are pretty much on our own."

"What do you mean 'on our own'?"

"Well, you and I... I mean essentially you and occasionally me," Ava said, with a smirk on her face.

"But I have no clue as to what's really going on."

"You read the documents I gave you, didn't you?"

"They were dead mute. Besides, I had a number of questions and clarifications I intended to ask Shumington and Necromonti about. I had even planned on completely giving up..."

"Well, I guess it's too late now. You're in it; whether you like it or not. As for your questions, luckily we still have Dr. Necromonti."

"If he survives..." I said with a sigh.

"Now, you are being pessimistic."

"No, just realistic."

I didn't want to sound pessimistic, but our enterprise had a rather shaky start. It seemed the terrorists had found us. They obviously had a good understanding of what the theory of 'pre-emptive strike' was. Instead of chasing the bad guys, we were being chased.

The Chinese food was delivered to the room and we sat to eat.

"How did you get involved in all this?" I asked Ava.

"I had just received my Bachelors of Science and I was doing some modeling jobs here and there to sustain my studies towards a Master…"

"And…?"

"I got tired of the futility of modeling; my studies were not exactly exciting either. So, one day, I saw an ad in the newspaper and I applied… and *voilà*!"

"I was expecting some tragic story of your parents being killed by a group of dangerous terrorists and you, in order to avenge them, had joined Interpol."

"Sorry for the disappointment."

After dinner, Ava went out, saying she had things to take care of. She forbade me to leave the room under any circumstance. I felt like a bird in a cage. It's when somebody prohibits me from doing something that I suddenly feel the itch to do it. Considering the situation, I decided to rely on her experience and follow her advice. I turned the TV set on and picked up the phone to call my apartment in order to check my voice messages.

The phone rang. At the second ring, before being oriented to my voice-messaging menu, to my utmost surprise, somebody picked-up:

"Hello, this is Haftemizan," a male voice said.

"Is this the… Balthazar residence," I asked, picking the first name that came to my mind.

"No, wrong number," the voice said before hanging up.

I don't have the gift of ubiquity. Ava was once again absolutely right. These guys are already in my home, searching for the documents and probably also looking for me. I decided to call the Police from my cell-phone. I told them that a burglary is taking place in my home while I am away. Hopefully, if they haven't already left by the time the Police arrive, they'll get a good scare and, if I am lucky, they'll be caught red-handed.

There wasn't much more I could do considering the circumstances - since I was banned from leaving the hotel room. So, I switched from channel to channel. I wasn't in the mood to watch a movie - that would have required too much focus. I settled on switching between a couple of those Cable news channels with back-to-back – should I say endless and often repetitive – talk shows. These shows may appear silly, and at times be utterly boring, but I like to watch them because they are something between a forum - in the Antique sense of it - and a pugilistic encounter, but with a sparkle of show-biz. Most of the talking heads are faces known on the circuit, moving tirelessly from set to set. I am so addicted to this type of spectacle that I sometimes surprise myself by watching them for hours, unable to unplug. The product may be bad, more than likely harmful for my mental sanity as well as for my health, but I still can't shed the habit. I am probably what you would call a 'political/news junky.'

I especially enjoy it when the anchors don't have the slightest clue regarding a topic and have to improvise. That's usually when they come up with some of the most flat, empty and stupid commentaries ever heard on television. I find it particularly funny when they attempt to have history's long dead personalities comment on today's events: "Do you think that Jesus would have approved of the legalization of gay marriage?" or "Do you think that, if Madison were alive today, he would be amending the Constitution?" or "Let me ask you this: what would MLK say about Rap music, if he were alive?"

I can assure you that if it ever happens that I am a guest and the host asks me one of these stupid questions, I would smile – no, no; you know I can't say the 'F' word on television, but it was the first to come to my mind too – and turn to him and say: "I have no idea; I don't have the gift of making the dead talk!" I think that it would be a memorable moment in television history...

After a couple of hours of trying to keep myself busy - so that I wouldn't think about what kind of damage the bad guys could be inflicting to my apartment - I finally fell asleep. The last twenty-four hours had been hectic. I think I deserved some rest.

I had not heard from Ava. I wasn't really worried for her, but she is my only link to the operation I am supposedly leading; should anything happen to her, I'd be in pretty bad shape.

At about 9:30 in the morning, the phone rang. I woke up and picked it up. It was Ava. She had spent the night working in her office reviewing all the files Shumington had on the case and made phone calls around the globe to gather additional information. She promised that she'd tell me more once she returned.

She returned to the hotel a little before 11 o'clock. I had just finished my belated breakfast and was getting ready to go down and ask the hotel if I could use one of their computers to check my e-mail. I was happy to see her. Not just because she was appealing, but also because she discovered new elements that could help to shed some light on the case.

"It's much more complicated than I thought," Ava said.
"How could it be?"

"I was looking in the files for the source of the tip that had allowed Erebus to uncover the devilish plot to acquire bio-weapons..."

"And...?"

"I was trying to figure out who the informant was but I couldn't find any reference."

"Perhaps because of the need for secrecy in order to protect that individual – whoever he may be," I suggested.

"With the degree of clearance that I have, I would have seen it," Ava said.

"Is there anybody else who would know about it?"

"Dr. Necromonti."

"And absolutely nobody else..."

"Well, there was a folder with an odd denomination on it – 'Beta 1' – and there was a note attached to it indicating that its content had been retrieved by the Big Boss."

"Here you go: you've got your other man now. Isn't this fantastic?"

I was happy about it because I knew it was multiplying - though in a meager way - our chances to see clearer in this otherwise obscure affair.

"The thing is that our Big Boss is based in Lyon, France, where our international headquarters are," Ava said.

"Can't they fax you the files?"

"You're not serious! These kinds of highly classified documents are never faxed; they travel by other means or not at all."

"Do we know if that 'Beta 1' file contains what we are looking for?"

"Excellent question, but I have no idea. I have sent a coded message so that, if at all possible, they'll tell us what the subject matter is without compromising the integrity and the security of its content."

"How soon can we expect a response on this?" I asked.

"It shouldn't be long. Now, let us see how Dr. Necromonti is doing," suggested Ava.

"I hope he is all right."

"I hope so, too; otherwise, it would be rather tragic."

Assem Akram

FourteenNinetyTwo@Hotmail.Com

As we walked the two blocks to the hospital, I informed Ava about what had happened at my apartment. Besides giving me the "I told you so" look, she said that I did the right thing and that we would eventually be able to go and assess the damage after we were done with Necromonti.

The hospital was not one of those huge complexes that have become almost the norm now. It was an older brick building with ceramic accents on the outside. We took the elevator to the second floor and ventured straight to the intensive care unit area. The smell of disinfectant was expectedly strong but it didn't really bother me: I expect a strong ether-type of smell in a hospital and I like it. In my mind, it equates to cleanliness – or the appearance of it. Likewise, I expect the nurses to be dressed in white and not those ugly pajama-like uniforms, with childish patterns such as Mickey Mouse or golf balls on them...

From a distance, in the contre-jour, I could distinguish the silhouette of a Police officer and I signaled it to Ava with a bit of distress. I feared that our visit was about to be cancelled or at least postponed for 'technical reasons.'

"Don't forget that in 'Interpol,' there is 'Police,' and I am a cop before anything else," Ava said.

And that was comforting, whereas so far my impression had been that we were avoiding the 'normal' authorities for the sake and the pursuit of our operation. Once at the door, Ava flashed some kind of police badge: "Interpol; we are expected." The officer nodded and let us in.

Inside the room, a nurse was standing as a doctor was busy examining Necromonti. The poor ailing Necromonti was surrounded by all kinds of vital equipment and monitors. Tubes were going in and out of almost every part of his body. Looking at the scene, we didn't know if we should have been optimistic, because we knew that at least he was alive, or pessimistic, because such an elaborate medical machinery meant that he was in a coma, just inches away from his final destination.

"What are the bets, Doc?" Ava asked.
"I am afraid your friend is in critical condition."
"How critical," I asked.
"Well, because of the position he was in," the Doctor proceeded to explain while tracing the trajectory with his pen, "the bullet entered his back from an angle and proceeded through his throat into his maxillary, before exiting his forehead."

I could easily imagine the bullet's journey, cutting through the flesh and drilling through the bones… Despite the appearance, the fact that he was shot at a distance of only a few inches probably helped him.

"He's doing okay," Ava said.
"I did not say that," the doctor said.
"But you just said that he was doing better than expected…"
"We're doing the best we can."

52

Somebody knocked at the door.

"Yes, what is it?" the Doc said, annoyed by the disturbance.

"Professor, the students are here," a man said as he peaked through the open door. "Should I let them in or should I ask them to wait for your visitors to leave?" The man was looking at us as if we were a nuisance.

"I am busy right now. Besides, the patient is in critical condition... We'll do a PowerPoint instead. I've got all the pictures and the X-rays. I'll see them in the conference room in ten minutes."

"Very well, Professor; we'll go there," the man said.

"I am sorry for this interruption, but the case is a bit unusual and - you know what it is - we have to form tomorrow's MDs," the Doc said.

Had he not added the last line about 'forming tomorrow's MDs,' I would have criticized his vulture-like, voyeuristic approach: our friend Necromonti is on his deathbed and this croaker has the audacity to invite a cohort of students to take a look at him as an object of medical curiosity!

"What are his chances of remission?" Ava said.

"Slim, I am afraid. His brain is damaged. As I told you, the bullet has cut through the frontal lobe; also his larynx and vocal cords are perforated. I don't want to sound too pessimistic, but there is a good chance that, if he survives, he will end up paralyzed and will need the help of a synthesizer to speak."

"Doc, that's not helpful," I commented with a bit of caustic – perhaps misplaced – humor.

Suddenly, something moved in Necromonti's bed.

"Can he hear us?" Ava asked.

"He probably will - I hope - but at this time he is heavily sedated and in a deep sleep."

Something moved in the bed. Necromonti's face was going through contortions, expressing pain and serenity consecutively, while attempting to move his right arm and hand.

"This is strange," the Doc whispered. "He seems to be moving his arm as if to draw our attention."

"Why would it be so strange?" I asked.

"For two simple reasons: one, he should not have control over his movements because of his cranial trauma; and the second reason is that he is loaded with enough drugs to put an elephant to sleep for a week without being able to move a hair on his trunk."

"He's probably dreaming," I suggested.

"That's probably the case," the Doc said.

Ava sat at Necromonti's bedside and gently took the hand he was trying to move. She pressured it, repeatedly. Then she got closer to his ear and started talking to him to the bewilderment of both the Doc and I. What the hell was she doing?

"Benvenisto, I know you can hear me. We are here; you're not alone. We won't let you down. Do you hear me, Benvenisto?"

She whispered in a voice so soft and suave that I was mesmerized, almost wishing that, at this instant, I were the one lying on that bed instead of Necromonti.

When the doctor was about to open his mouth to invite her to stop what she was doing, branding it as a futile exercise, she gave him a look so ferocious that he immediately cowered and left the room, silently signaling that he would be waiting outside. No doubt, Ava knew how to impose authority.

"Benvenisto, we need your help. We need you to be able to find the bad guys and uncover their plot. Shumington is dead. We are here, me and Haftemizan." As she said my name, she seized my hand and pressed it against Necromonti's palm. "Only you can help us track them. Haftemizan is here, as you wanted him to be. He's not going to let you down." Then she looked at me, with an expression that said, "Come on! Tell it to him now, please."

"Dr. Necromonti, this is Haftemizan," I said, complying with Ava's request. "We are here with you. We are very happy that you made it... Yes, Ava is right. I am going to use all my abilities to track down the bad guys and stop them before they endanger the planet: you can trust me.

"I had a million questions for you after I read the documents. I guess, it's because you and Shumington didn't want to address my irritating inquiries that you set up this murderous attack on yourselves... Jokes apart, Dr. Necromonti, we need your help to find out who they are. Give us at least one indication, a sign that would put our investigation on track, so that we can save time and therefore save money... I mean lives."

"You really are incorrigible! Even in the least favorable moment, you have to unleash your weird sense of humor," Ava said.

Despite admonishing me, I could sense that Ava was somehow appreciative that I went along with her idea, considering that I obviously doubted its soundness and that the

Doc, before he left the room, was staring at us as if we were two lunatics from another planet.

Imagine me, less than 48 hours earlier, I was just a consultant on international affairs, content with my semi-glamorous job, traveling here and there and selling in essence a few basic analyses in nice packaging. Now, I am involved in the hunt for a terrorist network - which evades me - and the two people who convinced me to help them have been shot. And at this moment, I am in a hospital room holding the hand of a moribund Italian expert and talking to him in the hope of resuscitating him... Isn't all of this too much? Shouldn't I ask someone to pinch me to see if it's real?

In the meantime, Ava's hand approached Necromonti's nostrils – at least the one nostril that did not have a tube in it. Between you and me, I think she is confusing Necromonti for a horse. Anyway, now she is rubbing her fingers on her neck and then placing them back in front of Necromonti's nasal orifice.

"It may end up being completely vain, but I am trying to appeal to some of his senses that are not solely dependent on the cortex," explained Ava, who could feel me staring at her with amused disbelief.
"What do you expect?" I asked.
"That he'll become aware of our presence in whatever layer of his mind or corner of his brain there is activity."

The doctor came back. "Now, if you'd excuse me, I have a presentation to make to my students. I am afraid you are going to have to leave, too. This patient needs a quiet environment."
"Sure, Doc; here is my card," Ava said. "Call me when he regains consciousness or, God forbid, should something uncalled for happen to him."

We were on our way out and the mood was not cheerful: we had not made any progress. Despite Ava's moment of "magic," Necromonti had not emerged from his coma and we still didn't have a clue as to whom we were chasing.

Ava's cell phone rang to the theme of 'Tomorrow Never Dies' – proof that she has a good sense of humor:

"Damn it!" Ava said.
"What is it? Did Necromonti die?"
"No, it's a message from the headquarters."
"What is it saying?"
"That the source is ...Necromonti."

She was literally stupefied. She stopped walking and stared at the text message.

"What do you mean?" I asked.
"Now, I understand...at least I think I do," Ava said.

It appeared that the clues were aligning themselves in her head and she was finally able to put the pieces of the puzzle together.

"Now that you've got it all figured out, maybe you can share it with me?" I suggested.
"Well, not everything; but at least I know that the only source of information we have is Necromonti."
"Great! The guy is dying or perhaps is already dead - despite sticking your fingers in his nose – and he is the only source of information we have. And how did Necromonti get wind of it? Was he part of the plot?"
"I don't know," Ava said.

"I guess he was. Believe me, there is no way someone would have been able to uncover information about transactions happening on the other side of the globe without being an insider."

"Again, I don't know."

"I don't see any other explanation. He must be a repenting former terrorist who made a deal with Interpol: the organization was giving him protection and a chance at a new life and, in exchange, he was giving Interpol the info it needed to foil a plot or bring down a network..."

"Very smart; you could be right," Ava said.

"...But since you guys failed to fulfill your part of the contract, he was executed mafia-style. His revenge is to do the same to you and die without giving you further information..."

"You are right about one thing: we failed to protect either of them." The tone of her voice was tinted with regret.

"By the way, what were you doing there at the time?" I asked.

"I was assigned to watch over them... over you."

"So, it happened before your eyes... Did you see the assassins?"

"No."

"What happened? Were you sleeping?" I asked half-jokingly.

"It's not much different than that: I was in the ladies room when I heard two detonations. No matter how fast I scurried to get back, it was too late. The killer had already left the scene."

"Ouch! That must have badly hurt your professional ego..."

"I am still digesting it. It's not easy, but you've got to rationalize and carry on."

Ava is decidedly tough. If I were in her shoes, it would take me at least a few weeks to sober up and I would probably carry the feeling of guilt for months if not for years on my shoulders. But she was calm and in control of her emotions, apparently feeling as guilty as if she had missed watering the plants.

We weren't even a block away from the hospital when Ava's cell phone rang again. The hospital informed her that Necromonti had regained consciousness. This was probably the best news I had heard in a long time. We both beamed with renewed optimism. We walked back to the hospital. If we had wings, we would have probably flown.

In the room, Necromonti had opened his eyes and, although he could not speak, his slow movements coupled with his facial expressions were much more than we expected. His long emaciated face looked as if it had been cropped out of an El Greco painting.

The Doc, a large smile on his face, was also in the room.

"Inspector, I have got to give it to you. I don't know what you did or how you did it, but you brought this man back to life," the Doc said to Ava.

"Are you mocking me, Doc," Ava said. She did not know whether he was being sincere or sarcastic.

"I am absolutely serious. This man was in a comatose state – half-dead by clinical standards – and his chances of recovery were pretty slim."

"Another victory for Eros over Thanatos," I said. All I got from them was a look of incomprehension.

We were all gathered around Necromonti's bed as if he were a newborn baby. His lethargic eyes browsed the room, apparently taking comfort in our presence at his side. When

Necromonti attempted to talk, an incomprehensible sound came out of his mouth. We could see how surprised he was, whereas we were not: the Doc had warned us ahead of time about his vocal cords. He tried a second time; but this time, the Doc, by a simple gesture, made him understand the problem. Necromonti shed a tear.

It was also evident that, for now, Necromonti did not have control over his movements. The doctor could not prognosticate if he would be able to recover his full mobility but, at this time, perhaps also due to the rather short lapse of time since the shooting and the surgery, his limbs were numb. All he could do was to move his arms a little bit.

"Let us bring Dr. Necromonti a laptop," I suggested. If he can move his arm, then he can press on a keyboard."

"Don't you think it's a bit premature? This gentleman needs to recover from at least two traumas..." the Doc pointed out.

"I would agree with the Doc on this one," Ava said.

"I understand your precautions," I said, before whispering to Ava: "Should I remind you that time is of essence in the endeavor we have undertaken. We have absolutely no idea if Necromonti will recover, or if he'll remain as he is now - or perhaps get worse..."

"You are too pessimistic," Ava said. "Look at him now; just half an hour ago, who would have thought..."

"Perhaps, but what if he were not to improve any time soon? We would then have lost precious days and probably months: are you willing to take the risk?"

"No, I guess you are right. We don't have much of a choice."

I did not feel guilty about it. After all, Necromonti and Shumington had scared me to death with the threat of a catastrophe of biblical proportions looming over our heads, if we didn't act fast enough…

The Doc volunteered to bring his own laptop and then we asked him to leave the room because whatever information would be obtained from Necromonti would be highly confidential and there could be no derogation. He complied uneasily, fearing for the wellbeing of his patient, and requested from us to act with caution and gentleness.

"Don't worry, Doc; he is much more precious to us than he is to you," I said to reassure him.

I quietly told Necromonti what we were planning to do: I would hold the laptop wide open with the screen towards him and the keypad held vertically at his fingertips so that he could press the keys effortlessly and at the same time monitor what he was writing. Ava lifted his right arm a little bit and held his hand to allow some mobility. But our attempt failed. The pile of equipment connected to Necromonti's body, added to his debility, was preventing him from seeing his own hand and giving the right impulse to press a key.

"Eureka," I said.
"What?" Ava asked.
"Do you remember the Doc telling us earlier that he was going to do a Power Point presentation for his students?"
"Yes."
"Well, we can borrow the projector and hook up the laptop to it," I said with the kind of proud excitement conferred only by some extraordinary discovery. "He'll be able to see

61

whatever he is typing blown out on the wall: isn't that a great idea or what?"

In a matter of minutes, the Doc arranged to bring the projector for us. I set it up and we were ready to start the experiment.

"All right, Dr. Necromonti; we are not going to bother you too much today. We are just going to ask a few questions which you can answer very briefly. Feel free to let us know when you are tired and we'll stop and come back tomorrow. We are very happy that you escaped the assassination attempt. Use the keyboard; Ava is at your side to assist you: see how lucky you are to have her on your side..."

Necromonti smiled and looked at Ava with an appreciative look. At this point, I realized that I was talking to Necromonti as if he were mentally challenged... But come to think of it, he may have not been so less than twenty-four hours earlier, but now he is totally challenged. So, my way of communicating with him is not so inappropriate and insulting after all.

"My first question is in regard to the killer: do you suspect anyone in particular?" I asked.

"Them," Necromonti painstakingly typed.

"Who are they? Can you tell us anything? Because in the papers you had given me earlier, there was nothing to indicate the identity of the bad guys."

Necromonti nodded, indicating that it was done on purpose.

"Apocalypse coming... Find them."

"I understand that - and I have agreed to help you, but you must give us more info. Who can help us, besides you?"

"I am…link."

"I understand, Doctor; but you have to reveal your source to us - it is too vital. We need additional information to progress."

"Source…dead," Necromonti typed.

"Damn it! Just what we needed: the informant is dead, too," I exclaimed with disappointment.

"Calm down, please," Ava insisted. "This is the time to control your emotions." It was a wise remark. I recognized that it was certainly not the time to further upset Necromonti.

"Source talks to me," Necromonti further typed.

What did he mean by that? I looked towards Ava for a hint, but she seemed as clueless as I was. Maybe he meant that the source used to talk to him only?

"We don't understand. Could you please elaborate?" I asked Necromonti.

"…Must trust source," he wrote in response.

Once again, Ava and I looked at each other not knowing how to digest the information Necromonti had just given us. His responses seemed off the mark. The Doc and Ava were right: it is too premature to try to get anything out of him. We failed to really enter into the equation the extremely powerful anesthetics and other painkillers they had him ingurgitate.

"He's in no condition to give us anything useful. I think our friend Benvenisto could use some rest. We'll come back tomorrow."

Ava smiled. "You're right," she agreed. "Let's leave Dr. Necromonti to recuperate, and tomorrow we'll quiz him relentlessly."

Before she was able to remove the notebook computer, Necromonti pressed the keyboard in an ultimate selfless effort. On the screen we could read a succession of four numbers: 1, 4, 9 and 2.

1, 4, 9 and 2... '1492'... Why did this number appear so familiar? Of course! That is the year America was discovered. But what did it have to do with these terrorists?

"Could you tell us a little bit more, *Dottore*?" I begged.

Necromonti would not respond. His eyes were shut. I panicked for a second, thinking he may be dead. But since the monitors did not go off to signal the failure of any of his vital organs, I was reassured. The poor man had probably passed out because he had spent all his strength to assist us. We quickly called the nurse and informed the Doc that we were done with his patient for the day.

"What did he mean by '1492'?" I wondered again.

"It could be that the terrorist group in question is targeting America," Ava said.

"I agree. That seems to be a very likely scenario. But then why not just say that? He could have written 'America' instead. I think there is something else behind this number. Or, maybe, in his delirium, he just remembered his ATM card's pin number," I suggested as a joke.

"You're right. Maybe we should steal his card and try. What do you think?" Ava said, with the same tongue in cheek tone.

"I knew most cops were no better than the thieves they are after, but I thought you were different. I am really disappointed, Inspector."

"You should be," she said. "You never know whom you're dealing with."

From the hospital, we took a cab to my apartment to assess the damage. From the outlook, it didn't seem that someone had broken in: the door was not damaged and I was able to use my key to open it. Once we got inside, there did not appear to be any chaotic disorder resulting from a hurried search. Everything seemed to be exactly where I had left them – at least, from what I could remember.

"Are you sure that you heard someone pick up your phone?"

"I know, by looking around, that there doesn't seem to be any tangible evidence that anyone has visited my flat. Perhaps, it was just a bad dream generated by anxiety?"

I decided to call the Police and ask them if they had indeed sent a dispatch last night after I called them. The officer on duty looked up my file and confirmed that two officers went there twenty minutes after I had called but did not see any trace of an infraction and, once they were able to get inside with the building attendant's key, everything looked absolutely fine.

"Did you hear that?" I asked Ava as I hung up the phone. "They did not find anything to corroborate my suspicion."

"Yes," she replied. "But let us not stop at how things look. You need to search for specific details. Look for your phone book, for example, or for your passport, and how about the Erebus papers? I am certain that's what they were looking for. I guess you didn't destroy them after you read them as instructed..."

"No worries - as my Australian friends would say. They are in the back of my car, in the trunk. I had a million questions to ask, so I had brought them with me to grill Shumington and Necromonti."

"God bless you!" Ava said with a sigh of relief. "Although, I should tell you that these documents were 'sanitized' and did not contain the most critical information."

"No wonder why I had so many questions. So, in essence, it wouldn't have mattered much if these guys had gotten hold of those documents," I said, both surprised and disappointed to witness how little trust they had placed in me.

"In essence: no." Ava was manifestly pleased to see me upset.

I carefully toured my apartment looking for something missing or visibly displaced. Meanwhile, Ava, an ultraviolet light in hand, scanned some objects, including the phone handset, looking for clues.

"Here," I called out.

"Were you able to find something?"

"My PC is on. I can hear the fan. I vividly recall turning it off after I was done with some back-ups."

"Let me look at it first for a second. It could be booby-trapped, or there could be some interesting evidence lying somewhere here."

Ava used her blue light to scan the computer from side to side, as well as the desk, the chair and the floor in the immediate perimeter, before allowing me to do anything.

Ava laughed. "That's a funny one," she said, when she saw my screen-saver representing a famous picture of Churchill, Roosevelt and Stalin in Yalta but touched up to include some pin-up babes, as if they were having a good time in a cabaret or at some strip joint.

I sat on my chair and moved the mouse very lightly. When the screen-saver faded away, a short message appeared: "Do not attempt to get in God's way!"

"That's a chilling warning," I said.

"Indeed. What is remarkable is that these guys have entered and left your apartment without leaving a single track behind." Ava seemed impressed by the degree of stealth the intruders had shown.

"Professional job," I pointed out, stating the obvious.

"They certainly knew exactly when you'd be out."

"Do you think I was under surveillance?"

"More than likely... I think that this time they just wanted to warn you."

"I get the message 10-4; believe me! I don't plan to get in 'God's way': who am I to do that...?"

"Their intent was to scare you and they've succeeded."

"Don't you think that it's a bit too much for a soft-spoken consultant on International Relations, whose only fault is to have written a damn book some years back that Necromonti happens to have read?"

I was furious; the kind of fury that inhabits a person who has the uncomfortable impression that he is helplessly trapped in an inextricable situation. Ava advised me to stop whining about it. She was right. I had *nolens-volens* renewed my promise to carry on Necromonti's quest. I am a man of my word – at least for the big things, I hope. I'll do what I've said I'd do. Besides, I was at a point of no return, now; so I had to think positively.

In the lower corner of my desktop, I saw a little icon signaling that I had new e-mail messages. For the last twenty-four hours, I had not been able to check my e-mail. Beside the usual junk, one immediately caught my eye: it was sent from 'fourteenninetytwo@hotmail.com.'

"Ava, look at this message! Look at the sender's name." Ava was wandering in the kitchen in search of something to eat – or perhaps checking if my dishes were done...

"How odd; open it! But be careful because it has an attachment."

"It's a JPG file. There is no risk of infection," I reassured her as I double-clicked on the tiny icon to download it.

The picture showed Necromonti on his hospital bed, exactly the way we had left him. Ava drew her cell phone from her pocket and called the hospital right away to see if anything had happened to Necromonti. While she was waiting, she forwarded the e-mail to some address with a long string of numbers and letters that did not make sense to me, for verification.

The hospital number wouldn't go through. So, we decided to return there without wasting a single minute. We hopped into my little convertible – my weekend glamour sports car. While I was zigzagging my way through the afternoon traffic, Ava called some guy named Ranjit and asked him to figure out who had registered the e-mail address 'fourteenninetytwo@hotmail.com.'

"I've forwarded the e-mail to the box...I understand... try your best," she told him.

At the hospital, there was no officer on duty at the door and Necromonti was missing.

"Where are they? Where is he?" Ava asked at the reception desk on the floor.

"Oh, here is the doctor: he'll tell you," the nurse said.

"Doc, what happened?" Ava said.

"I wanted to call you, but I couldn't find your card."

Just minutes after you left, he fell back in an intense coma. His pulmonary system completely stopped functioning and his brain's electrical activity slowed considerably. We tried everything in our power to resuscitate him, but it did not work. I am sorry."

That was a big blow. We were in very bad shape now. Our only link to the 'source' was gone before we were able to extract any valuable information from him.

"You did everything you could, Doc; I guess it was his destiny," Ava said.

"A tragedy," I added.

Assem Akram

May the Spirit of Ferdinand and Isabel Guide You

Naval Observatory, Washington DC

"Good evening, Sir."

"Good evening; have a seat. I have to finish one more page and I'll be with you."

"What is it, Sir?"

"Oh, hum… I am putting some final touches to this speech for Pretzel Boy."

"I see."

"Yes, good, excellent…that's exactly what I wanted," commented Dick as he read through the document in his hand.

"Is this for tomorrow's event, Mr. Vice President?"

"No, it's another one. I am always working ahead on a few speeches."

"I see. Very wise of you, Sir."

"It's laborious, but someone has to do it. We have a mission to accomplish and we cannot leave these things to amateurs."

"You're absolutely right, Sir; it would get out of hand then."

"Did you take care of it?"

"Affirmative; Sir!"

"Both of them?"

"With a slight delay; but, yes, Sir."

"So, it's all taken care of…"

"Albeit one little problem…"

"What is it?"

"Well, Sir, there is a third and even a fourth 'player' who seem to be involved somehow," the man said.

"Don't fuck this one up; I am warning you! You know what can happen to you if you screw this one?"

"I know, Mr. Vice President… But trust me; we checked everything and they don't have a clue as to what's going on."

"This is too big an affair to take any risks. If you feel that they are too nosy and are getting a little bit too warm, don't hesitate," the Vice President said, his thumb simulating the cutting of a throat.

"Understood, Sir!"

"You may leave now… And keep an eye on the third and fourth guy and make sure that there is no fifth or sixth or any other number of them…"

"Be assured, Sir! Good evening."

"May the Spirit of Ferdinand and Isabel guide you," finished Dick, as he watched the man exit the room.

"Sir, Mr. Joachim Azuelos is here," announced an usher.

"Yes, yes, excellent; bring him in, please," Dick said.

"Joachim, what a pleasure to see you. Come on in!"

The man was in his mid-fifties – perhaps closer to sixty - elegantly dressed, and leaning on a walking stick.

"I came as soon as I got your message," Joachim Azuelos said.

"I've got to tell you that I need your absolute discretion."

"What is it this time, Dick? You know you can always count on me."

"I know I can trust you. You and I have known each other since we were kids... Believe me; those bonds are rock-solid, irreplaceable."

"Sure, they are. So, what is it all about? I am starting to get excited like a high-school kid about to do something bad. It's not bad, is it?"

"Trust me, Joachim; this is something bigger than you and me. This is the real call of our generation. We are in a unique point in time where we are able to do it... God has given us the power and the will to do it in order to save mankind."

"I am sorry, but you lost me."

"What I am about to tell you is going to shake you at first; but when you are done digesting it, you'll think about what you can do for others and - never to be neglected - the benefit you'll draw from it, then you'll find it an excitingly attractive plan."

The phone rang.

"Yes? Hello."

"Dick, this is Pat."

"Hey, Pat! How are you doing? What's the weather like on the Hill?"

"Agreeable. The clouds are dissipating and there is hope for more sunshine."

"Excellent! Keep me updated on the forecast. I am with a friend right now... Our lunch is still on for tomorrow. We'll talk more when I see you then".

"Sure ... I get it ... Bye!"

"See you tomorrow, Pat," said Dick as he hung up. "I am sorry for the interruption," he apologized to Joachim.

"No problem at all."

"Where were we? Oh, yes, the plan…"

"Yes, the plan…?"

The Vice President's phone rang again.

"I am not going to take it this time, Joachim."

"No, no, go ahead."

"Good evening, Mr. President," Dick said as he picked up the phone.

"Have you finished readying my speech for tomorrow?"

"Yes, Mr. President."

"Good. And did you make sure that there are no complicated words that I can't spell - let alone attempt to pronounce them?"

"We've all learned our lesson, Sir. You won't find a single word that has more than three syllables in what I have concocted for you… And if they do, I have made sure to break them down for your convenience."

"You're my man! I knew there was a reason why I kept you for a second term."

"You're too kind, Mr. President"

"Do me a favor, Dick; send it over to me so I can familiarize myself with the text."

"Certainly, Mr. President; right away!"

"Oh, and one more thing: don't forget to replace the batteries before you go to sleep," giggled '43.'

"Don't worry, Mr. President; I won't forget," said Dick with a forced laughter.

"Nighty night!"

"Good night, Mr. President," said Dick before muttering "moron" as he hung up the phone.

"Did I hear you call him 'moron'?"

"Yes, I am afraid you did."

"I am not interfering in your personal relationship with the President, but it appears to me that what you said may be... inappropriate if not risky."

Dick frowned. "You're right in principle, but you have no idea what I have been enduring with Pretzel Boy, day and night, for years now!"

"I can guess," Joachim said.

"If it wasn't for..." Dick started saying before realizing that he was about to reveal too much on the true nature of his relations with '43.' "Ah... let's leave it here, old pal, and let's talk about our project."

Dick swiftly closed the chapter of his relationship with the President and offered some Cognac and some Belgian chocolates to his guest before explaining his plan:

"Listen very carefully and if you have a question, don't hesitate to interrupt me."

"Come on; spit it out, for God's sake!"

"You've said it! That's exactly what our plan is all about: for God's sake. In a few words, the plan is to save Humanity by saving the Middle-East from its plague of war and endless confrontation, which can only be achieved if the Holy Land returns under the protective wing of Christianity."

"How... why...?" asked Joachim Azuelos. This was like Hiroshima and Nagasaki at once.

"With a group of devout Christians, true followers of the Apostle of God, we've concluded that those Semitic tribes – the Arabs and the Jews – cannot come to terms and they are spoiling the Sacred Land, the land that saw Jesus brought to life to save Humanity from its sins."

"And what do you intend to do about it?"

75

"We believe that it is our destiny, as Americans, to take control of those lands so that our might in the service of our Lord Jesus brings peace to the entire region."

"Are you planning on invading the Palestinian territories, perhaps Syria, too? Is that your plan?"

"No, we are planning to take control of the Holy Land."

"Do you mean Jerusalem only?"

"Well, in fact, our plan is broader and includes Syria, parts of Lebanon, Palestine and Israel, all the way to the Sinai desert."

"I can't believe what I am hearing! Are you serious? You want to conquer that entire region?"

"If I may correct you, we are not going to 'conquer' but rather 'reconquer' the Holy Land."

"I see: it's the Reconquista redux!"

"How did you guess? Your smarts will always amaze me. To be very precise, the idea is that the Reconquista was not completed and we have a duty to finish it and bring the Pax Universalis under one God."

"Why would it be any of our business?" Joachim said.

"Because the same year the Reconquista was supposedly finished, Columbus discovered this Promised Land and that is an undeniable sign that the Lord has sent to tell us that we are the inheritors of Isabel and Ferdinand and that we ought to finish the task of 'Reconquista' to extend it to the Holy Land."

"This is pretty scary, Dick. I am not sure that it's such a good idea to revive centuries-old civilizational quarrels and be chastised around the world for being anti-Islamic."

"Trust me, Joachim; we will not be perceived as anti-Islamic because we are taking over our long-standing ally Israel as well."

"I am not sure how that can help: we'll be viewed as anti-Semitic altogether."

"Your analysis is perfectly correct and we have thought about it. Of course, we are not going to send our troops there with a banner proclaiming: "We are here to finish the Reconquista!" Come on; you know me better than that, Joachim! What I told you is the real motivation behind, which only a very select number of people know about. Officially, as the strongest nation on the surface of this earth, we'll be intervening over there to stop a war that would have just started between Arabs and Israelis."

"I see…"

"Believe me, once we've installed law and order, people in this country and outside of it will thank us. Think of the effect that our success will have on the world, in the region and here, at home."

"How so?"

"Well, with the newly found regional stability, the oil market will settle down and the consumers at home will see the immediate benefits of it. As you very well know, if you give our fellow Americans cheap oil at the pump, cheesy sitcoms and Sunday football on TV, they are content."

"I think that you're forcing the metaphor…"

"Perhaps, but you know what I mean. Plus, let us not forget that the majority of this country has a deep belief in evangelical values and when they see what we are doing over there and how their leaders can be useful, they'll back us. I can guarantee that."

"And what exactly will those 'Evangelicals' be doing over there?"

"Exactly what they've been doing under the radar for years: bringing the word of our Savior to the Jews."

"Do you mean to 'convert' them?"

"Absolutely; because then only the prophecy of the Messiah will be completed. It's our mission to bring the lost sheep back to the herd."

77

"Is the President with you on this?"

"He shares our views on the spiritual goal and the historical mission, but he may not be aware of all the 'technicalities,' if you will."

"And my guess is that those 'technicalities' include the kindling of the fire that will start the conflict you need for your stratagem to succeed: am I right?

Dick smiled. "You've got it all computed."

Joachim Azuelos sat back in his chair and looked around him for a second as he tried to digest the enormity and the boldness of the plan the Vice President had just lain out. He thought that this was so huge and so evil in essence that it could not succeed. But then again, he thought, this guy is known in certain circles as 'Machiavelli.' So, this plan, as bold and as dangerous as it may appear, might have some solid preparation behind it; otherwise he wouldn't be confiding the way he has. While Joachim Azuelos was thinking it over, Dick was staring at him with a look that said: "Come on, old pal; I know you want to do it. So, get on board!"

"Tell me exactly what you expect from me and also what's in it for me for taking part in this risky enterprise."

"Let me tell you first what would be in it for you: I need someone trustworthy, with your type of profile, to set up a consortium that would take over the water management of the entire region."

"That doesn't look too promising as a return on investment."

"You're a businessman; you know very well that water distribution companies around the world are some of the largest and most profitable companies in the long run. Besides, in this part of the world where water is scarce, whoever controls the water supply, controls life."

"You're right; so you benefit and I benefit."

"Let us put it this way: you'll benefit, and the friends that will be associated with you on this project will benefit as well."

"Give me a break. Are you saying that you are not going to gain from it? Remember that you're talking to me..."

"I'll benefit indirectly: if you win and they win, then I win something, too. I am not playing it innocent; you know how these things work..."

"I know. Now, what do you expect from me?"

"Twenty-five million odorless orphan dollars."

"That's a lot of money."

"That's the price-tag to join the club. Life is so expensive nowadays... Besides, we need to take care of some 'technicalities...'"

"All right; you'll get it. Just let me know how you want it."

"I knew I could count on you. I'll give you the details later... Oh, and one last word..."

"Yes, what is it?" Joachim said, as they were walking towards the door.

"This discussion never happened."

"Obviously."

The Following Day

"Good to see you, Senator," Dick said.

"Delighted to see you, too, Mr. Vice President," Patrick Jeremiah Gareth, the four-term senior Senator from the South, said.

"Pat, let me tell you that I am very happy with the way things are going under your leadership. You've been a solid backer of our agenda and I can assure you that I will personally make sure that the President knows about it."

The Vice-President enjoyed his position that enabled him to double his firm grip on the party to keep it neatly in line with the Administration's policy.

"Thank you, Dick; I am not sure if I deserve it, but I must confess that we've done a pretty good job circumventing those liberal whiners with our group and promote a truly patriotic agenda in jive with our conservative Christian values."

"And I've put a word to the Secretary of Homeland Security to include your district to be home to one of the four regional centers he's planning to set up by the end of the year; it'll give you a little boost locally."

Gareth rubbed his hands together. "Are you kidding? This means that my re-election is in the pocket."

"So, how is our little business going?" Dick said.

"Not too bad, I must say. Our group understands the challenges facing our new role on the international scene as well as the responsibilities bestowed upon our great nation by history and by God."

"I wouldn't have said it better. Pat, you are a true patriot," Dick said, before interrupting the conversation to allow lunch to be served.

"I asked the Chef to prepare some Middle-Eastern dishes for us; I thought you'd like that."

"Very thoughtful of you, Dick. I am going to try it, but I do not specially fancy this kind of spicy food; it upsets my stomach."

"Well, maybe you should try to get used to it. You know what they say: you've got to love it to have it."

"Yes, you're right. And I certainly wouldn't want to suffer from indigestion then…"

"I should tell you, Senator, that we've moved a few steps closer toward the completion of our goal."

"That's good news. Dick, you are a devilish mastermind - I mean... you are a God-sent mastermind."

"Would you like some more of this kabob?" offered the Vice President. "It's absolutely delicious: so moist, so juicy that it'll melt in your mouth."

"You're very kind; but I think I am going to take some more of this 'Ali Baba' thing I started with."

"The name is Baba Ghanouj, not Ali Baba," Dick corrected with a smile.

"If you say so..."

"There is something else I would like to share with you."

"I am listening, while I am trying this 'doormat' thing. What an odd name for a dish," the Senator said, forgetting his apprehension.

"Dolma not 'doormat,'" corrected the Vice President with a slight undertone of consternation this time.

"Duma [sic]... Oh, Jesus; this 'Duma' is so delicious. I wonder what's in the stuffing. I'm listening..."

"As you know, the presidential elections are fast approaching. The President has done his two terms and, therefore, cannot be re-elected, which leaves the horizon wide open for me to be the candidate of our party. God willing, with the new situation that will be prevailing by then, the American people will elect me – we've learned by now that, in times of war, they don't like to change course."

"This is simply brilliant! But I should tell you that this is something we had envisioned with the group, but then..." the Senator paused.

"...Then you thought that my health will probably prevent me from posing as a credible candidate for the ultimate job, isn't it?"

"You know it yourself better than we do: it is viewed as a handicap by the voters."

"And they are probably right. But if they can see that, they will also recognize that, despite the criticism of the alarmists, I've been standing by the President, without vacillating, throughout his two terms, and then they'll realize how rock-solid I am," Dick said, hitting the table with his fist.

"I was just echoing the gossip in the media. I know how healthy you are; you'll end up burying us all," Pat said, realizing he had struck a sensitive cord.

"It is a fact that I have this pace-maker implanted to my side," Dick said. "But it could be to your advantage…"

"God forbid! I would never wish you harm."

"That's not what I meant. Lately - as we are going forward with our plan - I've been doing a lot of thinking about the elections. A dinosaur of politics such as you knows perfectly how these things have to be meticulously planned months and years in advance."

"Yes, I know."

"With that in mind, I have put your name on my very short list of possible choices for a running-mate."

"That would be an honor and a privilege," the Senator said, about to jump off his chair and embrace the Vice President. "Wait till I tell my wife!"

"I thought we were very clear on this one, Pat: nothing, I insist, absolutely nothing of what we say or do should be revealed to anyone, including your wife, your mistress or whoever shares your bed."

Clearly, the Senator's comment burped out of enthusiasm was a faux pas. An usher brought in the phone.

"Who is it? I said that I am available for no one," Dick said, looking very annoyed.

"Sir, it's Colonel Bernardino..."

"Oh, yes; okay, I'll take it."

"Hello, hello...Bernie, can you hear me, Bernie...?"

"Mr. Vice President, I can barely hear you. The communication is very bad...I'll try to reach you another time."

"I hear that there was a sand storm hitting where you and your men are stationed: did it blow away all your equipment?"

"No, Sir; It did not. Everything is exactly where it is supposed to be."

"Great to hear that, Bernie. I wish you good luck. You and your men stay safe!"

"We will. Thank you, Sir".

"God bless you," the Vice President concluded.

"What a true patriot," the Senator thought. "He refuses to take any call, and yet his line is open for a soldier calling from the battlefront to tell him about a sand storm... That's just unheard of among our politicians." The senior Senator from the South was definitely impressed. But in the meanwhile, he wanted to rectify the disastrous impression he had just given to the Vice President:

"I usually... I mean, I never tell my wife anything... It was just a figure of speech - humor, if you will," the Senator said, still red out of confusion, remorseful for his puerile excitement.

"I cannot emphasize enough the need for absolute secrecy. This is no amateur enterprise. I don't want any unwarranted mistake to hamper a mission that has been bestowed upon us by God. We've come too far and I've spent too many years of my life preparing for this to allow some stupid imprudence get in the way of our success. Am I clear, Pat?"

"Perfectly clear! Rest assured that there is absolutely no risk of leakage on my side."

"My trust in you is unwavering; otherwise, we wouldn't be having this conversation," the Vice President said, before switching to "would you like some baklava?" to ease a little bit the atmosphere that had all of sudden gotten very tense.

"Yes, sure… Why not? The hell – I am sorry - the heck with my ramping diabetes."

"Life is full of risk," Dick commented with imperceptible sarcasm. "But watch yourself, Senator; the country needs you and, most importantly, we need you for the greater cause. Losing you would be tragic."

Point of No Return

Ava answered her cell phone. "Oh, hi, Sir; how are you doing? ... Yes, it is possible... We can be there in less than fifteen minutes."

"Who was it?" I asked.

"The Big Boss," she replied, frowning.

"You mean Interpol's boss?"

"Yes, he's in town and he wants to see us at the Willard, where he's staying."

"Do we have time to return to the hospital so I can get my car back before they tow it?"

"I am afraid not. Don't worry about your little 'toy car': we'll get it later. Now, we have an important appointment and we can't miss it."

The cabby wasn't really worried by the traffic or by the signs. Driving a large Crown Victoria, the man appeared to be talkative beyond exasperation. You know what the deal is with cab drivers? When you don't want to talk, because you have other things on your mind, you encounter one of the chattering, insatiable kind; and when you are in the mood and you feel like engaging in some type of conversation, the guy is mute or, at best, drops a "yes, Sir" or a "no, Sir" here and there throughout your soliloquy.

This one was not of the mute variety. He was from Afghanistan and - like almost three-quarters of the cabbies I've met - he was once a political refugee. In this case, he had left his country when the Soviets invaded it. The middle-aged man wore a dark blue beret and a gray, rather fashionable jacket, with a matching chiffon around his neck.

"Yes, now, I know where I've seen you." The cab driver stared at me through the rear mirror. "It was on C-Span!"

"I am impressed," I said. I was as much impressed that he recognized me as I was that he watched that rather confidential channel. I should confess that, on nights when I have difficulty sleeping, I tune to C-Span as a drug of choice.

"And... yes, now that I recall, I've also seen you once on CNN. Am I right?" yelled the cabby with enthusiasm as if he had won the lottery.

Ava smiled. "We've got a fan here."

"You know, lady; you look exactly like my daughter. She's pretty too, you know," the cabby said.

"I am sure she is," Ava replied.

"She just graduated from Georgetown, you know; she is very smart."

"You must be proud of her."

"Yes, Madame," the cabby said before turning to me. "Since you're an intelligent man and you know a lot about many things, let me tell you an interesting story that should be in every history book."

"Go ahead, please; I am listening."

"Did you know that I saw Brezhnev being slapped?" the cabby announced with pride.

"Are you kidding me?" I reacted with incredulity.

"I mean, not 'physically' slapped, you know, but 'politically' slapped... It was in Moscow, in 1976. I was a junior diplomat at the time, you know, and I happened to be part of the

86

delegation that was accompanying our President – Daoud - to the USSR…"

"Wasn't Daoud the King's cousin who abolished monarchy?" I pointed out, proud to show off my knowledge.

"Yes, you're right. He was one of a kind, you know! Not like those spineless weasels we have today, you know. I was there when Brezhnev complained to Daoud about several issues, including why he was opposing Cuba's membership to the Non-Aligned movement and why he had removed some of Moscow's allies from his government. That's when, my friend, Daoud stood up from his seat and said to Brezhnev: 'Shove it!' – pardon my language, lady."

"Really? Did he say that like this?" I asked. I was captivated by his narration and so seemed to be Ava.

"Well, you know, in essence, yes. In fact, he told Brezhnev that Afghanistan, you know, was a sovereign country and that the USSR had no business dictating to its president how to conduct his policies. He left the room and we followed right behind him – I should confess, with anguish in our stomachs, you know."

"That's a heck of a piece of history you witnessed! I am jealous; I wish I had been there, too," I said.

"And believe it or not, when Brezhnev almost ran after him to apologize, President Daoud did not wait and left the room: that guy was a man of honor and principle; not like this mindless puppet, you know, that Karzai guy we have in office in Kabul right now."

"What did the Soviets do after that? Did they let him get away with this affront?" I asked, curious.

"The KGB started preparing his downfall, you know… and you probably know the rest: the Communists, these SOB's - excuse my language - staged a coup d'Etat and killed him with all his family, including the kids, you know."

"How sad," Ava commented.

"Tragic," I added.

It was obvious that the man was marked for the rest of his life by this episode. His adrenaline rose and the tone of his voice modulated towards higher frequencies. As he was telling the story, perhaps overwhelmed by anger, as he recalled the past, at times he would stumble on words or pause to try to find the right one.

It's always difficult to joke or to express anger in a language that is not your native one. This reminds me of an episode once in Paris, where I was trying to chastise - in French, *s'il vous plait* - the server who kept bringing me back the same dish I had returned twice. Believe me; I was so enraged not to be able to properly express my frustration that I did not know whether to shoot the server or myself.

And just as we approached the hotel, the cabby turned open the sun visor on the passenger side. There was attached a faded black and white picture of a group.

"That's me, to the right" he pointed proudly. "In the middle, here, is President Daoud. Can you see?"
"Yes, I can see. When was the picture taken?" I asked.
"That's our delegation, in Moscow, at the Afghan Embassy, after the incident."
"That's indeed fascinating," I genuinely wondered. "You should write this," I suggested.
"I am just a cab driver, you know. Besides, I am too old. I shared this story with you because I've seen you and I know you are interested in world affairs. Maybe you can do something with it?"
"Thank you for your trust; but I should tell that I am no specialist of your country," I cautioned.

"Well, if not you, maybe someone you know - a student, a professor - may find it insightful… And I have many other stories like this one - many of which I have witnessed."

"I'll think about it and, if you give me a number where I can reach you, I'll get back to you."

"God bless you; my name is Shams," he said, before shaking my hand vigorously and giving me his card. To be courteous, I gave him one of mine in exchange and asked him to call me back to remind me the promise I had made to him - as it is very possible that I get overly busy and forget about it, or even get killed…

Shams seemed to be outright pleased by our encounter. I have a guess that this was not the first time he was telling this story to some complete stranger – that's the nature of his job - but this time, he was lucky to have found an attentive ear. In less than fifteen minutes - the time it took him to drive us to our destination - we learned more about this man, his life, his emotions and the tragedy of his country than we may know about ourselves.

"You are celebrity among cab drivers," Ava said.

"I don't even want to respond to this kind of pernicious remark coming from a cold-blooded international cop."

The elevator opened and perhaps half a dozen FBI agents were spread across the hallway leading to the room of Interpol's Big Boss. For those who haven't visited Washington, the Willard is one of the most luxurious hotels in town, located at a short distance from the White House.

"This is how Interpol spends international tax-payers' money?" I commented.

"What did you expect? That he books a room at a Motel 6 on New York Avenue?"

"Why not?" I responded half-jokingly.

After Ava flashed her badge and I was patted down, we were able to finally get into the suite.

"Welcome, Mr. Haftemizan; my name is Hector Metaxas. I am Interpol's Secretary General," the man, wearing a navy blue striped suit, said.

Metaxas was of medium corpulence and completely bald. His handshake was firm and his royal blue tie matched the color of his eyes as well as that of the mural tapestry adorning the room.

"It's a pleasure to meet you," I said.

"The pleasure is all mine; Shumington and Necromonti – God bless their souls – had immense trust in you. And Ava, here, who is one of the most brilliant of our agents, has told me of your courage and your wits."

"I think they've been too kind and have by far over-rated my humble person," I replied, covering myself in a shroud of partial false modesty.

"Believe me, Mr. Haftemizan; we know people at Interpol," Metaxas said with conviction. "And I know that, in you, we have found someone of great value and high determination, ready to do whatever it takes to save the world from an imminent threat."

"*Alea jacta est*, as they say," I responded with a grind of fatality.

"And I welcome your good judgment; you've made the right choice."

"I was not so sure about the whole affair, but after what happened to Shumington and Necromonti, I don't think I have much of a choice anymore."

"I know what you all have been through for the last couple of days or so. This is why I wanted to see you and assure you of our full backing and unwavering confidence."

Evidently, Metaxas is someone used to giving motivational speeches: empty in essence, but aimed at making you feel good for the moment. This is the kind of person who, regardless of what his profession may be – politician or Tupperware salesman - once on stage, is able to line up about thirty to forty pre-cooked sentences and recipes, before drying up. Anyhow, there is no reason for me to doubt the sincerity of Interpol's Big Boss at this moment.

"Thank you for your support; but to be sincere, we've reached a dead end: Shumington and Necromonti are gone and all we have are some meager clues divulged by Necromonti on his deathbed," I complained.

"He is right, Sir," Ava said. "We would very much appreciate it if you could shed some light for us."

"Yes, anything that would allow us to see the picture a little clearer would be most welcome. For instance, Necromonti – God bless his soul – told us that he was 'the source' and that we should 'trust the source': we are a bit confused!"

"I believe I can clarify this one a little for you. But before I start, I would like you to take a seat because, with what I am about to tell you, you are going to need it."

Metaxas was talking with the voice of someone who is - or was – a heavy smoker. A voice that was pleasant to the ears for its softness and yet annoying because it was accompanied by a constant wheezing. His back was to a large French window.

The afternoon's yellow light turning ochre still had enough reach to glide over his bald skull and blind us. All we could see was Metaxas' heavy silhouette sitting on the chair in front of us, one leg crossed over the other.

Ava sat to my left and I should say that this light unfairly accentuated her graceful features. The sun's rosy beams were piercing through her nacre blouse as if to caress her skin. The magic of the afternoon's evanescent luminescence had turned the fabric of her shirt diaphanous, offering to my appreciative sight the forms of the divine creation at its best. All right, enough lyricism now! We are here for serious business. I should not let myself become distracted... Okay; now, let us forget Ava and instead concentrate on what Interpol's Big Boss has to tell us. "Yes, that's what's important, not my libido, for God's sake," I told myself, trying to regain control of my weaker-self in order to concentrate on the topic before us.

"About eighteen months ago," Metaxas continued, "officials from the Italian Ministry of the Interior contacted Interpol's headquarters to inform us that they had credible evidence that a terrorist plot of importance was in the making. Rome was providing us with extraordinarily accurate actionable tips.

"I gave the mission to my agents at Erebus, since it fitted their assignment within Interpol. We were able to find out that, through several underground financial networks, a group, which we suspect has malevolent intentions, was able to purchase bio-hazardous material from two labs formerly part of the Soviet WMD program.

"Every time we put some hope in reaching those behind it, the trail turned cold. Anyhow, we started to become puzzled by the degree of accuracy of the information we were receiving, but Rome would not reveal the source. We initially thought that it was probably some kind of repentant deal, whereby a regretful former terrorist becomes informant in exchange for pardon and a new life with a new face..."

"That's what I thought, too... that it was a mafia type of deal," I interrupted.

"I went twice myself to the Viminale to ask the Italians to tell us about the informant. I explained to them that, in order to obtain more cooperation from the countries involved, we needed to provide them with some information and particularly whether there is a judicial case going on involving a witness... They perfectly know how things work at Interpol, but they still wouldn't cooperate."

"So, what did you do?" Ava asked, like a student following the argumentation of a revered professor.

"I had two options," Metaxas said. "Either drop the case altogether - and risk serious consequences - or threaten to lodge an official complaint through our board on the grounds that Italy was not complying with Interpol rules. I, of course, opted for the second option, in the hope that just the threat of an official complaint would bear its fruit.

"It took some time but my strategy worked in the end. One day, I received a call from the Archbishop of Lyon who told me that he had in his office a visitor who was eager to meet me."

"Who was it? Was it a trap?" I asked, absorbed by the story.

"Since the call came from the Archbishop personally, I knew that it was something important. And indeed it was. The visitor was an envoy from the Vatican - an itinerant Nuncio - who told me that they had been providing the information to the Italian Police all along and that their deal included that, under no circumstance, the source should be revealed."

"It's not difficult to understand why the Vatican's Curia doesn't want to appear as a suppletive to the Italian Police, especially on a subject as touchy as terrorism," I commented.

"Your analysis is correct, Mr. Haftemizan; but there is more to it. The Nuncio told me that the reason why they had insisted on so much secrecy was that, in fact, the information was coming from none other than a repenting dead terrorist who wanted to make amends and, for that purpose, had chosen to communicate through Dr. Necromonti."

"Now, I understand what Necromonti meant," I said, as my eyes lit up.

"Why Necromonti?" Ava said.

"Dr. Necromonti was a researcher working for the Vatican on paranormal, occultism and other witchcraft related subjects. He had the double advantage of being a scientist and a medium."

"He had a third advantage…" I joked. "He was working for the Holy Ghost - considering the circumstances, that was certainly very helpful."

"The Nuncio's revelations were indeed troubling," Metaxas said. "I know what you may be thinking at this time: you're thinking that we've all gone mad! That's exactly how I felt when the Nuncio told me the story. The amusing part of this is that it's because they knew the kind of reaction it would engender that they were so shy about the 'source.' Believe me; I am as far removed from religion and superstitions as one can be. As a Cartesian, if I hadn't witnessed the accuracy of the information we were getting, I wouldn't have bought a word of that 'I communicate with the dead' crap – sorry, I mean 'story.'"

"So, you are confirming that Necromonti had nothing to do with the terrorists and had not made a deal with the Police to become a repenting informant," I insisted to completely clear any subsisting doubt.

"I wish it were the case, believe me. That would have been much easier to explain and to report! Right now, I am having one of the most difficult tasks in the world trying to cover up where we were getting our information from."

94

"For sure, that's not exactly what we had learned about sources and informants during our training," Ava said.

"Whatever it is and however we perceive it, we cannot afford to drop the case. Let us not forget that this is only one part of the equation. The terrorists - plotting to commit something horrible - are absolutely real and we've got to figure out what they are up to in order to stop them. Needless to say, the credibility of the Erebus project on unconventional terrorism, that of Interpol and my own one are all on the line in this affair - not discounting the lives of thousands, perhaps millions of innocent people."

"Perhaps; but how can we make any progress if Necromonti was the only medium through whom the 'repentant spirit' was communicating now that he is dead?" I asked.

"And also," Ava added, "when I checked the files, it stated that you had the part regarding the informant; but then you sent me a message telling me that the source was Necromonti: would you have that folder now? Necromonti probably documented his sessions with the 'spirit.'"

"I don't have it," Metaxas said.

"Could you make it available to us?" Ava said.

"I don't think that it's going to be possible."

"I have all the clearances necessary to access it..."

"The issue is that there is no such file at all. It was part of our deal with the Vatican that there would not be any written records of Necromonti's interaction with the 'spirit.'"

"Has the spirit, by any chance, left a phone number where we can reach him in case of an emergency?" I dared to joke, considering our desperate situation.

Metaxas smiled. "I wish he had."

"Sir, what can you tell us about '1492'?" Ava said. "The last piece of information Necromonti gave us on his deathbed was the sequence of these four numbers: 1, 4, 9 and 2."

"I have absolutely no clue other than an educated guess, which is that they may be targeting the United States."

"That's what we thought, too."

"I have a scheduled meeting with FBI's Director, Rupert Molinero, just a few blocks away from here. And I will mention to him that he should be on the lookout," Metaxas said before adding: "It's not going to be an easy sale, considering the commitment we've made to the Holy See."

"Since Necromonti is dead, perhaps you're not bound by the same level of secrecy?" I suggested.

"We cannot afford to alienate anyone - especially, not those red-hat-wearing gentlemen-in-robe from the Vatican," Metaxas pointed out, raising his eyebrows and rolling his eyes as if to say: "tough crowd to deal with!"

"Since you mentioned that you were going to visit the FBI, I think they should definitely be aware of something, because the bad guys and their associates are already operating in here," I said.

"We are not a hundred percent sure if these events are related. At this point, all we have are assumptions."

"Perhaps, the Secretary General of Interpol is not completely attuned of everything that has happened," I said, turning to Ava who looked at me with the same stupor.

"Do not misunderstand me. As I told you earlier, I am well aware of what you've both endured and that is the main reason why I am here today. But it is my duty to caution you not to be led only by presumptions related to events that may have touched you personally. We are going to ask the authorities here to look into them - as they would do for any other criminal case. And until we hear back from them, I would urge extreme caution."

"I don't know what exactly is going on, but there is something fishy about this whole affair," I said. "I personally think that these guys are extremely well informed. They are tracking every one of our moves."

"Indeed, Sir; we are facing a bit of a paradoxical situation," Ava said, "whereby, as things stand right now, instead of us tracking the bad guys, they are the ones breathing the air behind our necks; and I can assure that this is not a pleasant sensation."

"I understand. I am urging you to use extreme prudence because I've already lost two of our most valuable assets and I don't want to lose two more."

"Understood, Sir," Ava said. "Thank you for your help. We'll keep you informed through the habitual channels."

"It was a pleasure meeting you, Mr. Haftemizan," Metaxas said, as he vigorously shook my hand.

"The pleasure is all mine," I replied.

"Good luck! We are counting on you," he concluded as we were exiting his suite.

"I don't know if it's just my impression," I commented, "but it seems to me that, towards the end of our conversation, Metaxas was a bit guarded, as if by not clearly addressing our suspicions, he was trying to tell us something."

"I sensed that, too," Ava said.

"Tragic," I commented.

"Why do you say that?" Ava asked, intrigued.

"I don't know; I felt that I had to…"

Anthrax and Red Wine

Bagram Air Base, Afghanistan

"Good evening, gentlemen! Fred, Larry," Dick greeted them as he shook hands with each man, respectively.

Fred and Larry were former Special Ops turned CIA contractors, operating on the fringes of what the law permits. His comrades in arms had dubbed Fred 'El Ladron' since he was reprimanded for his participation in some murky 'drug-for-arms' traffic during the Reagan Administration. As for Larry, he was nicknamed 'Chewbacca' because of his height, his wild beard and his unruly hair that made him resemble the popular Star Wars character.

"Good evening, Mr. Vice President."
"I apologize for the late hour, but I wanted the three of us to meet so that we can update our information about our little operation before my departure tomorrow morning. You know how these visits are short for security reasons…"
"Not a problem, Mr. Vice President," the two men said in unison.

They were sitting inside a container transformed into a 'presidential suite' of some sort, located inside one of the base's large hangars inherited from the time when the Soviets were occupying the country. A few of these units had been placed this way to host high-value visiting officials in a secure and relatively more comfortable environment.

Since the fall of the Taliban and the installation of a 'friendly government' in 2001, Dick was a frequent guest on these grounds battered by wind and covered with dust in summer and battered by the same wind and covered with snow in winter, at the heart of Afghanistan's highlands. Here, he felt a little bit like the father and the Ob/Gyn that – along with a few others – gave political birth to Hamed Karzai. He had come to check on the 'accomplishments' of his protégés and also to be close to the troops. He wanted to make them feel that he was there for them. Unlike Washington technocrats, who are often despised by those in the line of fire, Dick strived to build the kind of relationship of camaraderie that soldiers share only with those 'who've been there; who've done it.' From 'Desert Storm' to 'Enduring Freedom' to 'Iraqi Freedom,' Dick had patiently built trust with the men in khaki and he knew that he had a very strong, tightly knotted network of people he could count on for critical missions; the kind of missions that no other person, not even their direct hierarchy or the Commander in Chief would ever suspect existed.

As one can imagine, the comfort in the vice-presidential 'container suite' was somewhat Spartan. But to the two visitors, it was luxury compared to their everyday lot since they've been working in this harsh regional theatre of operation.

"Gentlemen, there is some hot coffee in the thermos, here, and the commander of the base has spoiled us with some baklavas. Help yourselves, please!"

"Thank you, Sir; a hot coffee wouldn't hurt," Fred 'El Ladron' said.

"You should really try these baklavas: they're excellent. My wife tells me to stop eating these Middle-Eastern pastries but I can't help myself."

"They sure are good, Sir," Larry 'Chewbacca' said.

"What is fascinating to me," marveled Dick, as he was licking his fingers after shoving a couple of baklavas down his throat, "is that you can find them from Morocco to right here, in Afghanistan. But there are no two countries that make them exactly the same."

"No wonder why these guys are losing it," El Ladron said.

The Vice President's cell phone rang to the tune of the Ride of the Valkyrie.

"Good evening, Dick; this is Condi."

"Good evening, Condi," Dick replied in a sleepy voice to make his interlocutor believe that he had just been awakened by her call.

"I am sorry to call you this late, but I am running into a bit of an impasse here, in Warsaw, and I need your advice."

"Not a problem. Yes, it's a little bit late here - half past midnight in Kabul - but don't mind... So, tell me; what is worrying you?"

"The Prime Minister wants to recall his troops from Iraq, advocating that they have fulfilled their duty beyond what they had promised."

"Tell the Prime minister that the Free World needs them to propagate Liberty and Democracy and yadda, yadda, yadda... you know, the usual speech...."

"I tried that line; but he says that as much as he would like to continue believing in it, opinion polls show that the Polish public resents him siding with us."

"All right; I got it: they are bargaining. Well, if that's not enough to convince them, promise them some robust economic incentives: that should do it."

"Can we afford to give them yet another package?"

"Between you and me, we don't really care because we are spending Joe Schmuck's tax money – that's how our system works," Dick replied with cynicism. "I will personally take care of it and it will be a piece of cake to pass it on the Senate floor: how do you like that, Condi?"

"To tell you the truth, I have tried the economic argument, too. But he is adamant. He says the elections are approaching and he asserts that he wouldn't have the slightest chance of winning if he doesn't pull out from Iraq."

Dick's face turned red. "What the fuck does he want? Tell those Polacks, who want to run away, that if it weren't for the CIA funneling loads of money to Solidarity, they'd still be shining Jaruzelski's boots with the thin skin of their asses today!"

"Ungrateful!" Condi said, equally disappointed.

"They owe us. They owe us big time!"

"I'll try my best. I'll use the 'carrot and the stick' approach with the hope that it will work once more. I'll keep you posted."

"Take care," concluded Dick.

"Oh, one more word before I hang up," added Condi. "Today, I got to visit the Chopin museum and then I was taken to a gourmet restaurant: it was fantastic!"

"And I guess you had a taste of their specialty: what is it called? … Oh, yes, yes, Beef Stroganoff…"

"Dick, that's a Russian specialty. I guess your area of expertise remains pastries..."

"All right, Madame Secretary; I got to go back to sleep now. I am flying early in the morning. I'll see you in Washington in a couple of days or so. "

Dick turned off his cell phone and focused on his two guests who had witnessed the conversation half-surprised, half-amused:

"We are on track, on schedule. Everyone is doing their part for the greater cause we've committed to. Harvesting time is near, my friends." Dick rubbed his hands together. "This being said; now, tell me, how are things progressing on your side? Fred, let's start with you."

"Very well, Sir. I think that, with my team, we've done a pretty good job. As part of the first phase, we have been able to disassemble the mobile launch vehicle we've acquired in Kazakhstan and transported it in pieces. We did this during a three-month period to evade any suspicion. The vehicle has been reassembled and is ready now."

"How about the missile...?"

"That's phase two, Sir; and as I am talking to you..." Fred 'El Ladron' explained, looking at his watch, "the last part of the SS-25 should have passed Hayraton at the Afghan-Uzbek border and on its way to its final destination."

"How long will it take your team to reassemble all the pieces and be ready?"

"Probably a week, but certainly not more than two weeks," Fred said with confidence.

"And for the final ingredients, we are counting on you, Larry."

"I think we are in good shape, Mr. Vice President: five million dollars goes a long way in the former Soviet Republics," 'Chewbacca' said.

"Have we gotten everything we had planned to 'spice up' things, if I may say it that way?" Dick said with a devilish smirk.

"Affirmative, Sir. I have already arranged the shipment of the Congo-Crimean Hemorrhagic Virus that we've acquired in

Tashkent to reach our base in Farah. If all goes as planned, Fred and his team should get it within forty-eight hours."

"What about the other one?" Dick asked.

"We've got it, too, Sir," Chewbacca said.

"Where is it? Did you bring it?"

"Yes, Sir; the Anthrax is in a case in the trunk of my jeep, waiting outside the base."

"How much of it?"

"Thirty pounds."

"Is it safe?"

"Yes, Sir; it's stored in three titanium canisters - designed to resist even an airplane crash. I've put the canisters in an ordinary looking case to elude any suspicion."

"I'll have someone pick it up so that it doesn't go through the security checks."

"Very well, Sir; thank you."

"All right, gentlemen; I think we've said all that needed to be said. Keep up the good work and your rewards - spiritual and moral - will be beyond your expectations," Dick said in a solemn tone as he accompanied them to the door. "And may the true spirit of Isabel and Ferdinand be with you."

"Good night, Sir," Fred and Larry said, in unison once again.

Dick smiled. "Gentlemen, one last detail that I almost forgot to mention. Your Bahamian bank accounts have been provisioned with half the total amount I had promised you: I am a man of my word."

"I never had a doubt, Sir," Fred 'El Ladron' said.

"*Magnifico*!" Larry 'Chewbacca' said.

The faces of the two men beamed with satisfaction. Dick deliberately released this piece of information at the last possible moment to enhance the theatrical effect. 'Chewbacca' and 'El Ladron' were so overwhelmed that they could not suppress their urge for mimicking a little victory dance in front of the Vice President.

For the two men, money was perhaps the first motivation to engage in such a hazardous operation, but their love of risk was just behind it. Dick wanted to ensure that money would be so large a bait - and palpable – that whenever a doubt would arise in their minds about the righteousness of what they were doing, the money argument would win over the debate without an ounce of doubt. And indeed, a million dollars was a considerable incentive for these two guys with many unpaid debts and as many unachieved dreams awaiting to be fulfilled.

As for the ideological argument - the 'unfinished Reconquista' line preached by the VP and his circle of conspirators – 'El Ladron' and 'Chewbacca' were not really able to gauge the validity of it from a variety of angles or in-depth. But one aspect of that plan struck a cord with them: it would put an end to the perpetual conflict of the Middle East, which they had witnessed first-hand. They sincerely believed that America's intervention and take-over would appease the region.

Green Zone, Baghdad

The Vice-President sat at the corner of a large room in one of Saddam Hussein's former presidential palaces. The edifice has been damaged by the initial assault and the scars from the American bombings were visible from the outside; inside, most of the ceremonial rooms were intact. This palace, with its classical European architectural style, the marble on the floor, the Corinthian columns, the detailed ornaments on the walls and the high ceilings, breathed an air of majesty. The furniture was somewhat damaged by US soldiers when they first invested the place, but at least this one, unlike some other Government buildings, did not undergo looting.

Dick sat alone, a cigar in one hand and a glass of Bordeaux in the other. His doctor had advised him – begged him, rather - to stop smoking and start drinking red wine because of his heart. It would seem that he listened - at least, to fifty per cent of his doctor's advice.

The space inside the room, the appeasing harmony of the architecture and the vision of Bruegel's Babylon revisited by some kitsch local artist plunged Dick into some reverie, quickly turning into an involuntary afternoon siesta.

"Sir, …hum, hum… Sir, Mr. Vice President!" yelled the officer in a voice that went crescendo in volume to make his presence noticed.
"Yes, what is it?" Dick said.
"Sir, your visitor - Colonel Bernardino – is here: should I let him in?" the officer asked, a bit embarrassed to find the Vice President napping.
"Yes, sure; let him in," Dick said, as he attempted to regain his senses.

A man in military fatigues, covered with dust, an attaché case in his hand and the recognizable antenna of a satellite phone hanging out of his shirt pocket, walked straight to Dick and shook his hand first and then embraced him.

"Bernie, old buddy; nice to see you again!"
"How long has it been?" Bernie said.
"Almost six months. You've lost a lot of weight!"

"I shall remind you that I've put my ass on the line for you, scouring every inch of that hellish Iraqi desert, working to set up 'you know what...'"

"Oh, yeah; that thing..." Dick said, deliberately dismissive, as if he were referring to some insignificant matter.

"Well, I can tell you that 'that thing' is ready and all we need now is the other 'thing.'"

"We can talk freely here; there is no risk," Dick said.

"All right... Good. We've managed to recuperate fifteen Al-Abbas missiles and set them up to point to the targets."

"So, where exactly have you set up the base?"

"It's in the Western most corner of the Anbar Province, very close to the Syrian border and not very far away from the Jordanian one: we figured that it would be the ideal location."

"Have you also taken the necessary precautions?"

"Sure; but let me tell you that with the kind of mess going on in this country at this time, nobody knows who is doing what and why...The location is an abandoned air-base that was partially destroyed during Desert Storm and was never repaired because it was in the 'no fly zone.' As for our cover, we are officially crisscrossing the area in search of WMDs and high-value terrorist ring leaders - if we ever come across any of them..."

"That's pretty solid," Dick said.

"When I said that you could trust me on this assignment, I meant that you could count on me to conduct a neat operation all the way to the last little detail."

"That's why you're on the President's 'A' list. Let me ask you this: how did you get the missiles to your base, or is it that they were already there?"

"No, there weren't any missiles there. In the course of the past several months, as part of our mission, we've taken possession of missiles from different locations and moved them to a central depot, where they are to be kept in waiting for the

Congress to fund their destruction. We would cook up the counts so that every time one or two vectors were not included in the inventory and we would quietly take them to our base – unnoticed."

"Brilliant. Hats off!"

"In the meanwhile, we maintain them and we keep them away from indiscreet eyes. Apart from my team, nobody has access to that site."

Suddenly, the bang from a big detonation resonated and shook the room. Dick stiffened as if he were paralyzed.

"It's nothing…" Bernie said.

"What do you mean: 'it's nothing'?"

"I mean that it's nothing unusual. It happens all the time here. Whatever it was, it exploded a good distance away from here."

"But it shook me in my bones; I thought they had hit the building. What the fuck do these people want? We've freed them from a brutal dictator and given them control over their destiny, yet these ungrateful bastards are siding with the terrorists against us."

"Let's just say that you and I are sitting in the exact same palace from where Saddam Hussein used to rule the lives of the Iraqis… You and the President have got to pay some attention on how you are being perceived in this part of the world if you want to win them over."

"There is no disagreement between you and me on this," Dick said, seizing the opportunity to fall back on his feet. "This is exactly why we have this plan. Once we have accomplished what we want to do, the Arabs won't be able to accuse us anymore of favoring the Israelis. They'll understand that we are treating them and the Israelis equally."

"You mean equally bad…"

Dick acted offended. "That's not what I meant."

Both men guffawed.

"Let us get back to our business," Dick said, trying to suppress his laughter. "I've got two bits of good news for you - actually three."

"I am always in favor of good news."

"The first half of the money we had promised you has been wired to your designated off-shore account. Second, I've brought you thirty pounds of Anthrax... and two bottles of your favorite wine: Saint-Emilion 1982."

Bernie smiled. "Are you serious? How did you remember the Saint-Emilion? Anthrax and red wine: that's a deadly association!"

"Do you see the box over there?" Dick said.

"Where did you get it from, you old rascal: Fort Detrick?" Bernie said.

"The Internet, like the wine... To be serious, it's coming from a former Soviet lab."

"You were able to get me in a matter of days what we haven't been able to find in more than six months in this damned country?"

"I can't say that it was easy. It took our guys several months to secure the channels and complete the transaction. What matters is that now you've got it. I think it's going to be fantastic."

"I think that it's going to be rather tragic," Bernie said with a sad voice, realizing that, now that they have the Anthrax, the day he'll be pushing the button and causing the tragic death of thousands of people is near and very real...

Assem Akram

The Nuncio

Florence, Italy

We traveled to Rome, then to Florence to see the Nuncio who had negotiated with Interpol the conditions of Dr. Necromonti's cooperation.

It took some negotiating skills and Metaxas' personal intervention to make the encounter possible. At first, the Vatican invoked its habitual – almost obsessive-compulsive – preference for absolute discretion to reject any request for a meeting. Then, perhaps weighing what its non-cooperation could cost in terms of human lives, as well as bad press if it came to be known that it knew something but didn't share it with others, the Holy See agreed. The Nuncio's name was Father Emilio Ungari.

At first, we were told to go to Rome and visit him in the Vatican's Curia. But once there, we were told that Father Ungari had left for Florence due to a family emergency. Fortunately for us, he had left a note telling us that if we really wanted to see him, we should travel to Florence and meet up with him there. Did he think that we negotiated laboriously for days to get the 'benediction' and then traveled across the Atlantic to say: "Oh, well; if he is not in Rome then we are going back home." He probably was our only chance to get some real information on what Necromonti knew but didn't find the time to tell us. So, we would follow Father Ungari to Heaven or Hell.

Father Emilio Ungari had accepted to receive us at his family home, on a hilltop overlooking the city of Florence, precisely in the locality of Fiesole. The house was ideally located on a large piazza with direct view over the entire city, including its famous Duomo. The beautiful morning sun made the entire Tuscan urban scenery encased in a valley look picture perfect.

Though it's not my first trip to Italy, it's a new discovery every time. I had the opportunity in the past to make short trips to Rome and Milan to participate in some tedious seminars and conferences, but I have never been able to travel for pleasure and take the time to thoroughly visit and enjoy the wealth of architectural marvels - let alone the beautiful girls - this land has to offer.

Since I mentioned the Italian girls, and Italy being a land of lands where each of its regions' female population has a distinct reputation, it reminds me of a short trip we made some years back to Venice from Milan, where we were participating at a week-long academic seminar: it was summertime and what I found striking was that, in the museums, the guardians were mostly young attractive girls. So much so that I did not know what to look at first: the paintings on the walls or the lively pieces of human harmony sitting at the corner of each room.

One thought leading to another, since I referred to the word 'harmony' – and that's the point I wanted to make – what I noticed was that, as beautiful and as neatly prepped these Venetian girls were, most of them had large feet. I am sure that those who study the evolution of human morphology in relation to its environment in space and in time might find this observation of some interest...

Father Ungari ushered us into the living room. He told us that his father and his younger sister were living in this ancestral home. Father Emilio Ungari was younger than I expected: he may have just reached the age of thirty-five: tall, even very tall, short hair, dressed in all-black with a rosary wrapped around his right hand and wrist.

"Thank you for agreeing to receive us despite the initial reticence," I started off saying.

"I should add," Ava said, "that you were gracious to do so despite the family emergency you are experiencing."

"I apologize that I forgot to mention that," I added, sincerely sorry to have been forgetful of that important detail. "We are by here twice as grateful to you! It goes without saying that we hope that the matter that drew you here was nothing serious."

"You are very welcome and thank you for your concern," Father Ungari said. "We have had a death in the family and you know how it is… that's the time you need those close to you to be around you."

"Yes, we know what you mean," I replied. "Our sympathy is with you."

"Thank you," Father Ungari said, bowing his head in sorrow.

I now realized that from his sister's demeanor, who opened the door, to Ungari and the atmosphere inside the house, everyone and every object seemed to be grieving the loss. Out of respect for their privacy, neither of us dared to ask whose loss they were mourning.

The room was a nice mixture of antique and modern furniture, including some typical pieces from the late sixties and early seventies. On the walls, there were some Christian memorabilia and insignia - one wouldn't have expected less from a family that had a priest in its midst. But also, hanging here and there, some autographed drawings showing well-known Italian actors such as Alberto Sordi, Marcello Mastroiani, or Vittorio Gassman - at least, the ones I was able to recognize.

"These portraits..." I dared to comment, pointing at one of them, "they must be very valuable."

"Indeed they are. My mother - God bless her soul - worked for many years as a costume designer at Cinecitta."

"I am sorry she passed away," I said, thinking that she was the one that had just died.

"My mother left us many years ago. Since then, my father has been reluctant to change the slightest little thing in the way the living room is arranged. For me, of course, it is not as difficult, because I live in Rome; but for my sister, who spends three hundred sixty-five days a year here, it's much harder."

Ava nodded. "I understand exactly what you mean. I went through the same kind of process after my father died. Then, one day, I decided that my life was turning sclerotic and that I needed to move out."

"If it weren't for my work, I wouldn't have left them alone," the priest said. "You know, for us, family is very important. Family is everything."

"Father, we really feel that we are two complete imbeciles, disturbing you in the privacy of your family home at such an importune time," I apologized.

"Don't worry; it will pass... What we have to discuss is beyond personal contingencies, no matter how painful they may be. If you allow me, I am going to get us some coffee: that will put us in the mood."

"Sure, thank you; we'd love some," I said.

"Did you notice?" Ava whispered as soon as our host left the room.

"What?" I responded in the same low voice.

"The resemblance!" she said, while gesticulating to make me understand that she was referring to Father Ungari.

"Resemblance to what, to whom...?" I asked a bit exasperated by her mute gesticulations.

"You are decidedly slow," Ava said, unnerved by my stubborn incomprehension. "Ungari, Necromonti... Necromonti, Ungari: can't you see how they resemble one another?"

"Oh, yes; you are right," I said, as I finally got to her point. "Excellent observation; although I think it's probably just a coincidence. All Italians may look the same to you..."

"Perhaps, but let us ask him?"

"I think it would be inappropriate."

"What would be 'inappropriate'?" Father Ungari said, after hearing the last part of my response to Ava.

"Oh, nothing... We were talking about something totally unrelated," I said.

Ava gave her best-wicked smile. "Mr. Haftemizan had noticed how much you resembled the late Dr. Necromonti, but he didn't know how to formulate it without offending you."

"Not exactly..." I tried to interject, looking at Ava in awe of her 'in your face' attitude.

"As somebody said once, there are no stupid questions; there are only stupid responses. Benvenisto was my brother: we were twins."

That's another Hiroshima! Ava and I stared at each other with stupefaction. Ungari pulled a picture from the family album showing both brothers in happier times: they undoubtedly were twins. The living room was filled with a smell of old wooden furniture.

"If I may ask," Ava said, "If you are twin brothers, how come your last names are different?"

"When we agreed that Benvenisto would collaborate on a temporary basis with Erebus, we thought it would be best to protect his real identity."

"I understand," I commented. "Besides, by doing so, you were preventing his name to be traced to the Vatican."

"It is not unreasonable to think of it that way, too," Father Emilio Ungari acknowledged in a circumlocution not unusual in the language spoken by the hierarchs at the Curia, trained to be masterful in the art of dialectic in a way not so dissimilar to what agile Marxist ideologues were able to do and - much closer to today's realities - what lawyers excel in.

"Father Ungari," Ava said, "We have come here in search of answers. Your late brother was able to give us some hints, but it wasn't enough. We need your help."

"We had a good start though..." I dared to interject, tongue in cheek.

"Benvenisto, God bless his soul, was a genius. At the age..."

"...Heck, yes, he was a genius!" Ungari's father suddenly burst into the room with a photo album in his hand, crying. "They've killed my son; they've murdered him... *Assasino, assasino!*"

"Father, how many times have I told you not to listen at the door? Misplaced curiosity is a sin," Ungari said.

"I don't care. If I go to Hell, at least I'll meet them there to make them suffer. They've killed my son... *Il mio figlio e morto!*"

"Dad, you are cursing and you are disturbing my guests. Please, leave! We have some serious business to take care of.

These honorable people have not traveled from so far to hear your complaints: please leave us now," Ungari said, seizing his father by the shoulders.

"I have to tell them... They have ruined our lives. Do you see these pictures?" he said, pointing at some photos from the album. "This one shows Emilio and Benvenisto, at the age of ten, giving a piano recital on television. Here they are at the age of fourteen – do you realize...fourteen - with Prime Minister Andreotti, who is congratulating them for being the youngest ones to get the baccalaureate in the entire peninsula."

"Dad, I am begging you; please, leave! You are making a fool of yourself..."

"It's all right; we understand your father's grievance," I said. "For the couple of times I had seen Benvenisto, he came across as a man of integrity and a very affable, knowledgeable person: we miss him already."

"So, you knew him?" his father asked.

"Regrettably, not well enough," I replied.

"Find his murderers, for the love of Mary!"

"I can promise you that we'll do our best," Ava said. "And I can tell you that an investigation is already under way."

Ava's words appeased the old man's revolt. He stopped weeping and left the room, tightly holding the album in his hand. He was obviously in need of some consoling, the kind that perhaps his own children could not provide.

"I sincerely apologize for this incident. It was not meant to happen," Father Emilio Ungari said.

Ava shrugged. "You don't have to apologize; he is going through a pretty painful time. We understand that."

"About this whole affair, the truth is," Ungari said, "that there never was communication with a dead man and my brother was not a specialist of paranormal phenomena or a medium."

That was another Hiroshima. Ungari's statement came as a shocker to us. Ava and I looked at each other, baffled.

"Wow!" I said. "What's next? Perhaps you are going to tell us that you are not a priest working for the Vatican, but you are an undercover cop working in the Curia because you like cross-dressing?"

"In the abyss I am right now, Mr. Haftemizan. I wish what you are saying were true! The truth is that Benvenisto was indeed my brother and that I got him involved in this story... Now, I can only blame myself for his death."

"Could you, please, shed some light for us?" I asked. "Because, frankly, we're lost... At least, I am lost."

"The source is a very well-connected person in Washington," Ungari started to tell us. "I had befriended him some years back when he came to Florence to study Italian culture through a program run here by the John Hopkins University. He was staying in a room rented to the University by my father – he's been doing this since the passing of my mother to add some butter in the everyday pasta, if you will.

"Our friendship developed throughout the years and, every summer since then, he spends some time here, bringing his little family along now that he's got one. I should stress that he is from a wealthy family and that his father has close business and personal ties with the present White House occupants.

"One day, my friend called me at work and asked me if I was planning on spending the weekend in Florence with the family? And as I said yes, he told me that he was on a business trip and that he would drop by to say hello. He was sitting exactly where you are sitting right now when he told me that he may have uncovered an unbelievable plot, but that he would only tell me about it if I could give him the assurance that he would be covered by the same type of discretionary privilege as someone going to a confessional would receive. As a friend and as a catholic priest, I could not refuse him.

"He told me that while going through the financial statements of his father - for whom he works - he had noticed several very large cash withdrawals from various accounts at home and abroad. He did not pay attention to it otherwise until, one day, he saw his father – who was not aware that his son was there at that moment - gave a bag loaded with cash to a man he did not know. At first, he thought that maybe the money was for one of those 'special' political contributions that he made from time to time. But then, when he heard them saying goodbye using a rather uncommon farewell - 'may the true spirit of Ferdinand and Isabel be with you' - he understood that something fishy was going on.

"Later that day, he confronted his father, with whom he had a very close relationship. Upon his son's insistence, the father finally gave in and told him what he was involved with – at least, from what he knew of it - presenting it as a 'philanthropic' project aimed at putting an end to the endemic violence in the Middle-East.

"It didn't take him long to understand that his father had been lured into something that, based on the type of secrecy and unofficial proceedings involving high officials surrounding it, looked highly suspicious. Armed with that piece of information and a few details, because he knew that I was involved with the diplomacy of the Vatican and because he trusted me, he came to see me and asked me to do something about it, as long his identity and that of his father remained undisclosed."

"Which is easily understandable," I said. "He didn't want to appear as betraying his father and, at the same time, he didn't want his father to go through any trouble - which could cost him his life, based on what those people are capable of."

"Did he, or his father, reveal the name of the person who got him involved in the first place?" Ava asked.

"No, he didn't tell me. Our understanding was that if he were to reveal that vital piece of information, it would immediately put him at risk of being tracked and he would more than likely pay the price with his life."

"So, how did your brother get dragged into this?" I asked.

"Well, because of the particular nature of the issue and all the perquisites outlined by my friend, I could not go to the Police myself. Besides, my position at the Curia would have made it delicate. After much brainstorming and the benediction of my superiors in Rome, we pulled together this little stratagem by which we used Benvenisto – God bless his soul."

"And he became the smoke-screen," I commented.

"He was a brave and deeply loving human being, always enraged by inequality and injustice. So, when I suggested the idea to him, he jumped in right away, without the slightest hesitation and... now, how I regret to have involved him in this... my dear brother."

"We understand how difficult it must be for you," Ava said. "But if it can be of any help to you, the day they were assassinated, I was there to protect them and I lamentably failed!"

"This means that it was meant to be: *fatalitas*," Ungari said with hopelessness.

"*Maktoub*, as Arabs would put it," I added.

"Yes, perhaps; we have to concede that we are not much in this world," Ungari commented.

120

"We thought that we had an invincible plan with so many layers that it would be very difficult for anyone to uncover the whistle-blower: my friend was passing to me whatever information he was able to obtain surreptitiously from his father's dealings; I would then pass on the tip to the fake 'Dr. Necromonti,' who would pretend to have received it from a 'spirit'; he would then communicate it to the *Carabinieri*, who would share it with Interpol."

"It's indeed very smart... even very alembicated in conception," I remarked.

"But on Interpol's insistence, we had to agree to have 'Dr. Necromonti' collaborate directly with them, exposing Benvenisto unreasonably."

"I apologize on behalf of Interpol," Ava said, feeling the guilt on behalf of her organization. "Had we known..."

"You don't need to apologize. But then I should tell that my brother enjoyed it. He wanted to do it. He felt personally concerned by the plot and wanted to do whatever he could to uncover it and stop it."

"Did he tell you anything specific? Did he - or do you - have any thoughts as to what's cooking?" I asked.

"Nothing specific...that's why they went to find you to help figure it all out."

I felt the jab directed at me when he said that; but considering the circumstances, I decided to let it die.

"One thing is certain," I said. "Based on what we know – i.e. big money, big guys in Washington, the special hand-shake referring to Ferdinand and Isabel, and not discounting their so far fruitful quest for such cute bio-weapons as the Congo-Crimean Hemorrhagic Fever or Anthrax - if any action is initiated, it's more than likely originating from the West to impact the East and not vice-versa."

"I agree with you," Ungari said.

"If we could get your friend to talk and tell us who 'recruited' his father and what exactly he had told him on how they are planning to 'pacify' the Middle East, then we would be making a decisive leap forward."

"You're putting me in a very delicate situation..." the priest said.

"I know, Father; but I don't think we have much of a choice at this point."

"It's an issue of conscience as much as one of professional ethics for me," Ungari said.

"I can understand that," I conceded, "but you have to put into the equation that many innocent souls may perish as a result of our failure to foil whatever crazy plot is brewing."

"All right; I'll do my best. I'll talk to my friend. I hope he'll understand."

"That's the kind of attitude I like!" I said. "We are taking you with us: get packed and get your passport."

"Hold on; I can't leave just like that!"

"Don't you worry; it's for a good cause. You'll call your boss from the airport.... once we've passed the check-in."

The Fourth Rome

White House, Washington DC

"Gentlemen, I can see that you've all made it and I appreciate that," the President said. "Let us start with a prayer, shall we: Dear Lord, we thank you for your kindness for you have blessed us as a Nation, as a country, as a group. We are here gathered today to thank you for you have chosen us to accomplish the extraordinary task of spreading the word of Jesus and make your peace shine again over the Holy Land. Lord, you have chosen us to make of this city – Washington - the Fourth Rome to pursue your son's evangelical mission. Help us to be truthful to your word and to prevail for your greatest glory."

"So help us God!" the participants, sitting at the conference table, said in unison.

"May the true spirit of Isabel and Ferdinand be with you, Mr. President," said Dick.

"Thank you. Now, let us start our briefing," the President said.

"Certainly, Mr. President. I shall remind everyone that our discussion here shall remain entirely off the record: no pen, no paper. If you need to remember something, use your memory cells and don't count on anyone to corroborate your statements outside of this room."

Beside the President and the VP, there were half a dozen people present in the room, constituting the core, the inner circle of operation '1492.'

"First of all, on behalf of the President and myself, I would like to congratulate all of you on an outstanding job…" Dick began to utter before being interrupted by the President.

"Hold on, Dick; you are telling my part here!" the President joked, causing laughter among the small audience. "You'll do the explanation, so let me take care of the congratulations."

Dick smiled. "I am sorry, Mr. President; I didn't realize I was trespassing my boundaries."

"In all seriousness, you've all done a terrific job so far, which puts us only inches away from the realization of our ultimate goal. I am very proud of you. Dick will give you some insights on the details of the plan in a few minutes.

"Right now, let me tell you this, gentlemen: most of you present here know one another but, more than likely, ignored everything of others' involvement in this highly secret operation until this moment - if not, then we have a serious problem on our hands!"

Some in the attendance laughed.

"We have reached a point of no return in our commitment. If all goes as planned, we will be celebrated *Urbis et Orbis*, in this world as in the next one, as saviors, as true Christians who have heard the word of Jesus and, as his devoted disciples, have taken upon themselves to finish spreading it in order to bring about the implementation of the *Pax Universalis*.

"The key to achieving this ultimate goal and accomplishing our mission on earth lays with the stabilization of the Holy Land, which can only be achieved by us, the mightiest power this earth has ever known. It is our mission to bring back that sacred land under the wing of Christianity.

"For decades, we have tried to bring to terms Arabs and Hebrews in order for them to live in harmony on the land that witnessed the birth of Jesus, but all in vain! We've allocated resources, we've put efforts, we've sacrificed lives so that these cousins, these Semitic tribes of yesterday, can make peace and live in harmony as nations of today, without success.

"The Good Lord has bestowed this extraordinary task upon us, Americans, ever since in 1492 Columbus discovered this land the same year Ferdinand and Isabel finished the Reconquista, throwing the last Arab Muslims out of Christian Spain. That year, the flame was passed on from Spain to America to bring to completion the Reconquista all the way to the Holy Land. For all these centuries, the flame was dormant but alive; now is the time to revive it."

As soon as the President finished his allocution, the men who had been listening intently, stood up and clapped exuberantly to manifest their approval. Dick was bedazzled by the oratorical skills '43' had just demonstrated. Although his intervention was carefully scripted, '43' himself could not believe how good he had been this time, as if he had been transported by what he had to say, not even mispronouncing a single word, not even the Latin ones.

"I completely forgot," the President said. "I have to make an important satellite appearance. I leave you with Dick for the continuation. I'll be back in a *momentito* – see, how I am improving my Spanish," he said, as he left the room promptly.

The President's sortie was a theatrical arrangement set up earlier between the two men. He did not have anything specific scheduled, but they had agreed that it would not be very clever to involve him in the part of their discussions where details on how war would be provoked were going to be outlined. The President would reappear following the discussion of the conspiracy's 'technical' and other dirty little details.

"All right, gentlemen," Dick said, "here is the plan – but before I start, I am inviting you to taste these delicious little baklavas I have specially brought for you from Baghdad. Please, help yourselves and enjoy!

"We are going to provoke a war that would constitute the pretext for our intervention. Unfortunately, this is the only solution. As things stand right now, most if not all of the countries in the region are either so absorbed dealing with their internal problems or militarily so backward that it is almost impossible to expect any of them to have the guts to attack Israel any time soon. If we were to wait for them to give us a reason to intervene and put our plan to work, we may wait indefinitely. This is why we've come up with the idea of provoking the war, which has the great advantage of enabling us to intervene on our terms and on our timetable.

"In our scenario, we are targeting Israel in a converging and simultaneous attack from two directions, which should prompt Tsahal to retaliate immediately against the aggressors. At which point, we will intervene militarily to impose a cessation of hostilities and – officially, to avoid a major international conflict. And, for this effort, we will receive the benediction of the UN and that of the International community.

"On D-Day, we'll have one SS-25 launched from Western Afghanistan, loaded with a deadly biological load carrying the Congo-Crimean Hemorrhagic Fever. And, calculated to impact simultaneously on the Israeli soil, we'll launch fifteen Al-Abbas missiles from Western Iraq, some of them carrying Anthrax.

"As you can easily guess, this is going to have a very large psychological as well as real physical impact on the populations targeted, even though in terms of actual casualties, the number will proportionally be low immediately after the attack - perhaps in the hundreds. But in the following days, as the organisms complete their incubation period, we will probably have tens of thousands of additional casualties, which will make our presence even more required and therefore, legitimized."

"If we attack Israel from Afghanistan and Iraq, which we occupy and are *de facto* our allies," asked one attendant, "how would it be seen as credible?"

"You've raised a very good point here," Dick said. "We have set up our launch sites in a very astute manner: in Afghanistan, it's very close to the Iranian border and in Iraq, it's just miles away from the Syrian frontier, making it appear as though the attacks are coming from Iran and Syria. Besides, bear in mind that the first line of defense of the Israelis are the Patriot systems we've provided to them..."

"Very ingenuous!" commented another attendant. "The Patriots can only detect incoming missiles at about one hundred and fifty miles of their approach, so Israel won't figure out with exactitude the point of origin... only the direction from which they are coming."

"Exactly; and for that piece of information, they would have to rely on our satellite intelligence, which we can give them with some delay and put the blame of the attack on some dangerous terrorists of the Al-Qaeda variety. By then, it would be too late to prevent the first confrontation between them."

"This is indeed very clever, Mr. Vice President; but how about our men? Won't they be exposed to the contamination?"

"Our troops have all the equipment necessary to face this kind of situation. Besides, one or two generals, whom I've talked to, have told me that they would welcome a situation where they can put to the test their ability to cope with a chemical or bio attack. They had hoped to do it in Iraq, but it did not happen."

"Isn't there a risk that the Anthrax will be traced back to Fort Detrick?"

"No, I can guarantee you that it won't happen," Dick said.

"You seem pretty confident about it…"

"Yes, I am."

"How so, if I may ask?"

"Simply because it's a different one; we've obtained this one from a former Soviet lab."

"You'll never stop to amaze us, Dick!"

"Do we have the capability," asked yet another one, "to contain the diseases we are instilling over there? Because if everyone has to wear those suffocating protective gears and masks, I can guarantee that it will have a pretty negative effect on the morale of our troops."

"He is right," added another one. "And you know how hot it can get in those places…"

"We have a vaccine for the Anthrax and an antidote – though in limited supply - for the Congo-Crimean Fever."

"…Which means that our men will only need to wear masks and latex gloves: is this correct?"

"Absolutely; at least, until we are done cordoning off the areas affected by the impacts and put in quarantine those infected. Then those areas will need to be sanitized. The troops busy in other capacities will be risk-free - at least, as much as a war situation permits."

"Dick - although I have an idea about the 'why' - I would like you to tell us why we are assuming that the Patriots will not pulverize all the vectors?"

"First of all, the *casus belli* for the Israelis will be the attack itself, not its success or even less its aftermath. Israel's aviation will take off only minutes after the first Patriot has detected the missiles on its radar and we can be assured that, in less than a couple of hours, they will be striking objectives in Iran and Syria. If they ask us our consent as an ally, we will tell them that, whereas we cannot officially approve of any retaliation without determining clearly who the culprits are, unofficially, we cannot oppose Israel's right to self-defense.

"Second, our Patriots have proven not to be that efficient. During Desert Storm, they had a number of misses. Even with the upgrades and the improvements since then, the system retains weaknesses. This is why we will be concentrating our salvo on one area, in synchrony, to confuse the Patriots' detection system."

"Brilliant!"

"Sheer genius!"

"Remember, gentlemen, all we need is the initial spark to get rolling."

"That's like being a pyromaniac fireman," one said with a smile, realizing how devilish the entire plan was.

The meeting ended with some last exchanges on the different hypotheses and eventualities and how to deal with them.

"Gentlemen," the President said, having just returned. "I am sure Dick has answered all your questions and you know now what is expected of you. I expect great things from great men; so should you. Our great destiny lies ahead of us. God bless you all!"

A cellular phone rang to the tune of the 'Macarena,' drawing the attention of everyone in the room, amused by the easily recognizable melody.

"Whose phone is it?" asked one.

"Oh, it's my personal cell phone," the President said. "The girls have downloaded this ring-tone for me: I kinda like it: it's fun; it's dynamic and it reminds me of my hay days," he added with a wink.

"Nostalgia, Mr. President," one commented.

"No, it's called the 'Macarena.'"

"May the true spirit of Isabel and Ferdinand be with you," the Vice President said.

"Amen," '43' added emphatically, as the participants filed out of the room.

"Mr. President, the Secretary of State is on line two," the assistant said.

"I am busy right now. Tell her that I am in an important meeting and that I'll call her back later."

"She insists, Mr. President."

At that point, '43' looked toward Dick to seek his approval; the latter nodded with exasperation.

"Hello, Condi; are you enjoying your trip in Italy? How do you like my good friend Berlusconi? Is he a stand-up guy or what?"

"Mr. President, I am afraid the atmosphere has changed here. Berlusconi faces a tough challenge from the opposition."

"Maybe I can help him? Perhaps, I can go there and tell the Italian public how much Berlusconi has been helpful by sending his troops to Iraq and by staying the course in the fight against Evil."

"I will tell him, Mr. President. But I think that, considering the way things have shifted on the Italian scene, it may not help him all that much. He is facing a difficult election ahead and, on the contrary, he is trying to…"

"What is he trying to do?"

"He is trying to distance himself from us?"

"If he is doing some political maneuvering, it's okay by me – we have all done that – as long as his troops stay with us in Iraq."

"I am afraid, Mr. President, that he is hinting to a pullout."

"He can't do that to me!" said '43,' offended and resenting it as a personal betrayal.

"I think there are career considerations that are heavily coming to play here," Condi said. "Besides, as you may well know, he is embattled in some old judicial cases that are haunting him. And if he no longer is an elected official, he becomes prosecutable: this is something that he certainly doesn't want to happen."

"No wonder why Rome has lost the battle for Christianity!"

"May I, Mr. President?" whispered Dick, who was still standing there and growing impatient.

"Sure; go ahead," '43' said as he passed the phone to the Vice President.

"Hello, Condi; this is Dick."

"Hello, Dick; how are you?"

"Fairly good, thanks for asking. Listen! Tell that fucking suntanned Macaroni bastard that he owes us big time; that if it weren't for us, they'd still be polishing Mussolini's boots with the thin skin of their fat asses!"

"Dick is right; they owe us big time!" '43' said, taking heart at his Vice President's argument.

"Their military sucks anyway," Dick added.

"When I think that I invited this guy to Crawford and that Laura prepared lasagna for him...Ungrateful!" '43' said with indignation.

"I'll try my best, Mr. President; and I'll keep you informed as to whether I am able to reverse a course, which I am afraid may be inalterable."

"I know you can do it, Condi. I trust you. And if they really want to weasel their way out of the coalition, go to neighboring Monaco and try to bring those guys in," '43' said.

"Excellent idea, Mr. President," Dick said. "They can't refuse: these guys owe us big time."

"Dick is right," '43' said. "Remind me what exactly we did for them?"

"We gave them Grace Kelly, Mr. President," Dick said with assurance.

"Oh, yes... All right... Was she a pro athlete that we traded?"

"Of some sort, Mr. President," Dick said, not wanting his boss to look bad.

"All right, 'Brown Sugar,' bye, now! ...And remember to go easy on the minestrone..."

Cabin Pressure

In the airplane

We took off from the à-propos named Amerigo Vespucci airport, with additional luggage: Father Emilio Ungari, whom we had almost forced to accompany us. Our flight was from Florence to Milan and on to Washington. The Al Italia plane was not overly packed, but its configuration was made for maximum occupancy, which means that there was really not much legroom for us, poor passengers. Ungari sat about five rows behind us.

As the plane prepared for take-off, I fell asleep only to reemerge minutes later. I should tell you that, for some odd reason, perhaps related to variation in air pressure, I fall asleep in a matter of seconds at take-off and at landing. And to be honest, I even look forward to it because it's a short but strangely pleasing moment of complete black out. Now that I think about it, this could well be an unconsciously self-provoked snooze to avoid the annoyance of a flight's two worst moments.

"Sir… Sir! What would you like: tea or coffee?" the flight attendant asked as I was suddenly coming back to my senses.
"I'll have some coffee; I definitely need to wake up."

"That was amazing," Ava said, looking at me as if I were a curiosity. "I was talking to you and in a quarter of a second you dozed-off: was I so boring?"

"Oh, I am sorry; I didn't realize."

"I guess you're taking one of those medicines to avoid becoming sick…"

"I used to - many years ago… Now, I don't have to because my body has come up with its own preventive measure."

"What do you mean?"

"Exactly what you saw…"

"Sure," Ava said with incredulity.

Ava set to review the notes she had taken from the conversation with Ungari and update her files on her laptop while reviewing her e-mail: that's what I call multi-tasking. Meanwhile, I decided to watch a movie to kill time - transatlantic flights are so tedious. All the movies for selection were old. I settled for one of the 'Matrix' sequels, but quickly turned it off: I had forgotten how insipid this movie was. Instead, I decided to watch the Marx Brothers' 'Room Service.' These old classics are still good entertainment, but after a few minutes of it dubbed in Italian, I got tired and turned it off. I think the issue was not with the movies but with me. I was tired and the constant background noise of the engines made it hard to focus on anything.

"By the way," I asked Ava, "did you ever watch that movie with Vittorio Gassman where he was playing the double role of a normal guy and that of an insane uncle sequestrated in a room?"

"I don't believe I have. I haven't watched many Italian movies."

"Once I remember the name, I'll let you know; you really have to watch it."

"Sure."

"How about 'Dark Eyes' with Marcello Mastroiani...?" Just as I asked her whether she had seen the film, I was taken by laughter remembering – although with not much accuracy - some of the scenes where Mastroiani was trying to seduce some lady in a spa and, for that purpose, he was using an arsenal of charming ruses. There was a scene in particular where Mastroiani, who had been faking a leg injury to draw the attention of the lady he was courting, ran like everyone else in the panic following a light earth jolt. The lady saw him and asked him how come he was able to walk again with such ease? Mastroiani responded with aplomb that the earthquake had miraculously healed his leg...

"No, I haven't either," Ava replied, feeling guilty for not being more versed in this type of cinephilia.

"Rent it; you won't regret it," I suggested. "Or, maybe, I'll rent it and I'll lend it to you... I feel like seeing it again after so many years."

"All right, that's a deal."

"Perhaps, we can do a 'dinner and a movie' kind of deal?" I dropped in, just to see how she would react.

"I'll bring the dessert," Ava replied casually.

A little further into the flight, I thought it would be nice to visit Father Ungari in the back where he was sitting. Of everyone involved, he has been the worst hit by the series of unfortunate events that lead to the death of his twin brother; and he has been the one who has taken personal, professional and ethical risks in order to uncover the plot.

"Do you mind, Father, if I sit here?"

"Not at all, please, you're most welcome!" Ungari said. "...And if you could call me Emilio, you would honor me."

"The honor would be mine, Emilio," I replied, quite happy to drop the formalities. "So, how are things? Pretty unsavory, I guess."

"You've guessed right. No matter how I try to convince myself, mixing reason and my profound belief in destiny, I still can't get over this feeling of guilt that is devouring me."

"I can perfectly understand what is going on in your brain..." I said, with an air of sadness. But since I didn't want to harp on the topic - for which unfortunately there was not much I could do - I immediately diverted the subject: "Quid of the Vatican's interest in this peculiar case, which seems, from a naïve point of view, outside the traditional boundaries of the Holy See?"

"You are absolutely right, Signor Haftemizan; but the truth of the matter is that, based on the elements we have been able to gather so far, we fear that there might be something cataclysmic in the making that would not only cost lives but would put in jeopardy the relations between major religions and therefore between civilizations, countries and nations."

"You mean a war between religions?" I asked, troubled.

"Yes, exactly - I mean... of some sort. As you probably know, for the last several decades, the Vatican has made the inter-faith dialogue a major pillar of its policy, especially John-Paul II, who did more than any of his predecessors in this area. And I am confident that His Holiness will continue in the same direction.

"For some years now, whereas the Catholic Church has almost abandoned any type of active proselytism, some of the US-based Protestant churches are acting otherwise, often correlating charitable activities with religious proselytism."

"I see what you're referring to," I acknowledged, willing to demonstrate that I am not completely ignorant of the issue. "I recall... some years ago, there was the case, in Afghanistan, of two girls caught proselytizing under the harsh conservative Taliban rule: their story was all over the media in America."

"Can you imagine how detached from reality and how dangerously naïve these people can be? What they did was a little bit similar to some mullah coming to the Vatican and attempting to surreptitiously convert some of our people here. Their irresponsible activities back-lash on all honestly sincere Christian caritative organizations and, by extension, brings suspicion on all western NGOs working in Islamic societies and even in other places such as India or Sri Lanka, where Hinduism and Buddhism are predominant."

"But, if you allow me to be the Devil's advocate here, isn't the work of catholic missionary groups, such as the one founded by Mother Teresa, also resented for being proselyte?"

"I had a feeling that you would bring Mother Teresa up, signor Haftemizan... Yes, she was accused of proselytizing and of many other things. But I would tell you in all honesty that her order may have had some activities that could be confused with proselytism, but the very profound nature of it was not. If it were the case, she could have never been a Nobel Prize recipient."

"You're probably right; but as I warned you, I am acting as the Devil's advocate," I said with a smile, sensing that the subject was irritating Emilio.

"In essence, you are right though: some catholic groups have been accused of exercising some type of religious proselytism. But I can assure you that they are very infinitesimal in number and that they are doing so in defiance of the Vatican."

"To continue in my role as the Devil's advocate – without you trying to exorcize me, Emilio – there are Islamic and Buddhist groups who openly proselytize in Western Christian countries: so why not the other way around?"

"You're playing your part so well that I may very well end up practicing an exorcism on you," Father Ungari said, smiling. "To be serious, first of all, two wrongs don't make a right. Second, in most if not in all Occidental countries, for good or for bad, the Church has been separated from the State. Therefore, officially, there is no monopoly and there are no privileges granted to one religion over another. And, last but not least, Vatican II has definitely banished any propention to hunt on other religions' territories and attempt to convert their faithful to Christianity."

"You made your case," I acknowledged.

"What's worse is that the situation has considerably deteriorated since Signor Bush is in the White House: with him, the most radical aisle of the Evangelical movement, represented by individuals such as Jerry Falwell and Pat Robertson, have virtually gained access to the briefcase that carries the nuclear code – the 'nuclear football' as you call it in Washington jargon!"

"I understand your worry," I said. "But perhaps you are exaggerating a tiny bit…"

"Barely; Mr. Bush relies a lot on his so-called spiritual guides and I can assure you that they do not provide good advice… Their ideas are dangerous."

"I concur. I think that this White House is under the influence of a conjunction of negative influences that proceed mainly from three sources that I call the 'War Party,' the 'Big Business Party' and the 'Evangelical Party.' The policy brought forward by Bush, as a result of the interaction between these three interest groups, is not perceived as very positive to many, to put it in euphemistical terms."

"You are being kind. The results are not only 'not positive,' they are furthermore catastrophic," Ungari said. "In my capacity as a Nuncio, I travel a lot, attend seminars and conferences and get to meet leaders and scholars from the Islamic world. I can tell you that the Invasion of Iraq – and to a large extend that of Afghanistan – has worried them greatly. Even some of the most moderate ones relate it to the crusades or – at best – to the colonial times. All the groundwork that we've been paving for decades from both sides has been compromised by the inconsiderate policies of Signor Bush and his acolytes."

"We agree on this one, too," I said. "That's what I've been telling these guys in Washington: with their lame policies, they have pushed tens, hundreds, perhaps thousands of youngsters in the arms of extremist organizations, including the kind run by Bin Laden, Al-Zarqawi or any other ring leader we haven't heard of yet... But, alas, these stubborn bigwigs of the Administration in Washington don't want to hear any dissonant voice."

"*Signor* Haftemizan, I am a man of religion and as such I ask you to trust me when I say that the worst fanatics and the most dangerous people are the 'born again' kind, whether they are Christian, Muslim, Jew, Hindu or whatever... Usually, when they rediscover religion, they do it through the type of channels that brainwash them with misconceptions and narrow-minded views. The first thing these people do is attempting to impose their intolerant views on everyone else."

"I think that it's all the more difficult to give the appearance of a balanced American foreign policy in the Middle-East that a bunch of radical Evangelicals, with connections to this White House, are staunch backers of Israel and make hateful comments about Muslims in general and Arabs in particular," I said, referring to Pat Robertson who once declared that Islam was 'extreme and violent.'

"I know, from following this issue closely, that you are absolutely right on this one," Emilio agreed. "But one important thing that some radical rabbis, who have made an informal pact with some of the most zealot Evangelical pastors, need to realize is that these Evangelicals may appear to be very pro-Zionist - and in some instances *plus royalistes que le roi* - but, in the end, their interest is similar to that of the ranchero who wants his cattle to feed well and get fat...."

"Very true..." I agreed. "I should tell you that I have witnessed first hand what you just said: about two years ago, I was in Jerusalem to participate in an international symposium on the future of the Middle East. On Sabbath, I saw a group of American Evangelicals in the Old City's Jewish quarter distributing copies of the New Testament to pedestrians passing by …"

"Although, very unfortunately, this is not new," Emilio lamented. "But since the arrival of *signor* Bush at the White House - and even more so since his re-election - these groups have been largely emboldened. They disgrace Christianity!"

I understood why the Vatican was so worried about something happening that would jeopardize the precarious equilibrium that had been finally reached between the three major monotheist religions. I understood the difference between a Catholic Church, matured over centuries and in search of harmony with other believers in an increasingly materialistic world, and a multitude of small Evangelical churches born into the New World and fed with the messianic spirit of the pioneers, full of their own certitudes and ignorant of the convictions of others.

"Emilio, I am very pleased to have met you," I said as I extended my hand to shake his. "You are a man of conviction and a man of religion. Though, I should tell you that I have never met an ecclesiastic who was so open-minded and with his feet so firmly grounded in this world's realities. You could be a professor of International Relations at a university."

"Thank you, signor Haftemizan. I appreciate very much these nice words. They are all the more valuable to me that they are coming from you," he said, visibly touched by my praise. "You know, one has to be very open-minded when living among actors and artists," he said, referring to his mother's employment with Cinecitta. "I should also tell you, signor Haftemizan, that our backgrounds are not so dissimilar: in parallel to Theology and Christian History, I have also studied Political Science and International Relations."

No wonder why the Vatican recruited him as a diplomatic emissary: he was the perfect candidate.

We chatted a little longer about subjects of lesser importance. Then, as I noticed Emilio's eyes surreptitiously closing from time to time, I went back to my seat to allow him to get some rest.

When I got back to my seat, Ava had fallen asleep and had taken advantage of me being away to occupy the entire row. What to do? I didn't want to disturb her; so I wondered around the aisles to see if I could find any empty seat. Unfortunately for me, everyone had taken advantage of whatever empty space was available to stretch his or her limbs and take a nap. When I reached our row again, Ava was in the exact same position I had left her, so I decided to go to the toilet to freshen-up a little, hoping that by the time I'd get back, she would have awakened. In the end, I saw no other solution than to gently flex her legs up and quickly drop myself in the last of the three seats on the row.

Ava's head was resting on the armrest by the window. She was in the fetal position, hardly covered by one of those light blankets provided by the airliner. I pushed my seat backwards to make myself as comfortable as possible, put the headphones on and decided to watch whatever was on the little LCD screen in front of me. I couldn't help glancing at Ava, whose beauty was even more accentuated by the innocent look that sleep conferred on her. I browsed the few channels available and, almost naturally, I settled on a news channel.

As I said earlier, I am a news-junky. I can watch the news to go to sleep – as a somniferous drug – or I can watch or listen to it to wake up with my morning coffee. And, yes, I have had the news on while I was doing it… It may not be the most romantic background sound around, but it all depends on the time of the day and the setting, if you know what I mean... Please, forgive my digression here, but, hey, it is a part of our lives – maybe not that of Father Emilio Ungari's, but that is his sacerdotal choice – and as much as I would like to avoid telling you anything about it in this story, it still manages to instill itself somehow.

Speaking of which, while I was quietly watching the news, Ava turned around, on her back and, obviously without realizing what she was doing - since she was asleep - she stretched, extending her legs and lodging her feet between my legs, inserting her toes under my left thigh. At first, I was uncomfortable, as if I were pinned down. I couldn't move, fearing that the slightest movement would awaken her. But after a few moments, the inadvertent contact of her feet with my sensitive area resulted in transforming the discomfort into the kind of comfort that I did not want to occur and, considering the situation, even less to display. So, I swiftly unfolded the table in front of me and pulled the blanket to cover my emotion.

My improvised camouflage was not the best one could find, but since everyone was more or less asleep and the cabin lights were off, I can say that honor was safe. Twice I tried to gently remove her feet, but in her sleep she would just put them back where they were. To fight off my emotion, I tried to concentrate on the news. And just as I had succeeded to empty my brain of any sensual thoughts – watching the financial news helped a lot - she tossed and turned again facing down with her feet positioned in an even more compromising way. I had to do something, because otherwise if she woke up and noticed the physical state, it would have put me – in fact, most likely both of us – in a very uncomfortable position. So, in a quick and coordinated manner, I pushed her legs back, crossed mine and loudly cleared my throat in the hope that she would wake up: thankfully, it worked!

"Oh, I am so sorry," she said, a bit confused, as she emerged. "I've taken all the space."

"No, no, you're welcome; you did well. Did you get some rest?" I asked with a false air of interest.

"Yes, thank you; although, at first I was cold, not very comfortable... Then my feet warmed up, as if someone had wrapped them with a heating pad. It was so comfortable, so enjoyable... I was warm... Then after that, I slept pretty well!"

"I see..."

"The sensation was so real that I dreamt I was sitting in front of a chimney after a long trek in the snow and that I had wrapped my hands and my feet around a cup of hot drink to warm me up."

"A bit cliché... but a dream is a dream," I commented.

Ava straightened her shirt, pulled back her hair and tied it with a rubber band, then grabbed her purse and stood up to go and freshen up. In normal circumstances, I would have moved out of the way or lifted myself up and back to allow her to maneuver through the very narrow aisle; but this time, I couldn't stir without inelegantly exposing the visible expression of my carnal emotion – I know, I am using a lot of periphrases to avoid the word 'erection.' Instead, I tried to twist my body in a way that a contortionist would not disapprove to allow her to pass through.

Judging by the naughty smile on her face, once she had passed the obstacle I constituted, I understood that she had more than likely uncovered what I had desperately attempted to dissimulate. Despite the appearances, I acted as if nothing had happened and put the headphones back on to signal that I was absorbed by the news running on TV.

When Ava came back, she smiled and was friendlier in her interaction with me. I didn't know if I should attribute this to the good rest she had, or to the fact that she had realized that, despite my noticeable emotion, I had behaved very gentlemanly? Whatever the reason, from that point on, the tension between us had receded perceptibly – rather, it had moved from one territory to another.

Another half an hour and we're there! These transatlantic flights tend to be lengthy and tiresome. The plane had started to decrease altitude and the cabin was at times briskly shaken by turbulences. That's when I blacked out again. No turbulence for me, please: I'm allergic to it; it makes me sick. I'll see you after the landing…

"Wake up… wake up!" I heard a voice telling me with insistence. It was Ava, looking at me with amused amazement.

"Have we landed yet?"

"You really are incredible. You dozed off the minute we commenced to descend on Washington."

"I told you: that's how my system works… Do you believe me now?"

"I don't think there is much room left for doubt. What do you have: a built-in timer of some sort or what?"

"I have no idea; but it works just fine for me."

Once we reached the terminal, just outside the mobile connection bridge, we decided to wait for Emilio before passing through customs. Nearly fifteen minutes passed without sighting Emilio. We looked around, just in the improbable case he would have exited without us noticing, but he was nowhere to be seen. Ten minutes later, the last passengers exited the plane and now it was the cabin crew's turn to leave and for the cleaning one to dash in to prep the plane for the next flight. Ava and I looked at one another to signal that there was something wrong.

"Excuse me, Sir," I asked a man standing at the entrance of the tunnel holding a walkie-talkie in his hand. "We traveled on this flight with a friend and it's been more than twenty-five minute since we've been waiting for him to come out. He is more than likely asleep and didn't realize that we have landed."

"All right, I understand; may I see your tickets for a second?" asked the man who wanted to make sure that we were on that flight and that we didn't have any ill intentions – post '9/11' oblige. "You probably missed him, or he came out before you did. The crew always checks for passengers left behind."

"But how about if he were in the toilet and they didn't see him?" Ava asked.

"Is your friend old?"

"No," Ava replied.

"Is he on medication?" the man inquired further.

"We don't know," I answered.

"Has your friend recently suffered from a stroke?"

"We don't know," I repeated with a sigh of exasperation this time. "Can't we just go in and see for ourselves if he is there?"

"All right, all right; let us go and check…"

"*Jack, Jack*" called a voice from the walkie-talkie.

"10-2" replied the man.

"*Jack, this is Incarnacion: could you come in? We have got a situation here.*"

"10-4; I am on my way," he said before looking at us and inviting us to follow him.

I understood right away that something was wrong. We rushed to reach the cabin. Each step we took was creating a loud echo inside the covered mobile bridge. While the cleaning crew was busy collecting the trash and vacuuming the ground, two staff members were standing before Emilio's seat.

"We found him here; but he's not sleeping," said the cleaning lady who seemed shaken. "I think he's dead."

Father Emilio Ungari was seated upright, his head resting to one side and a blanket partially covering his body. From the outset, anybody would have believed that he was just asleep. Ava was quick to check his pulse, hoping that Emilio had just passed out, that he was still alive. But alas, the reality was otherwise. Ava shook her head to signal that he was definitely dead.

"Sir, could you call the airport Police. This man is dead," Ava said, flashing her own police badge.

"So, this is your friend?" the man asked to confirm.

"Damn it! Why is this happening to me?" Ava yelled, trying to control her emotion.

"We chatted for a good while just a few hours ago, during the flight. He was doing just fine," I recalled. "He was preparing to sleep when I left him."

"I saw him, too, not long before the landing, when I went to powder my nose. He was in this exact same position, so I thought that he was sound asleep."

"He is indefinitely asleep now," I muttered.

"This is tragic. We've lost a very precious source… What are we going to do?"

"It's not just tragic, it's another Hiroshima!" I emphasized before suggesting: "We can start by finding his friend."

"That's what I had in mind, too," Ava said. "You can leave now, if you want to; I'll deal with the Police. I'll catch up with you later."

"Are you sure?"

"Definitely; it's pointless for you stay too… I'll call you."

146

I was really sad to see Emilio dead. I didn't know how to react. He was a person with whom I had more in common that I thought possible, considering that we come from seemingly different backgrounds. Although I didn't know immediately what might have provoked his death, I had a guess that it was not a natural cause – the probability of which would be infinitesimal considering the circumstances of the case we are involved in.

Emilio and his twin brother Benvenisto had both been sacrificed for the cause of Humanity and the preservation of what they valued: understanding and harmony between religions and cultures.

However noble their sacrifice may be, the real issue that tortures me at this time is: who is going to tell Emilio's poor father that his other son has been assassinated in the airplane while traveling with us; that Emilio has lost his life in the same quest that has already cost him one son. That doesn't sound good! I am afraid that when Mr. Ungari learns the bad news, if he doesn't succumb to a heart-attack, he might very well travel over the oceans to avenge the murders of his two sons - starting with shooting our brains out! And, frankly, I wouldn't blame him for doing so, for the calamity that has inflicted his family is not so dissimilar from the ones often depicted in Greek tragedies.

Sea Turtle Enchilada

"God, don't I look fat? Look at all this saggy flesh covering me from side to side: it is repulsive. Gone are the days when I was in the college football team. I had quite a success with some of the chicks. Look at me now: no hair, over-sized eye-glasses, obese stomach, bunioned feet, a pace-maker in my chest and, on top of it all, I can't even take any of those lozenge-shaped little blue pills from time to time to... let's say... to relieve the tension...

Not very sexy! ...Whereas Lynne's still got it. She is not overweight and I can see some of these guys lurking at her... God, what I wouldn't give to lose a couple of dozen pounds and rejuvenate a little."

"Honey, are you ready? It's getting late."

"I look overly fat in this suit!"

"Then wear the other one that I've pulled out from the closet for you."

"The dark one...?"

"Yes, come on, honey; we are expected."

"We'll be there on time. You know how much I hate these so called intimate dinners with them."

"I know, honey; but we don't have much of a choice: we've committed... and he's your boss."

"But he's so ignorant, so childish... and I am not into frat jokes: I have passed the age for that. Besides, I've heard all of them tens of times," Dick said with exasperation.

"Stop whining, honey. Do you think I like chatting with his wife? She's even worse. All she knows is talking about house-keeping matters and her happy days in rural Texas..."

"I know."

"Just remember one thing, honey; the two of you are in this together. You need each other. Don't let personal considerations and likeability factors get in the way of the greater cause you want to serve."

"You are right, honey; you are always a good judge. Let's go! The car is waiting for us."

The White House, Private Quarters

"Mr. President, the Secretary of State wants to speak to you from London."

"I am busy right now. Tell her that I am having a family dinner with the Vice-President and his wife and that I'll call her back later... or first thing in the morning."

"She claims it's important, Mr. President."

"All right, then; pass it to me here."

"Hello, Madame Secretary; 'how do you do?', as the Brits would say. Are you enjoying your trip to the United-Kickdom [sic]? How do you like our good friend Tony? Is he a great guy or what?"

"Mr. President, I am afraid the mood has changed here. Prime Minister Blair is facing a harsh challenge from the Tories and from within his own party..."

"Our prayers are with him, but I know he is a steadfast leader and he will overcome this challenge, too, as he has done it in the past."

"I am afraid it's very serious this time."

"Then, maybe I can go there and tell the English public how much he has been helpful in the cause of fighting terrorism and spreading democracy and liberty."

"I will tell him, Mr. President," Condi said. "But I think that, considering the way things have shifted on the British political scene, it may not help him."

"I don't understand. What does Tony want then?"

"He would like to take some distance vis-à-vis the American ally…"

"If he is undertaking some political maneuvering to appease his electorate, it is fine by me – we've all done that - as long as his troops stay with us in Iraq."

"I am afraid, Mr. President, that he is hinting to a partial withdrawal."

"How many: a few dozens or perhaps a few hundreds?"

"I am afraid he's got in mind something like…half."

"He can't do that to me!"

"I think, Mr. President, that we have to admit that there are national issues that are heavily coming into play here. Besides, as you may well know, he is jockeying with rivals from within the Labor who are squeezing him from the left side."

"No wonder why the Brits lost all their colonies!" the President said.

"May I, Mr. President?" offered an irritated Dick who wanted to intervene in the conversation.

"Sure, go for it."

"Hello, Condi; this is Dick."

"Hello, Dick; how is your health…? Are you doing better now?" Condi asked with some genuine concern.

"Fairly better, thanks for asking. Look, tell that fucking elephant-eared mint pudding-eating bastard that he owes us big time; that if it weren't for us, they'd be polishing Hitler's boots with the thin skin of their royal asses."

"Dick is right; they owe us big time," '43' said. He loved it when his Vice President said things that he couldn't because of his position and probably also because he was brought up that way.

"Their food sucks anyway," Dick said.

"When I think that I invited this guy to Crawford and Laura prepared a 'steak and kidney pudding' for him: ungrateful."

"I'll try my best, Mr. President," Condi said. "I'll keep you informed whether I have been able to reverse a course, which I am afraid seems already cast in the mold."

"I know you can do it, Condi. I trust you for that. And if they really want to weasel their way out of the coalition, go to… go to Afghanistan and try to bring those guys in," '43' said. "Why not, after all…?"

"Excellent idea, Mr. President; they can't refuse: these guys owe us big time," Dick said.

"Dick is right. Remind me what exactly we did for them?"

"We bombed out the Taliban and brought in Karzai," Dick said.

"Absolutely; Karzai owes us big time! Of all, he is in no position to say no."

"But the problem is that he's got no army," Condi said.

"I don't buy that. I am sure he can round some thugs that we can equip and make them look as though they belong to a regular army. Think about it: we've liberated them and now, to show their appreciation, they are sending their men in uniform to help us succeed in Iraq. Am I great or what?"

"This is brilliant, Mr. President," Dick said. "I am going to personally call Karzai to tell him what we want and I'll tell Rumsfeld to instruct his men in Kabul to do what is necessary for this to happen ASAP."

"Condi, did you hear what we just said?" '43' asked.

"Yes, Mr. President."

"Call up Rumsfeld and get with him on this ASAP. That's a done deal. The next thing I want to see are images of Afghan soldiers sent by Karzai climbing down the plane in Baghdad... Make sure to bring in the media."

"Very well, Sir."

"And Condi, while in London, try the 'Queen's pudding...!'"

London – The Savoy

"Sure, Mr. President," Condi said, as she hung up the phone.

"Sure, you dim-witted moron!" Collin had heard the entire exchange on speakerphone. "I'll shove the Queen's pudding down his throat with my bare hands."

Condi laughed. "Collin, come on!"

"Didn't I tell you that these guys were messing around with you?"

"I'd love to concede, Collin, and say that you were right all along, but..."

"They are using you the way they used me," the General interrupted. "They'll use your credibility to advance their own agenda. They'll put you front and center on the stage; they'll make you the focus of the media's attention and in the meanwhile, in the secrecy of their little meetings, they'll devise behind your back and expect you to be an empty suit."

"I was in some of the meetings you are referring to, and to which you were not invited, and..." Condi said, feeling that the jab from her predecessor was directed at her.

"Yes, indeed you were... But let's forget about the past."

"What I meant to say is that there were some meetings where only those involved at the highest level were participating and..."

"Are you kidding me? Secretary of State is the most senior position in the Administration after the President and his VP."

"You're right," Condi said. "The truth is that they excluded you from the inner circle because you were not in agreement on the war with the rest of us."

"That doesn't cut it. Despite my disagreement, I served faithfully, like a solider, to the point of losing my credibility nationally and internationally. People make fun of me: everywhere I go to deliver a speech - like I did yesterday here, in London, at the Royal Institute of International Affairs - inevitably, somebody in the audience stands up and asks if I have any other of those Power Point presentations to delight the audience with? And they all laugh," Collin said, shaking his head.

"I understand, but you have got to have faith in the spread of Democracy and Liberty..."

"Stop the nonsense, Condi. You're really naïve if you believe that's the motivation behind this team's agenda. They're telling you to go blab about grandiloquent values, but their real agenda is a retrograde one... And I can guarantee you, Condi, that you're good as long as you don't make waves and go along with the flow, but the minute you do otherwise, you're over, done, you're history."

"Maybe you're exaggerating a little. The President may not be very smart but he is sincere in his willingness to fight Evil around the world. And Dick is so nice to me; I always consult him on important issues.... He is really like a mentor to me."

"Exactly my point..."

"I guess you're right: I often feel that I am being coached a little bit too closely," Condi said. "But you know what? They have got their agenda and I've got mine: they are using me and I am using them to reach my goal."

"...Been there; done that!" the General commented with a smirk.

"What do you mean?"

"What I mean is that, in the end, you're going to be too conservative for the Democrats and too liberal for a good many within the Republican Party: you won't even make it through the primaries..."

"You're looking too far into the future for me, Collin. Perhaps my ambitions are a tiny bit smaller than that."

"Whatever your plans are, as somebody who's got only good intentions towards you, I wanted to seize the opportunity while we are both in this city to reiterate my friendly advice of caution to you. Now, you do whatever you want with it."

"I know; I appreciate it so much... You are an angel, Collin," Condi said with affection.

"There are no angels in Politics, dear."

"Am I not one?" Condi said, trying to appear angelic in her facial expression.

"Very cute; but you are part of the pack of wolves: Cheney, Rumsfeld, Wolfowitz, Perle and the rest of them - including the President. I still have scars from your vicious bites on my back and on my leg. Beware of one thing though, Condi..."

"What?"

"That the pack doesn't turn against you..."

"I'll be vigilant," Condi said, as she kissed the General goodbye.

Collin winked. "Of course, this conversation never happened."

"Of course. When do you leave London?"

"I am staying one more day, doing some shopping and some visiting, and then I'll be flying to Paris to attend a book party for the launch of the French edition of my memoirs. How about you...?"

"I've been traveling a lot recently; I am exhausted! I am heading home tomorrow."

"Have a safe trip."

"Thanks; you too..."

"Oh, I completely forgot to give you this," Collin said, as he pulled a CD from his pocket.

"What is it?"

"I got it for you last night from the Royal Philharmonic Orchestra."

"Thank you so much; you are an angel!"

The White House, Private Quarters

The President was disappointed. "I can't believe it. After all we did for these Brits, Tony is letting us down half way through our journey."

"It certainly is a disappointment, especially since we were counting on them a great deal to relieve more of our troops for 'you know what,'" Dick said.

"George, honey, come on; it's not the end of the world," Laura said, to cheer up the two men who were demoralized.

"We've got a great evening ahead of us. Look at this sea turtle enchilada I've had the chef prepare for us…"

"Great; this looks delicious," Lynne said with forced enthusiasm.

"That looks like a rare delicacy." Dick said.

"It's made after a recipe the wife of our great friend Vicente Fox gave me when she visited here."

"Sorry to correct you, sweetheart, but it's 'ex-great friend' Vicente Fox…" interrupted '43.' "The ideas he gave me about legalizing all illegal Mexicans got me in trouble: I am steering clear from him."

"You made a wise-decision, Mr. President; he could have cost us the entire South in the past elections. I don't deny that it certainly is a smart idea to grow the Latino electorate in order to destabilize and balance the Black vote anchored on the Democratic side, but I think it's still a bit premature."

"Hey, don't blame me! It was Karl's idea," '43'said.

"I know that," Dick said. "Fortunately, we were able to put the issue to rest before it got out of hand and distorted by the liberal media."

"By the way, Lynne, thank you so much for bringing something for desert," Laura said.

"You're welcome. But I should tell you that it was Dick's idea."

"I thought it would be a good idea to bring some of those appetizing baklavas for you to taste from my stopover in Baghdad. I hope you'll like them."

"See how great it is," '43' said. "We've freed the Iraqis and now their 'balkavuwa' [sic] can travel around the world without any constraint whatsoever."

"It certainly is extraordinary," Dick said.

Dick could not show his consternation. But his wife Lynne couldn't restrain a smile that didn't go unnoticed by '43':

"Why are you smiling, Lynne?"

"I was just thinking about your memorable joke the other day when you reminded Dick not to forget to replace his pace-maker's batteries before he goes to sleep: that was hilarious."

"Oh, yes; you liked it? That was a good one."

"My husband is so full of talent – and humor is one of them - that I don't know what I have done to deserve him," Laura said.

"That's what I keep telling Dick, too," Lynne said.

"Since we are having fun here, let me tell you what I did the other day – and I think, Dick, that you're going to be proud of me," '43' started to recount with visible amusement. "I was expecting Condi, and just before she walks in, I very visibly displayed a CD I got from the 'Blind Boys of Alabama' when they performed here a couple of years back."

"What did Condi say when she saw it?" Lynne asked.

"Nothing; but I could see in her eyes that she was impressed and very pleased."

"I am sure she was very impressed," Laura said.

"I think my credit is at an all time high with her and she'll keep working faithfully for us," '43' remarked. "What do you think, Dick?"

"I wouldn't have done it better myself, Mr. President. You're becoming a master in the art of manipulation. If only we could have you elected for a third term."

"I know; don't you agree? It's a shame," Laura said.

"Won't you take some more of this sea turtle enchilada?" the First Lady asked, playing her role of host, which she performed with delectation and dedication.

"It was delicious; I am going to reserve some room for the baklavas, though," Dick said.

"Heck, no! He doesn't want some more and neither do I," '43' pestered. "Forgive me, honey, but this thing tastes like crap."

"I found it to be very good," Lynne said. "The chili is perhaps masking a little bit too much the sweetness of the sea-turtle flesh but, other than that, I think it's… it's… an unusually terrific dish. Isn't it, honey?"

"Absolutely; and I think we should get the recipe from Laura so that we can treat our guests and family to it," Dick said.

"Honey, if you're still hungry, I'll ask the kitchen to prepare something: do you want a hamburger?" Laura said.

"Naaaah, it's all right; don't bother, sweetheart. I'll get some pretzels instead…"

Later that night, the phone inside the Vice-President's car rang:

"Good evening, Mr. President."

"Did you watch the news?"

"No, we have not arrived yet. Why… what's happening?"

"I just saw in the news that the wife of our good friend Senator Gareth has apparently been killed in a car accident involving a truck."

"That's very sad news, Mr. President. She was a very nice person. Lynne and I had them over on numerous occasions."

"I knew you were good buddies; that's why I called you right away."

"Thank you, Mr. President. I'll call Senator Gareth first thing in the morning."

"All right, *buenas noches* now."

"Good night, Mr. President."

"Oh, and one more thing, Dick…"

"Yes, Mr. President…?"

"Don't forget to replace the batteries before you go to sleep," '43' giggled, obviously getting a kick out of his recurring and questionable joke.

"Sure, Mr. President," Dick said, forcing himself to laugh, then turning to his wife: "Why in hell did you tell Pretzel Boy that his joke about my pace-maker was funny?"

"Forgive me, honey; but when he said that Iraqi baklavas – that he couldn't even pronounce correctly - could now travel freely around the world thanks to our intervention, it was so stupid that I nearly burst into laughter. Though I held myself, I couldn't suppress a smile that didn't go unnoticed."

"So you had to use me as a subterfuge…"

"I am sorry, honey pie," she said and kissed him on his cheek, "but that was better than a diplomatic gaffe that would have very negatively impacted on your relations with '43' at a time when you need one another more than ever."

"You're right once again, honey: the consequences could have been tragic for our plan."

The Red Door

From the airport I went straight to my apartment. It really felt good to unload everything and drop on my bed. The entire trip had been emotionally and physically draining: over all, a few hours short of five days for a transatlantic journey... My entire body ached and I still had the echo of the awful rumbling engine noise in my ears. I was too tired even to get up for an Alka-Seltzer. It was the early afternoon and the jet-lag syndrome had perturbed my inner horologe.

I was lying flat, motionless, eyes shut on my bed, but I could not sleep. Soon, I was overwhelmed by a sentiment of uneasiness. In a succession of images, I could see Ungari – the father – bursting into the living room and showing us pictures of his sons; then the vision of Necromonti's face in the Moroccan restaurant while he was giving us a lesson in the science of 'pasta recognition'; followed by that of his brother Emilio - an ecclesiastic - giving me a lesson in tolerance, and a few hours later the same Emilio, inert, in a deserted airplane... As these and other images invaded my mind in a disorderly manner, the same question tortured me: how are we going to tell his father that Emilio too is dead? My apprehension was that the old man would either completely burn the fuses and wind up in an asylum, or decide to commit suicide, devastated by the news. Either way, I felt for him but I also felt immensely guilty because I was the one who had pressed Emilio to accompany us.

161

Later That Day

We had opted to meet at 'The Two Hassans.' I sat at the exact same place as the first - and the last - time I had dinner with Shumington and Necromonti in this restaurant. I went there early on purpose to observe the restaurant more thoroughly and try to recreate in my head what had happened that funest night – at least, funest for the others, if not for me...

Because it was earlier in the day, there still was some light outside and not many customers had arrived yet. The restaurant's owner was a gray-haired man of medium height. He limped towards me and, peering over his thin reading glasses, he asked if he could offer me something to drink on the house before my company shows up.

"Sure; it's very kind of you. Thank you," I said.
"You're welcome. We like our customers. You know, Morocco is known for the hospitality of its people," he said as he filled a tiny cup with mint tea and placed it in front of me.
"Without a doubt," I responded. Obviously, I was not going to say anything contrary, considering the situation! Then I followed up by asking a question that was tickling me since the other evening: "Sir, may I ask you - without appearing too curious - why you have named your restaurant 'The Two Hassans'? Is 'Hassan' your last name?"
"No, not at all, I don't mind," he said, as he let himself fall down on the seat in front of me. "I like you, *ya Sidi*! You know why?"
"...Very nice of you...I have no idea."

162

"Sidi, I like you because, in almost twenty years - since I've opened this restaurant - nobody has ever asked me this question."

"That's incredible!"

"...But that doesn't mean that I haven't told the story to many people on my own initiative..." he laughed. "I love to make people uncomfortable by imposing a conversation on a political topic – when I say 'political,' I mean 'foreign policy' - that they don't want to hear about."

"Certainly not me, Sir; you can go ahead."

At that point, I understood that he was not going to tell me that he had named his establishment this way to reflect his involvement in a shared business with his brother or a homonymous individual. He told me that the reason for naming his restaurant 'The Two Hassans' was to refer to the duplicity of Hassan II, the father of the current monarch, who reigned for decades over Morocco.

He told me that, as a young graduate freshly back from Paris with some dreams and a lot of enthusiasm for his country, he once made the mistake of criticizing the king for not allowing political parties. As a result, he was promptly thrown in jail and kept there for five years, almost incommunicado. After being released, he decided to move to the United States where a cousin of his lived.

For him, there were indeed two Hassans: one was the 'Hassan' friend of the West, cozy with its leaders and even its intelligentsia, constantly patted on the back for being 'modernist' and 'visionary'; then there was the other 'Hassan': the ruler that he and others like him had experienced from the inside; a man who would not give political freedom to his subjects and who

163

would mercilessly throw his critics in jail and allow his secret services to mistreat them.

"Even here, Sidi, the secret services of His Majesty came after me and asked me why I had called my restaurant 'The Two Hassans,'" the owner said with a smile.

"You can't be serious! They came all the way from Morocco to torture you – I mean to question you?" Indeed the word 'torture' was not very well chosen on my part…

"No need to come especially for me. They have a section here at the Embassy that spies on nationals – or former nationals - and if they find that they are conducting 'subversive' activities not to the taste of 'His Majesty,' they use a whole arsenal of means of persuasion, including pressuring family members back home."

"So, what happened when they showed up?"

"What do you think?" he laughed. "I told them that I had baptized – so to speak – my restaurant in honor of His Majesty Hassan II and his illustrious predecessor Sultan Hassan I, who ruled in the late 19th Century. They returned to the embassy convinced that there is no more fervent backer of the Alaouite dynasty than me!"

"You tricked them well," I said, appreciative of the finesse he had demonstrated to fend off their suspicion.

"Whom did you trick?" Ava asked, as she arrived.

"Nobody, lady. I'll tell you this story another time: the dinner will be on me," the owner said, as he stood up to leave the seat for Ava. "Now, if you'll excuse me, I have some customers to attend to."

"Thank you for enlightening me," I said.

"My pleasure!" the owner replied as he slowly drifted away with his head held high.

Ava wore a beige linen skirt and a top of the same color, enhanced with monochromatic embroidery: casual yet elegant. Incidentally, because of the warm weather, I had on a suit of the same fabric, but a shade lighter.

"I can see that you got my e-mail," I said jokingly.

It took Ava a few seconds to figure out what I was referring to and laugh.

"So, what exactly were you two talking about?"

"I can't tell you. Didn't he promise you a dinner and a conversation?"

"Yes, sure…" Ava said, raising her eyebrows.

"He was serious about it. I think you should set a date with him."

"All right; forget about it," she said.

"Were you able to find anything interesting pertaining to Emilio's death?" I asked.

"Nothing substantial; local and federal authorities are investigating Father Ungari's death and I have made a request to get access the list of passengers on the flight."

"Do we have anything on the cause of his death?"

"There is no bullet, no apparent injuries: in summary, no visible physical damage. They are now looking for pathological or toxicological causes."

"Do you think he was poisoned?"

"I won't exclude anything until we have further details."

I had ordered Couscous – nothing original - and Ava, probably considering it to be too spicy, ordered some salad instead, much to the waiter's chagrin.

"How do you like it?" I asked.

165

"I hate it!"

"Why? The food is not good?"

"No, that's not it."

"You don't like the ambiance?" I pressed on.

"No, not the reason either..."

"Then what is it? Perhaps, you did not like the waiter's attitude?"

"This place brings back bad memories that are still quite fresh..."

"I perfectly understand how you may feel, but see it as a means to exorcise the feeling of guilt you have," I suggested.

"That's a way to put it..."

"I really mean it! I wanted us to meet here because, in a very peculiar manner, now I feel a connection with this place. Necromonti and Shumington were sitting at this very table, waiting for me to arrive, when they were gunned down. I feel that this is where destiny has given me another chance in my absence."

"Good for you! I also have a 'connection' with this place that I would like to forget ASAP."

Ava understandably closed the door for my glozing on the topic of coming to terms with past failures and on that of unloading some of the responsibilities on destiny's intervention in shaping what we are and what we become. It is not difficult to understand her uneasiness: after all, who wants to remember his or her past failures?

"By the way," I said in an attempt to switch subjects, "have you heard back from that guy?"

"What guy?"

"The one that you called on our way to the hospital to ask him to inquire about the e-mail account from which Necromonti's pictures were sent."

"Oh yes, Ranjit... He actually left a message saying that the account was created from a public computer and all the information in it was made up, untraceable."

"That's too bad, because I have received another message from those guys."

"Really?" Ava said with excitement.

"I checked my e-mail at home today and among the tons of Spam – and also friends' and work-related correspondence, which I haven't addressed for some time now – there was an e-mail from that 'fourteenninetytwo@hotmail.com' address."

"What did it say?" asked Ava.

"Not much..."

"Do you mean that it was empty?" she pursued.

"Here is what it contained," I said as I pulled the printout of a picture from my pocket.

The image showed a white car crushed by a truck in front of a house, as though the car was exiting the driveway backward and had not seen the incoming truck.

"Why did they send you the picture of a traffic accident?"

"I have no idea. But one thing is certain: it's not innocent. There is a message in this that we have to decipher."

"You're right. The last time, they sent you a picture of Necromonti on his hospital bed and, by the time we reached the place, he was already dead," Ava said.

"Then the obvious question is: who did they kill this time?" I asked.

"Did you look very carefully at the car and at the background?"

"Yes, I did... at least as much as possible: why?"

"I was just trying to see if you would have recognized anything familiar."

"I thought of it, too... that they may have targeted somebody very close to me, such as a family member or a friend, but from what I can see in this picture, I don't recognize anything."

"Whose vehicle could it be?" I wondered. "The picture is taken from an angle that prevents us from being able to distinguish any valuable clues such as tags, stickers on the windshield, or anything that could help us identify the automobile and consequently all the information related to it – including who the owner might be.

"If we can dare to draw a pattern based on the last experience, we can prognosticate that the accident has more than likely occurred today and that whoever was in the car has been transformed into unanimated ground meat."

"Very elegant way of putting it. I am glad that I ordered a salad," Ava said, in a rhetorical reprobation of my humorous metaphor.

"Let us watch the local news tonight for any clues," I suggested.

"I agree. I will also check the various police and traffic websites."

The next action item on our agenda was to track Emilio's friend. Ava planned to go to John Hopkins University to find a list of the students who frequented its center in Florence and, from among them, find the few who had resided at the Ungari home. Ava seemed pretty confident about the outcome of this piece of investigation but much less about the cooperation of that person once we find him. I would tend to agree with her assessment: it will be extraordinarily difficult to persuade him to take a stance that will more than likely be detrimental and even possibly fatal to his father – not discounting the danger he would personally be exposed to.

After dinner, Ava suggested that I accompany her to her place because my own apartment may be unsafe. The people who had previously surreptitiously searched my apartment had in effect now sent another warning to me when they e-mailed the second picture.

"These people – whoever they are – are extremely well informed and very professional," Ava said. "We can't take any risks."

"But I like my flat...!" I protested.

"I am sure you do, but the rate of casualties around this investigation is so unbelievably high that we can't afford to take further risks," she asserted before adding with a smile: "Don't worry; I am a good host."

"I am sure you are... but the thing is that, at home, I can get some work done; I can watch TV till late hours without bothering anyone; I am free to do whatever I want to..."

"I understand; hopefully it's only going to be for a couple of nights... Believe me; I love my privacy as well!"

I took my car to a public parking and rode with Ava to her apartment. She had a flat in a downtown four-story condominium. Looking at the building, it appeared very similar to the one I was taken to when I first encountered Shumington and Necromonti. I couldn't remember the street number but I recall that it had a '7' in it. All these buildings look very similar though: maybe I am mistaken; maybe it was somewhere else...

"Ava, don't mind me asking you this, but the building where you live looks strangely a lot like the one you took me to for my 'recruitment interview.'"

"You've got a good sense of observation," she said with a smile.

169

"Was that empty office space your apartment? Or, are we going there instead of your apartment?"

"That was on the third floor and I live just above, on the top level. The third floor condo's owners are good friends of mine and I show it from time to time to potential buyers."

"I see: you were completely part of the conspiracy."

"Guilty; Your Honor," Ava responded with a smile.

We climbed the stairs past the third floor where I recognized the particular Japanese-red color of the door. Arriving on the fourth floor, I was struck to see that Ava's door was of a dark, deep blue - almost black - color, in stark contrast with the pale white of the surrounding walls. Though different, both colors – Japanese red and dark blue - reflect strength and self-confidence in their own way.

"Did you choose the color of your door?" I asked, intrigued by the unusual choice.

"Yes, I did."

"Why this dark blue, black...? I am curious."

"I don't know; I painted it this way because I felt like it. Why? You don't like it?"

"Oh, no, it's very nice... I like this color a lot. I guess it would be interesting to know what the psychological ramifications of such a choice are..."

"Sure, Dr. Freud!"

In contrast, her apartment was all white, bright as it can be, except for the inside of the entrance door that was - interestingly enough - of the same Japanese red color as the one on the third floor. The apartment was airy, spacious and not overcrowded by too many pieces of furniture. As I sat on the sofa while Ava went to prepare some chamomile tea to calm our nerves, my eyes instinctively browsed her living room – as I guess anyone in the same situation would do – looking for elements that would help better discern my hostess's personality. All right, I give it to you: it equates to curiosity and curiosity is almost a sin, but only if it is misplaced.

Some old pictures hanging on the walls caught my attention. As I went closer to get a better look, I found out that they were portraits of people dressed in some type of Caucasian outfits - very similar to the ones I had seen in some books - and others whose appearance looked more Central-Asian. I had a hard time conceiving the type of connection Ava may have had with these fellows, but it was more than likely because she was related to them. I also noticed a beautiful sword displayed on top of an Arts and Crafts style armoire; but, out of politeness, I did not remove it from its boxed pedestal to take a closer look. The sheath was made of silver with gold tracings and adorned with what seemed to be lapis lazuli and emerald inserts.

"This must be worth a fortune," I commented, as Ava returned with the tea.

"The value is more sentimental than anything else. This sword belonged to my grandfather on my father's side. He had received it from the Emir of Bukhara as a token for service rendered."

"Wow, I am impressed!" I exclaimed. "So your grandparents were from Bukhara? That's fascinating! You never told me that."

"What did you want me to say: 'Hi, I am Ava; my grandparents are from Bukhara'?"

"What kind of service had he rendered to receive this as a gift from the Emir?"

"I don't recall exactly what my father told me, but I think that my grandfather had fought bravely against the advancing Bolshevik forces…"

171

"That was some time in the 1920s, if I am not mistaken."

"Probably," she nodded, before continuing: "When my grandfather went to the Emir's court to tell him that he had been able to inflict a defeat to the Russians – even though it was a temporary one, the Emir was so elated that he gave him his sword as a token of his gratitude."

"Who would have thought that?" I marveled, staring at her as if she were some kind of curiosity.

"What do you mean?"

"Well, I mean that… who would have thought that Inspector Ava – our Inspector Ava - from Interpol had such a fascinating family background," I said. "So, these pictures, here, represent your grandparents and your Bukhariot roots…"

"Some of them, yes; the others are from my maternal side."

"If I am not mistaken, they are dressed in some type of Caucasian outfits."

"You guessed right. My grandparents, from my mother's side, were a mixture of Chechen and Daghestanian. My grandfather was a member of the second Independent Government of the Northern Caucasus Montagnards…"

"That's a pretty explosive mixture!" I humorized.

"You bet it was! Both sides of my family gave the Russians – Czarist and Bolshevik - a hard time and they paid for it by being forced into exile for the rest of their lives. Both sides had settled in Turkey and frequented the same ever-growing circle of Caucasian and Central Asian nobilities who had lost their ancestral lands to the Bolshevik hydra. That's how my parents met as kids before marrying and finally migrating to Paris, London and then to New York."

"Quite a journey…" I said and immediately regretted the platitude of my comment.

Here is Ava, telling me about the extraordinary conjunction of historical events that make up her family background, and all I could come up with to say is "quite a journey," as if they'd traveled from Philly to Atlantic City!

"Yes, indeed," she sighed. "Would you like some sugar with your chamomile?"

"No, thanks. So, what do you think of the current situation in the Caucasus?" I pressed her on a more contemporaneous topic.

"I am no Geostrategy specialist or historian, but what I can tell you is that these barbaric Russians have been trying to tame that region for centuries without totally succeeding. Hopefully, the Chechens will overcome this dark phase, too."

"Interesting," I commented, noting that despite many generations, she has kept a vivid rancor against the Russians – but who wouldn't if placed in her position? "I presume you parents are still alive."

"My father passed away and my mother is driving me nuts!" she smiled.

"Oh, yes; now that you're telling me, I recall you mentioning it to Father Ungari."

"Yes, but she is doing much better now: she travels a lot and that has eased our relationship a bit."

"Where is she traveling to: Florida, the Bahamas...?"

"Oh, no; those are good destinations for me," she laughed. "My mother travels a lot to Paris, Cairo and Ankara where she has some old relatives with whom she loves to spend time."

"You can't blame her; that must remind her of her childhood... of the days she met your father."

"As long as she is happy..." Ava commented with fatality before bursting into laughter.

"What? What is it...? Why are you laughing?" I asked.

"She never stops amazing me! Just the other day, my mom calls me in the middle of the night and tells me that it's the end of the world because it's one o'clock and the sky is pitch black. It turned out that she had taken one too many sleeping pills and when she had awakened, she had no notion of whether it was night or day."

"That's worrisomely funny."

"The funniest thing is that she had walked through the hallways of her apartment building in search of survivors," giggled Ava.

"I didn't know what the end of the world would be like, but now I have a pretty good idea: it's filled with confused old people wandering around in their pajamas..." I said.

"That's not nice; my mom is not insane!"

"God forbid! I wouldn't dare... But I would seriously suggest that you ask your mom's doctor to reduce her prescription for sleeping pills, because this kind of dysphasia can produce violent anxiety attacks with the potential to cause a fatal heart-attack."

"Thanks for the advice. I'll try... if she allows me," Ava said, raising her eyebrows to signal that it would not be easy to convince her mother.

We spent a few more minutes scrutinizing with minutia the pictures of Ava's ancestors. It was interesting to see on the one side the transition between the very formal pictures of some eighty or so years ago that resembled official court portraits - very rigid in composition and in tenure, but nevertheless very valuable - and the pictures taken a few decades later with personal photo cameras, capturing much more the private life of the people they were portraying.

After looking at all those pictures and benefiting from Ava's enlightening commentaries, I almost had the illusion that I knew these people; I almost felt like family. To be more accurate, I wish I had known these people with extraordinary lives of a bygone era. I had visions of them in extraordinary horse battles, charging the Red Army's advancing troops in a desperate attempt to preserve their freedom, their land, and their historical and cultural personae.

"Now, I know where your fierce warrior instincts and overconfident demeanor come from," I commented, not without a hint of sarcasm.

"Now, you know," she replied with a smile.

"From now on, I am not going to dare to make any jokes for fear of you beheading me with this magnificent Bukhariot sword."

"You're right; I might just do that, because your humorizing - often untimely - can occasionally be truly annoying," she said playfully, affecting discomfort.

"It would be tragic and comic at the same time if you'd do that," I exclaimed with a smile. "Newspaper headers would read: 'Man decapitated for making ill-perceived jokes.' The news of it would be instantly posted on the Drudge Report and replicated on websites around the world."

"Then don't give me a reason to do it."

These Baklavas Will Kill You

Naval Observatory, Washington DC

"Good to see you, Condi."

"Happy to see you, too, Dick," Condi said. She had known the Vice-President at least since the Bush '41' era and more than likely from the Reagan Administration time.

It was not insignificant that Dick received her in the more private setting of his residence and furthermore in the sunroom, his favorite spot in the house. The space exuded the kind of coziness that fitted perfectly what Dick had in mind when he invited Condi for afternoon tea. Dick had carefully displayed on the coffee table a couple of African art books that he had purposely purchased for this occasion.

"Condi, let me tell you that I am very happy with the way things are progressing under your guidance at the Department of State. You've been a tremendous promoter of our agenda and I can assure you that I always personally make sure that the President is aware of it."

"Thank you, Dick. I am not sure if I deserve it, but I must confess that we've done a pretty good job circumventing those

Euro-liberal whiners and advancing a truly American agenda in jive with our conservative values."

"You bet you did," Dick said, "and I've put a word to the Secretary of Homeland Security to include Birmingham as home for one of the four regional centers he's planning to set up by the end of the year; it'll give you a little boost locally, although, you don't need it. But, hey, if the folks at home are not happy, then nobody's happy."

"Are you kidding, Dick? It's very useful. There are always some nosy journalists who are looking for skeletons in the closet. They usually like to drop by your hometown in search of some juicy stories. So, if the local folks are happy because I've brought them jobs, then they are not going to badmouth me." Condi said, her eyes gleaming with satisfaction.

"So, how are things going?" Dick asked.

"Well, not too bad, I must say. The Department understands the challenges facing our new role on the international scene and the responsibilities bestowed upon our great nation by history and by God."

"I wouldn't have said it better, Condi; you are a true patriot," Dick said, before interrupting the conversation to allow the collation to be served.

"I asked them to get us some French pastries to accompany the tea; I thought you'd like that."

"Very thoughtful of you; you know my weakness. Although, I try to keep away from this kind of temptation..."

"You don't have to love the French to love their food," Dick said.

"Yes, you're right. I remember in the days before the Iraq war, we had so much vilipended the French that it was impossible for me to go to some of my favorite French restaurants without causing a scandal if someone spotted me. So, to appease my cravings for real gourmet food, I would ask a girlfriend of mine to order takeout for me."

"Would you like some more of this one? I think it's called a Napoleon. It's absolutely delicious; so moist, so juicy that it melts in your mouth in the blink of an eye."

"Thank you, but I think I am going to take some of this Mille-Feuilles now."

"To leave food for a minute, I would like to talk to you about a little plan, which, if all goes well, would be incredibly rewarding for the both of us," Dick said, in an assured voice.

"I am listening, Dick, while I am trying this Religieuse thing."

"As you know, the presidential elections are fast approaching and the President has done his two terms, which leaves the horizon wide-open for a new candidate."

"I am flattered, Dick, but I don't think I deserve the honor to lead our Party to a new victory: there are better qualified people than me."

"There is nobody better qualified than you, Condi. But as you and I have discussed the issue in the past, you know that the country, including our party, is not ready to elect a black president."

"I know that; isn't it sad?"

"It is - and you know how I feel about it - this is why I have a plan."

"What is it?"

"My plan is that you and I form a ticket: I give confidence to the WASP majority, use my clout over the party to crush any contender and raise more money than anyone has ever seen and…"

"Why would you need me then?" Condi interrupted.

"You are going to bring a lot to the table; you'll bring in the black vote and the women's vote: that's what will make the difference and assure our success in a landslide."

"This is simply brilliant!" Condi said. "It would be an honor and a privilege to be on your side."

"Wait; that was not the best part: I have more…"

"Can it get any better than that?"

"The best part is that – and I think you're going to like this one – after two years, I pretext my heart condition to resign and you become…"

"…The first Black President in United States' History!" Condi yelled in a voice that went crescendo in pitch and in joy.

"And you'll be in an extraordinarily favorable position to win the next election two years later…" Dick added.

"You are not serious, Dick. You are just trying to get me."

"I am dead serious! Do I look like somebody who makes practical jokes?"

"Wow! I can't believe this," Condi said, as she stood up with tears in her eyes to embrace Dick. "But you have to promise me one thing…"

"Sure; just tell me."

"That, even after I become President, you'll be around to back me up and help me."

"Of course, I will. Now, would you like some baklavas instead of Champagne to celebrate our historic understanding? I had them specially prepared for the 'bouquet final.'"

"That's unusual… The heck with my diet! I am so happy that I'd eat all of them!"

"Don't choke on it," Dick said with imperceptible sarcasm, "and watch yourself, Condi; the country needs you and, most importantly, I need you for our greater design."

"Don't worry; nothing in this world will prevent me from reaching that moment. We are going to make it happen," she said with her fist clenched as a sign of determination.

"I cannot emphasize enough the need for absolute secrecy," Dick said. "It's between you and me and nobody else."

"Not even the President?"

"I think it wouldn't be wise to include him – or anybody else, for that matter - in our strategy at this stage… or at any stage."

"I understand; we'll take our little secret to the grave," Condi said, still overwhelmed by her joy.

"That's what I like about you: we understand each other so perfectly." Dick said.

After Condi left, Dick sat back in his chair and reflected on the victory he had just scored. Sipping a cup of tea, he looked beyond the bay window to the future he was building one brick at a time.

It took patience and a lot of strategizing to manipulate the different elements that contribute – knowingly or unknowingly – to the realization of '1492,' bearing in mind that one of the *sine qua non* conditions for success is that most of the 'stake-holders' remain ignorant of one another's involvement.

Unlike '43,' Dick was not of the most feverish religious type. Whereas for the President, Christianity was foremostly understood in its religious aspect, Dick viewed it more through its civilizational characterization. He did not adhere entirely to the rhetoric put forward by '43' and the Evangelicals but – strategy *oblige* - he played along with them to serve his own agenda. Besides, the difference in their concepts had more to do with nuances than chiasms. So, as a strategist of talent, he played to each the type of tune they wanted to hear, hoping that, in the end, he would direct the symphony that he had patiently composed, attracting the admiration of US and World audiences for his own glory.

"Honey, do you want some more pastry?" Lynne asked, waking him from his reveries.

"Hum... what? Oh no, thanks. You know I hate French pastries. I'll have some baklava instead, if there is any left."

"You're killing yourself with these damned Middle-Eastern pastries: they are full of fat and sugar."

"I know, honey; just one more."

"After all, it is your health...! I was just reminding you what your doctor told you..."

"I know what he told me: he advised me to drink tea - a lot of tea. That's exactly what I am doing, look." Dick showed off his cup filled with green tea.

"That's very good, honey; but he also asked you to cut down these poisonous sweets you've become addicted to."

"Sure, honey; I am doing my best. But with the kind of intense permanent brainstorming that I have to do, I need to absorb sugars. Besides, the tea I am drinking helps me lower my cholesterol and my diabetes. I am not doing that bad, honey; stop worrying senselessly!"

"Again, it's your health... I am going to the kitchen to see how things are moving along. Don't forget that we have guests tonight."

"What a pest," Dick said after she left. He hated it when his wife talked to him as if he were a little kid. The fact that she has a PhD and he dropped out before getting his made her think that he is no match to her intellectually. This otherwise insignificant little factor has always had a lingering effect on their relationship: as a result, Dick has developed a bit of a complex, forgetful of his own outstanding political career. So, when Lynne admonishes him for things as banal as what to eat and what not to eat, Dick resents it beyond normal.

Probably because his wife had upset him, Dick remembered the days when he was attracted to Condi. Though he was too shy to have ever made any overt attempts to court her, he had a recurrent dream in which they are torridly interlaced in the Oval Office when an usher opens wide the double doors and a handful of stunned visiting foreign dignitaries, accompanied by his own wife, enter the room... And that's when his sensually sweet, torrid, dream turns into a tragic nightmare!

The Senator's Wife

I had not slept well and woke up early in the morning. For one, it's always difficult to sleep well in a new bed due to the orientation, the bedding itself, and – believe it or not – the smell of the sheets; and two, perhaps influenced by what I had witnessed lastly with my share of tragic occurrences, I had nightmares involving members of my family whose deaths I was witnessing without being able to act or even move.

It was raining outside and, because of the early hour, the street below Ava's apartment was deserted; it felt like a winter Sunday morning in London, rather gloomy. I decided that it would be nice to prepare breakfast. I found my way around her kitchen and set up the table, but didn't start to make the scrambled eggs or toast the bread because I thought that, by the time she would wake up, they would be cold. I checked outside her door, looking for a newspaper, but I was out of luck. Since I hadn't slept very well, I was not in the mood for a book. After browsing once again over the pictures of Ava's ancestors, I sank into the sofa and turned on the TV.

I am keen on watching - or alternatively listening on the radio - a show named "Imus in the Morning," which is a mixture of entertaining politics and news. What I find exhilarating about this show is that you never know whom the 'I-man' is going to insult or – to quote an expression often used on air – 'suck up' to. In a time of phony political correctness and reverence, those who dare to appear on his show – apart from a very short list of favorites – never know if the lion is going to turn into a jackal or a domesticated cat.

The other day, Imus hung up the phone - with a digitally added screechy noise effect to make it a more strident rejection - on a notorious New York attorney who, despite the mocking he is subjected to, has been a returning guest, probably believing that there is no bad publicity, only publicity... Senators, congressmen, presidential candidates, former presidents and current Vice-Presidents, media moguls, reporters, anchors, athletes, show-biz personalities, etc: they all get their due on this show – and often rightly so...

I like this spirit of bravado. I've had enough of the obsequious flatteries; enough of the subdued reverence to the political establishment; and enough of the of the 'kiss the hand you cannot cut off' philosophy! Question first whether the hand that you are asked to kiss is worthy or not. In any case, a good handshake - or an accolade - is always preferable to a kiss of the hand. Pardon my pestering on this subject but I hate submissiveness.

I was calmly sitting there, having a rather good time watching the media pundits and the politicos being joyfully hodge-podged and grilled when suddenly something small and alive hit my legs and disappeared in the dark under the armoire. A cat stared at me, ready to do it again. I saw only glowing eyes: to Ava's little feline pet, I was a stranger intruding in a world it owned. But since I had experienced similar crises of jealousy in the past, I didn't worry too much and acted as if nothing had happened; to the contrary, trying to talk to the little feline to appease the tension. The cat did one or two more rounds from one corner of the room to the other before it eventually calmed down and disappeared.

"Good morning; I see that you are an early bird!" Ava said, apparently having had an excellent night of sleep - unlike me.

"Good morning to you."

"I am impressed!" she exclaimed as she reached the kitchen and saw that everything was ready for breakfast.

"It's really nothing; I had time to kill so I thought I might as well be helpful."

"It's very kind of you. By the way, have you seen my little bundle of fur?"

"What do you mean?"

"My little bundle of joy... the real owner of this house."

"I believe he has surreptitiously introduced himself to me."

"Did he? Was he nice to you?"

"Let us say that he manifested a little bit of displeasure to have a guest staying overnight without his prior approval."

"Rostam, come here! Where are you?"

The cat finally showed up and rubbed itself against my legs before jumping on the seat to my right. The feline was a stunningly beautiful animal, reddish in color, looking more like a miniaturized version of a cougar or a lion.

"Is this a domestic cat? I have never seen anything like it."

"Yes, it's of the Abyssinian breed."

"Just amazing! It almost makes me feel like getting one."

187

From where I sat, I had a direct view of the TV that was still on in the living room. Suddenly, the pictures of a car accident drew my attention.

"Ava, look at that!" I yelled, pointing my finger at the TV screen.

"What is it?" she replied with astonishment before turning around to see.

"The images of the accident: don't they look very similar to the picture sent by the bad guys?"

"You know, all traffic accidents look more or less the same," Ava said, playing it down.

"Look! Here is the picture… Look at the truck and look at the car: they are definitely the same!"

"You're right! Let me increase the volume so we can hear what they are saying."

« … *As I said, Jenny, we don't know the exact circumstances of the accident that caused the death of Senator Patrick Gareth's wife late yesterday afternoon, but we are waiting here in front of the Senator's home, hoping for a comment. Now back to you Jenny…*»

« *Lisa, do we know who caused the accident… whose fault was it: the truck driver or the Senator's wife?* »

«*We do not have that information yet. The Police are investigating and said that they would probably release a report later in the day.* »

«*All right; thank you, Lisa… And we'll keep you updated on this tragic traffic accident that has caused the death of Senator Gareth's wife.*

«*Now, on to some more jovial news: National Zoo authorities are announcing that the giant panda Jiang Qing gave birth last night to the little Zhao Ziang …* »

"Now, we know. But why would they kill the wife of a prominent Senator?" Ava wondered aloud as she turned off the TV.

"There is only one way to find out…"

US Senate, Russell Building

"First of all, Senator, I wanted to thank you for accepting to receive us in such a short notice and under these tragic circumstances," Ava started to say.

"You're welcome! When my staff told me that you wanted to see me but would not give the reason, at first I balked – because, as you can guess, we have to be careful here - but when I saw the name of Mr. Haftemizan, I immediately gave my consent."

"That's very kind of you, Sir," I said.

"I've read a couple of your books." The Senator seemed to be a genuinely amicable person. "You may not remember this, but we also met once in the green room of a TV show and we had a nice exchange."

"Yes, now that you mention it…" I lied as if I remembered.

Senator Gareth's office was overcrowded with pictures chronicling his long career. Eagle-themed objects of all kinds were everywhere: from the light on the desk to the knob on the door, from the bookcase's frontispiece to the big ring on his finger. I am sure that if he were permitted to keep a live eagle in a cage in his office, he would certainly have one... Oh, I forgot to tell you about the funniest piece of all: a large – very large -

marble nameplate right in the middle of his desk, facing the visitors: just in case whoever was able to get an appointment and go through a drastic screening did not know who the guy sitting in front of him was… I personally think that this sign has nothing to do with practicalities, but rather with the affirmation of an ego commensurate to the ambitions of the Senator.

"Senator, we have come to talk to you about the death of your wife," Ava said. "What happened is tragic but we wanted to tell you that there is more to it than just a traffic accident."

"What do you mean?" the Senator said.

"Look at this, Senator." Ava placed a print out of the picture I had received by e-mail on his desk.

"So?" said the Senator, not impressed. "This is a picture of the accident."

"It's not just any picture. It's a picture Haftemizan has received by e-mail."

"I am sorry, but I still don't see what you mean… Maybe I am a little bit slow today, considering the circumstances. Could you be kind enough to tell me what exactly you expect me to guess?"

"We understand perfectly, Senator, what you're going through and we are very thankful that you've accepted to see us," I said to acknowledge the circumstances and give the man credit for his courtesy. "The *hic* here is that this picture was taken only seconds after the accident and minutes before the Police or any rescue team were able to reach the location."

"Why would somebody take a picture of the accident and send it to you?" The Senator scratched his head. "…Unless you were somehow involved…. Unless you had an affair with my wife and whoever took the picture is blackmailing you … and you've come to me to… to blackmail me!" The Senator had a string of negative conclusions popping up in his mind and infuriating him.

"Senator, I am sure your wife – God bless her soul – was a beautiful lady but I did not know her; nor have I ever seen her. We are here to tell you that your wife's death may have resulted from foul play."

"What?"

"We suspect that the picture was taken by somebody who was directly involved in the murder of your wife," Ava said.

"How could it be a murder? Unless you mean that she was the victim of an involuntary manslaughter?"

"No, Sir, we mean real, premeditated murder," Ava said. "The picture was sent by an individual - or a group - that had done something similar as recently as a few days ago. Without revealing the details of our investigation, we know that it's not innocent. We know that it is a murder."

"But why...?" The Senator sat back in his chair, overwhelmed by incomprehension. "Who are those people? Why would they kill my wife? We have no connection whatsoever with Mr. Haftemizan; unless I am missing something here..."

"Have you received any threats lately?" Ava asked.

"No, not a single one - from what I know - but I'll ask my staff."

"There must be a link..." I started to explain. "Here is what we can tell you in summary: we are pursuing on behalf of Interpol an investigation into the plans of a group that we suspect is plotting some large scale terrorist action and these people are not happy with us being nosy... But I have to stop here, Senator. I can't tell you more about it," I interrupted my explanation to avoid leaking any vital information.

"We would like you to ask the Police to open a criminal investigation into your wife's death," Ava said. "But unfortunately you cannot cite what we told you - at least not at this time - because we are onto something much larger."

"Whatever we shared with you today is under the seal of complete confidentiality," I stressed.

"Yes, I understand. You can trust me for that, but I still don't comprehend why I am being indirectly targeted – if such is the case!"

"Think about it, Senator," I suggested as we were on our way out. "Review your recent activities; make a list of the people you've met recently and with whom you've had a strident, perhaps, personal disagreement or confrontation. I would also suggest that you think about sensitive policy issues and 'things like that' - as Arnold would say - and give us a call if you find anything, even the tiniest little link."

"Sure," the Senator said, preoccupied.

"Thank you for your time, Senator; and again: our condolences," Ava said, concluding our meeting with Senator Gareth.

"Do you have any idea who the terrorists are?" the Senator asked, as we began to exit his office.

"We don't know exactly, but we have reasons to believe that their plot has something to do with '1492,'" Ava said, before closing the door behind her.

Washington DC, FBI Headquarters

"Mother of Jesus!" the man said, as he examined intelligence reports he had received. Jack was tasked with creating a digest of all relevant information with highlights for the Director, who would, after careful review, pass it on to the President in a rotating process and in alternation with the DCI and the 'Intelligence Czar.' Although it was late - almost 10 PM – Jack picked up the phone and called his boss:

"Sir, I'm glad you are still here," Jack said.

"Where the hell could I be?" Rupert Molinero said. "Since 9/11, I have no family life, no vacation, no holiday and it seems as if I am sleeping in this damned office every night. I feel like the terrorists we keep in birdcages in Guantanamo are freer than I am!"

"I'll be right over, Sir." Jack said.

The files he put on the Director's desk were essentially made up of communication transcripts picked up by the NSA as well as excerpts from reports filed by various agents implanted on the ground.

"If I had the time and the patience to read all the so-called 'sensational' intelligence we get from the CIA and the other agencies, I wouldn't need you and a dozen like you to compile them for me," Rupert Molinero said with impatience. "So, why don't you just tell me what it's all about?"

"Very well, sir. In summary, Iranian and Syrian authorities are worried that we are going to attack them."

"How so...?"

"Well, sir, it's not totally clear at this time, but it seems that the intelligence services of both Teheran and Damascus have collected information hinting at the preparation of attacks being launched against them from neighboring countries that we currently occupy."

"It doesn't make sense. We have no immediate plan for attacking them... We certainly have contingency plans and computerized simulations - as we have for most places in the world for when and if the need arises - but, from what I know, there is nothing very serious on the table at this time," FBI Director Molinero commented before pausing, "...and if there were something, I would have been informed; right?"

"Without a doubt, Sir!" Jack said to reassure his boss so that he didn't think he had been left out of the loop.

"Or, perhaps - come to think about it - our guys may have picked up, with some delay - desperately tardy translations *oblige* - the stir and the speculations that the Administration's recent firm declarations on Syria and Iran have caused..."

"It might be the case; I don't know for sure. But the reports seem to indicate that their spies have noticed suspicious movements in the vicinity of their respective borders - with Iraq, in the case of Syria; with Afghanistan, in the case of Iran."

"This is odd. I think there is something going on that we are unaware of. We have to be very cautious," Molinero said.

"I agree, Sir; there is something fishy about it."

"Let us keep this quiet until we are able to steer things clear... Actually, I am going to call Porter right now."

"I agree, Sir; excellent idea!"

The repetitive "I agree, Sir" coming out of Jack's mouth triggered a quick reflection in Molinero's head – with a zest of reaction - on the subject of boss-to-employee relations, concluding at first that Jack was not much more than a sycophant, readily agreeing with whatever his superior was saying. Then, in an exercise of internal dialectic, he revised his view, taking into consideration that his position of power was de facto conducive of a certain form of sycophantism and, second, that in the exchange they just had, there was no room for expressing opinions and therefore not much room for disagreement.

The conversation Molinero had with his counterpart Porter Floss at the head of the CIA did not shed any light on what he suspected could be something significant. What astonished him more was that Floss was clueless:

"I don't know, Rupert. It's the middle of the night and I am dead tired..."

"My guy saw the information in the classified reports coming from your agency: you must have seen it," Molinero insisted with a tad of exasperation.

"I didn't see it; or if I saw it, I didn't pay attention...There is too much traffic, too many reports, too much to read, too much to digest...I am tired...I told the President that I can't do this anymore...I want my life back!"

"Quit whining, Porter, for God's sake! Do you think that I have time to read every little piece that circulates under the radar? Believe me, Porter; I hate my job as much as you do – especially since 9/11 - and I would quit in the blink of an eye if I could."

"Why don't you do it?"

"The President doesn't want me to. He says that if I leave at this critical hour, it would equate to a betrayal... Well, you've got to do what you've got to do!" Molinero said with fatalism.

"I may very well die before I can quit," Porter said.

"Don't tempt the devil!"

"You know what I miss the most, Rupert?"

"No, what? The sharks off the beaches of Naples, because you find them friendlier than the ones roaming Washington's murky waters..." Molinero said.

Floss laughed. "You almost got it. I miss the boating, the fishing, the *fare-niente*, the good time..."

"...And the superb creatures cruising on the beaches... I know what you mean..." Molinero joked.

"I knew I shouldn't have listened to my wife..." Floss said.

"Welcome to my world, Porter. There is one thing you should know: wives hate to see their husbands having a good time. They'd do anything to empty your surroundings and build in the vacuum their own wall of suffocating love and possessiveness. Besides, they want to be able to tell their girlfriends 'my husband is a big shot: did you see him on TV the other day?'... I think you were having too much of a good time and that's what betrayed you."

"How do you know?" Floss was flabbergasted by what his counterpart had just guessed. "You just described in few words what I am living, damn it!"

"Part of our job at the FBI is psychological profiling. So, over the years, you become expert in reading into situations and comportments..."

"I wish I had known you more on a personal level before... You could have saved me from this misery!"

"Come on, Porter; don't let yourself down like this! We're in this together and, to cite one of our very own Dear Leader's favorite quotes: 'we will prevail!'" Molinero said, attempting to boost the morale of his suffering colleague.

"I guess you're right; I shouldn't be so demoralized. After all, I am servicing the nation at a critical time and the President has entrusted me with his confidence," Porter Floss reasoned. "As for this issue, I'll look into it, Rupert; and I'll let you know what I discover."

"Thanks, Porter; but use extra discretion: there is something fishy about this. If you find something, let us consult one another before we do anything: do you agree?"

"I agree; do you mean absolutely nobody?"

"Yes, absolutely n-o-b-o-d-y! Or else, I'll have you eat Dick's famous baklavas or ask Don to throw you in jail at Abu-Ghraib: whichever is worse."

Porter laughed. "Don't tell me Dick treated you with baklavas too...?"

"Every time I see him," Molinero said, laughing irrepressibly with nervous snorts.

"Tragic," Porter Floss commented.

Passed Damocles

Ava was able to gather the information allowing us to identify Father Emilio Ungari's friend, the discreet whistle-blower – so to speak – who had been the primary relay of information permitting Interpol to get involved in the investigation of the plot dubbed '1492.'

Some astute research on the Internet had allowed us to find his address. We decided to pay him a little visit. It would have certainly been more courteous to call ahead to make an appointment, but then we figured that perhaps he would deny us such a privilege and act as if he didn't know what it was all about. To avoid wasting precious time, we decided to show up at his door – a little bit cavalierly perhaps, but efficient. Besides, nothing can replace a nice chat between friends of friends in the friend's home...

The house was one of those late Eighteenth Century villas in Georgetown, made of red bricks and very appealing in appearance. Emilio was right when he said that his friend belonged to a wealthy family: this piece of real estate must be worth millions. We walked passed the bricked alley surrounded by trees and rang the doorbell repeatedly, but nobody answered. We decided that we would stick around until somebody shows up.

197

We hadn't yet reached the car when we saw the person we were looking for walk in front of us and pass through the wide open entrance gate. Ava elbowed me and we turned around and followed him.

"Jim Azuelos," Ava called.

"Yes, what is it?" The man seemed a bit surprised.

"We are friends of Father Emilio Ungari," Ava said. "Can we take a minute of your time?"

"Oh, uh… Sure… Come on in," the man said, this time seriously discountenanced.

By mentioning Emilio's name, Jim Azuelos understood right away that we were neither itinerant sales people nor a couple of lunatic Jehovah's Witnesses. He opened the door and let us in the large foyer before leading us to a formal reception room. As we were about to sit down, he changed his mind and invited us to follow him into the patio garden. He was obviously made uncomfortable by our visit.

"We'll be more at ease in here," he said. "So, how can I help you?"

Ava started. "We are friends of Father Emilio Ungari – so to speak – and we are here to seek your help."

"If you are working for a charitable organization he is sponsoring, please give me your dossier and I'll make sure that my father pays the proper attention to it," Jim Azuelos responded.

"I think there might be a misunderstanding: we are not here to seek a donation; we are here to ask you about 'you know what'…" I said in an attempt to clarify the reason for our presence.

"I am sorry, but I don't understand what you are talking about. Besides, I don't even know who you are!"

"You're absolutely right. How uncivil of us! Go ahead, Ava, tell Mr. Azuelos who we are, please," I said, leaving the responsibility to Ava, in case she planned on shielding our real identities.

"I work for Interpol and here is my card," she said, as she handed Jim Azuelos a visit card and flashed her badge. "And this is Mr. Haftemizan..."

"It's all right," our host interrupted, "I know who he is."

"Really," Ava said, tired of seeing me being recognized by our interviewees – in fact, it was the second time only.

"Sure; I once attended a speech he gave at JHU and another time I got a signed copy of his book when he was promoting it at Politics and Prose."

"So, it was you..." I joked.

"Yes, that was I," Jim Azuelos responded, keeping up with the humoristic tone.

It may appear strange to some of you, but this simple connection between our host and me changed radically the atmosphere of our encounter, which went from painfully tense to somewhat agreeable and almost friendly.

"Would you like something to drink? I can make you some coffee – Italian style: I have an espresso machine - or I have some home-made iced-tea..."

"I'll have some iced-tea," Ava said.

"I'll opt for the espresso, if it's not too much trouble," I replied.

"No, not at all! Actually, I was going to make one for myself."

Our host was a tall, mid-thirty, rare-haired, elegantly dressed young man with agreeable manners, and perhaps even a little bit shy – I noticed that he was embarrassed to look at Ava when speaking with her, probably intimidated by her attractive demeanor.

"Mr. Azuelos, you do know why we are here…?" Ava said.

"Call me, Jim, please… And if you could give me a hint, that would certainly help me," he said, pledging ignorance.

"Jim, here is the issue: we are working on a case your friend Father Emilio Ungari had informed Interpol of. And if I may add, at this time, we know more than you would like us to know and less than we would like to know," I said to clear his mind from any type of confusion as to the nature of our visit.

"Why did he send you to me?"

"He would have told you that himself but…."

"I knew I shouldn't have trusted an ecclesiastic, friend or not."

"…He is dead!" I finished my sentence with a dramatic effect, pausing to savor the reaction on his face – a bit sadistic, isn't it?

"What? Emilio is dead?" Jim reacted, shocked.

We went on to explain what had happened during the last hectic days, including how his good friend Emilio had more than likely been the target of an assassination by some sort of poisoning while traveling with us.

"Are you sure Emilio has been assassinated and not victim of a heart attack or something similar?"

"We are not a hundred per cent sure because we are still waiting for the results of the necropsy but, from what we have seen lastly, there is little doubt about it," Ava said.

"That means that I am next in line!"

"We are all potentially 'next in line'..." I pointed out, to give him some comfort but also to relate a basic truth.

"I think not... I think that I am probably on top of the list," Jim said.

"Why would you think of yourself as the next victim? It's certainly possible, but at this time, you have no indication that they have uncovered who you are and even less what you've done," Ava said.

"If you guys were able to track me so easily, then..."

"Non obstante the fact that we are exceptionally gifted hound dogs... you're probably right," I concurred.

"Don't you see? They have been able to go up layer by layer: Emilio's brother, then Emilio himself; now, it's my turn and surely enough the next victim will be my father!"

"Your senses of logic and deduction are pretty startling," I commented. "But I would suggest that you do not jump too fast to conclusions, because we are not there yet."

"Perhaps, but I can already feel the Sword of Damocles hanging over my head," Jim said, wrapping his hands around his own neck as if he were being strangled - instead of impaled...

"I hate to play the realist-pessimist here, but we are beyond the Damocles situation: at this stage, whatever you do or do not do – and I am using the very clever logical suite you just laid out a minute ago - you are on the hit list," I remarked.

"He is right," Ava said. "And this is why you need to help us as much as you can."

"I am certainly ready to help you out, but convincing my father is going to be a demiurgic enterprise."

"Jim, we know you are a smart and sensible man; we know you can do it and I have a guess that you know very well how to skillfully pull your father's strings - every son knows how to do it," I said, not without humor and not without truth in it.

Ava's cell phone rang to the theme of 'Tomorrow Never Dies' – persistent proof that she has a good sense of humor. She looked at the LCD screen, recognized the caller, took the call and walked a little further for privacy. In the meanwhile, Jim and I engaged in banal chatter to kill time.

"You have a very nice place here," I said, sitting back and enjoying the view from every angle.

"Thanks, it's indeed very nice, but it's not mine: it's my parents'."

"I thought you lived here."

"I do live here; I love its 'secluded and yet in the heart of town' aspect... I live over there, right behind you." Jim pointed at a one-storey brick building with two wide double doors. "This was initially a carriage house, which throughout the years has served as a warehouse, a workshop, a garage - and everything in between - and now it's an in-law suite."

"Very nice," I said. "You have all the convenience of being with family while enjoying your privacy: it's like the Vatican in Rome..."

Jim smiled. "I must say that I am not totally dissatisfied with this little arrangement."

While chatting with Jim, I periodically glanced at Ava talking on the phone, trying to guess from her body language whether the call was of any special relevance to our investigation.

I don't know if it's just me or if you were sitting in my place you'd be sharing my point of view, but I couldn't help being moved once again by the grace of Ava's movements and the harmonious proportions of her body. Her phone stuck to her ear, she was genuflected, scrapping notes on a small pad that she was holding in place on her leg with the help of her auricular finger. To maintain her balance, she kept moving in a circular fashion, drawing a circle on the white-pebbled ground. The amazing thing is that she made the utmost simple khaki pants, white t-shirt and sandals combination she was wearing look like an haute-couture fashion arrangement. By the way she was bent, with her hair pulled back, in the middle of the boxed garden at the end of the patio, she looked like a Rodin sculpture, the result of a careful study in feminine harmony – minus the turn-of-century callipygian bottom, of course.

"Poisoning," Ava exclaimed, as she returned to her seat.

"Are they a hundred per cent certain?" I asked, guessing that she was referring to Emilio's death.

"Affirmative; without the shadow of a doubt. They said he was poisoned with some type of pesticide," Ava confirmed in an authoritative way.

"A pesticide?" Jim and I wondered in unison.

"That's what the autopsy revealed. That's why it took them so long to figure it out. The product is odorless, tasteless and acts slowly. If it is ingurgitated by a human, it makes the death appear as though the victim has had a heart-attack."

"These guys are really good!" I marveled, before pausing for a second and doing a silent handclap.

"Now, there is no more permissible doubt: we know who is next on their list," Jim said, unexpectedly joyful.

"You are not suicidal, are you?" I asked, surprised by his mood, which was not the type of reaction one would expect from someone who has just realized that he could be history at any minute.

"No, Mr. Haftemizan. The mask that you are seeing at this moment is probably out of nervousness… I beg your pardon but all this is not an everyday occurrence for me. If I seem to be acting odd, please forgive me," Jim said, before standing up and adding: "I should be fine in a couple of minutes."

Jim Azuelos appeared to be on the verge of a psychological meltdown. He walked in a resolute pace, head down, towards the house, stopped in front of the large French doors, took a deep breath - as if he were going to dive and swim under water - opened the double-doors in an ample, quiet movement before quickly shutting them behind him. To our complete bedazzlement, he repeated the same suite of movements twice, with a pause in between, where he would stand still, take a deep breath and move his arms up and down – again, as if he were in a swimming pool, ready to take a dive... When he came back, he looked amazingly serene. However bizarre his method of relaxation may have been, it worked and I can even say that it worked rather fast!

"I sincerely apologize for my disruptive behavior," Jim said, a large smile forming on his face as he fell back in his seat. "Now, I am fine."

"It's perfectly all right," Ava said.

"Absolutely," I concurred. "And by the way, Jim, one of these days you'll have to teach me your method for instant relaxation: I've never seen anything like it!"

"You could certainly use it," Ava smirked.

"Sure; come on by one day and I'll be honored to show you - if I am still alive."

"May I ask you something?" I said, looking straight at Jim.

"Sure; go ahead, shoot," Jim replied, ready for some tough questions.

"Forgive my curiosity, but how come you took this position? I guess it must have been a difficult choice."

"What do you mean?"

"It must have been difficult to make the decision of revealing what was going on under the radar in your own home," I attempted to clarify.

"Well, yes and no. It was indeed difficult to make a decision on triggering a process that could be ill-perceived by my father but, since the purpose was that it ultimately benefits him as well as the world we live in, my hesitation did not last too long."

Ava was blunt. "Why didn't you go straight to the Police?"

"I guess the dilemma was not resolved after all. It's never resolved when you're dealing with family members and friends... That's perhaps why I decided to go through this odd path, through my friend Emilio, who was one of the most brilliant and ethical human beings I've ever come across in my life."

"Indeed, he was a good man," I said, to add to the eulogy. "For the short time I had the privilege of knowing him, he came across as a humanist, a dignified and stand-up guy."

"I knew what he was doing for the Vatican. So, I thought that he could be the trusted friend who would shield me and my father from any spill while helping to uncover what was going on, naively hoping that I would be able to have it both ways."

"...Thwart some ugly, gloomy design and conserve the trust of your father..." I commented sardonically.

"Yes, exactly; but here you are, proof that I have tragically failed."

"Don't blame yourself," Ava said. "If it weren't for you, we would still be in the dark."

"She's absolutely right: don't beat yourself up! This is not the time for the mea culpas," I said to refocus our attention to where it should be. "The real culprits are on the loose and about to commit some ugly actions and that's what we have to worry about; otherwise, we'll have an immense tragedy on our hands."

Madame Secretary

Naval Observatory, Washington DC

"Dick, I meant to ask you…."

"Yes, honey?"

"Are you sure you are doing the right thing by keeping Don out of the loop?"

"Which 'Don'…?"

"Rumsfeld…"

"Oh, absolutely; honey!"

"Isn't he your pal? Besides, he has served this Administration faithfully… I feel guilty about it."

"This is precisely why we don't want him to know ahead of time."

"I don't understand…"

"Well, Don is a good soldier but he's good as long as his mind is not clouded with ideological considerations. During the entire pre-Iraq War period, I had him circumvented by guys like Wolfowitz and Perle, otherwise it would have been a blunder!"

"You two go back a long way: if he discovers that you've included in your plan men who were his subordinates and not him, he will be mad as hell and, honestly, honey, you can't blame him…"

"First off, he is in my plan, but he doesn't know it yet; secondly, Wolfowitz and Perle are not in my plan - at least not in its entirety," Dick explained with a devilish smile.

"What do you mean? They are either in or out... Or is it the same deal as for Rumsfeld: they don't know it yet?"

"Well, honey, the thing is - to talk in a 'rumsfeldian' way - that they are more 'in' than some, but less 'in' than some others, whereas they think that they are much more 'in' than the ones who think that they are totally 'in'...."

"Stop, honey; you're killing me, ha... ha...ha...ha; this is too hilarious!" Lynne said, about to collapse due to uncontrollable laughter.

"Come on, honey! Don't laugh at our Secretary of Defense," Dick said, laughing nervously without being able to put an end to it.

"Seriously, now that you have your senses back, could you translate to me what your 'rumsfeldian' piece of dialectic meant?"

"I thought it was pretty clear, though."

"Enough now, Dick...! Tell me what you meant," Lynne begged.

The Vice-President's cell phone rang – always to the sound of the same transporting Wagnerian tune.

"Saved by the bell! I've got to take this one, honey: it's the President."

"Dick, old pal, how are you doing today? Still hiding in your 'undisclosed location'?"

"Good afternoon to you, Mr. President. Yes, Sir, that's where I happen to be right now."

"You marauder..."

"How can I serve you, Mr. President?"

"I am sure you are surprised that I am using the word 'marauder,' aren't you? Well, that's a word Laura just taught me."

"I am impressed. Although, it is used to my detriment," Dick replied, playing along.

"Get used to it, old pal; because, from now on, you'll hear more of these. Laura and I have made a deal: she's going to teach her jolly husband a new word a day."

"I am ready, and I think that I am going to be forced to have my dictionary on hand so that I am not a 'child left behind,'" Dick said.

"All right; bye, now! Talk to you later..."

"Have a good afternoon, Mr. President," Dick turned his cell phone off and muttered "moron" for the billionth time.

Department of State, Washington DC

I was sitting in the Secretary of State's office, in Foggy Bottom. You may wonder what the hell was I doing there. Let me tell you: in the morning, I had received a call from the Secretary's office telling me that Madame Secretary wanted to consult me on some international issues. Obviously, it was difficult for me to say no. I had done it a couple of times with her predecessors and if I had refused, my gesture could have been interpreted in many ways – all undoubtedly negative. So, I decided to show up. After all, it's always good for my professional image to drop here and there in the conversation that the Secretary of State has asked my views on matters of importance. That will literally ulcerate some of my colleagues, and I am already getting a kick out of it.

I know for a fact that politicians work odd hours and sometimes very late at night, but I thought there were some limitations as to when the appointments were set-up for non-politicians: I am tired and I am hungry – without being too scatological, I've finished digesting my lunch and returned it to Mother Nature hours ago…

"…I am afraid you did, Madame Secretary," I replied with assurance.

The emphatic answer I had just given was in response to the Secretary's inquiry as to whether her Administration had mismanaged the Iraqi conflict.

"Interesting you should say that…" she started to say, appearing pensive, before continuing: "You know that you and I share more than our knowledge of international issues…"

"Yes, I am sure we do," I politely replied, unaware of what exactly she was referring to.

"You may not recall, but you and I have met before," she continued.

"Really?" I tried to unsuccessfully revive my memory.

"It was at a big fundraiser dinner at the Castle some years back…"

"Which one…? Because every year I participate in a couple of such events…"

"It was about five or six years ago and…you were very busy courting some Italian old lady."

"Oh, now I see…" My memory suddenly jump-started with this mention. "You're referring to Countess Dal Ri: what an extraordinary woman!"

"I am sure she was extraordinary," the Secretary snapped with innuendo.

"So, where did we meet?" I asked, aware of the sensitivity she was showing.

"I was sitting to your right."

"Yes, of course; now I remember... What a memorable evening it was!" I said enthusiastically, trying to conceal that I had absolutely no recollection that she's been seated next to me.

"Sure; you remember..." she commented defiantly and not buying it.

I was a bit discountenanced by the direction our conversation was heading, which seemed to be much more a jealousy scene than an expert exchange on burning international issues of the day.

While talking, the Secretary looked at me straight in the eyes, relaying to me a not too subtle message of ... yes... a message of sensual attraction! She sat across the sofa, crossing and uncrossing her legs while smiling, which I could easily interpret as another sign of her keen interest in me. She certainly is an attractive woman – I should add that, in women, too, power and position, add to the appeal - but, as far as I recall, I had not been asked to show up at the Department of State for a romantic date.

I felt that I was prey... that I was being chased by this feline woman who was exhibiting unexpectedly predatory behavior. You know how it is with us, men: we love chasing and we hate to be chased. It may be flattering to be pursued, but since it puts us in an atypical situation, we don't know how to react when it happens.

Incidentally, that is exactly where I stood: I didn't know what to do? Run away or jump on her since she was clearly making it understood that she wanted something to happen. But think about it: what if I read all the signs wrong and my reading of the 'geography of the tender' is all misconstrued? Then I would be in a very uncomfortable position, where I would have made a terrible faux pas while visiting the Secretary of State in her office – officially for an exchange of views. I'll be the laugh of the town and my colleagues would joke about it for decades... And, perhaps, someone will even write on my epitaph: 'He, who ridiculed himself by inappropriately making advances to the Secretary of State, lies here.' That would indeed be a Nagasaki for me.

As I was pondering all the consequences that my-out-of-the-boundaries action could create and persuading myself that I was being delusional, the Secretary had surreptitiously moved closer to me.

"Kiss me, stupid!" she said as she jumped on me to administer a deep French kiss, to my extreme amazement.

"Madame Secretary, what are you doing? This is not reasonable," I attempted to say, while she was holding my face and passionately gluing her lips to mine.

"I like you; and I've liked you ever since I saw you that day … Now, you tell me who do you prefer: that old countess or me?"

"Seriously, this is not reasonable, Condofelizza," I protested once more as I started to take pleasure in our luscious interlude.

"Don't call me Condofelizza while we are doing this; keep calling me 'Madame Secretary,' stupid," she said, as we rolled over and down on the ground.

"What if somebody enters, Madame Secretary?"

"Don't you worry; I've given instructions," she said.

She was obviously getting a kick out of doing this in her office – symbol of her power – with someone who had ignored her in the past and who would submit himself to her forceful desire and to her position by calling her 'Madame Secretary,' while doing it. I'll spare you the psychoanalytical part of this but there would undoubtedly be a lot to say.

Our torrid corps-a-corps lasted for a good hour. She knew exactly what she wanted and I was not unhappy to serve her whims as much as I could. Her firm, athletic, perfumed and lotioned up body was a real delectation and, to tell you the truth, it was an intense, lustful, carnal experience between two consenting adults. I'll omit the details, but I can tell you that it was a 'heated exchange' - to use in a parabolic way an expression otherwise often used in political debates.

Now, I know that all the gossip spread in Washington about her being "frosty" - or even that she is a lesbian - are unfounded - at least from the perspective of my own empirical experience. The sad thing is that I won't be able to share the details of this fling with anyone, because as the saying goes: 'What happens in the State Department, stays in the State Department' – or maybe it is something a bit different? Forgive me if, considering the rush I just went through, I can't remember it exactly…

"Wow! If I knew, I would have never spent that evening chatting with the old Countess and instead I would have courted you," I said.

"Very funny… Now, you know what you missed!" She put her clothes back on and walked toward her office's private bathroom.

"Madame Secretary, you are one incredible piece of …deliciousness," I said, unable to find a better adjective to describe her.

"It's okay; now, you can call me Condi," she suggested in a very serene voice: the kind of tone that signals a degree of intimacy between two people who know each other very well.

"No, it's all right. I want to continue calling you 'Madame Secretary': after all, it gives me more pleasure too," I said seriously before bursting into laughter.

"You are something…" she commented with a smile.

"And you are something else," I said.

It was unwise for me to stay any longer. So, we decided that I would leave and that she would join me at my apartment ASAP for a 'follow up' dinner. She formally accompanied me to her office door and asked one of the ushers to show me the way out, bidding me farewell in a very neutral and courteous fashion, as de rigueur in such circumstances and as she would do with any other visitor.

Haftemizan's Apartment

Condi had been able to lose her Secret Service detail by going home first and then arriving at my place, using subterfuges that only she knows.

On my way home, I had stopped at a nearby trattoria and picked up some freshly cooked pasta – fettuccine – and some extraordinary Roman onion soup that is the specialty of that place. We sat at the dining table, eating and conversing.

"This is really great food. Did you prepare it?"

"No, I picked it up from a trattoria close by that is pretty reputable."

"This is so good," she kept saying as she devoured the onion soup with obvious delectation. "I've never had onion soup like this one before."

"The family that owns the place is from Rome and they say that it's a specialty from their region."

"I guess you've found this great place because you're not the cooking kind of guy..."

"Actually, I am. I get tired of carry-out food, and - time permitting - I like to prepare a nice home-cooked meal now and then."

"Really?" she laughed in disbelief. "What...? Fry two eggs in a pan or heat up in the microwave the take-out food from the previous day...?"

"Since you are underestimating me, Madame Secretary, let me give you a little something to taste and you tell me how you like it..."

I quickly took from the refrigerator a small portion of a dish I had prepared just the day before and warmed it up in a deep pan for just twenty seconds with one drop of olive oil and served it in a large white plate to make it look appealing.

"Wow!" she exclaimed, "this is absolutely, incredibly, fantastically delicious!"

"I told you... I am no chef but I am not too shabby either," I said proudly.

"I don't believe it; you did not cook this... This is too elaborate. You are trying to trick me: I won't fall for that," she said with a smile, persistent in doubting my abilities.

"I have no reason to lie to you..."

"Well, then you've got to give me the recipe for this chicken," she said adamantly, with the kind of certitude that doesn't accept a 'no' for an answer.

"I am afraid I can't."

"What?"

"In short, this is a recipe a friend of mine has passed on to me under strict copyright rules – if I may say."

"What do you mean: is this some kind of invention or what?"

"What I mean is that I am in no way authorized to reveal his secret; otherwise, he has threatened to go medieval on me!"

"This is very funny," Condi laughed.

"This is not a joke; I take his word very seriously: once he actually threw out some nosy guests who were trying to sneak behind him to see what ingredients he was using…"

"Come on; how can you tell me 'no' after what we've shared?" she said, with a disarming smile and using her charms on me.

"Believe me; I would love to, but I've made a promise and I can't break it – although, you have a lot of leverage over me, Madame Secretary."

"Well, too bad for you! Because now that you've made me taste it, I am addicted: you'll have to make me some every time I feel like it…"

"Your wish is my command, milady! Anytime you feel like it…" I responded with a smile in a way that was at least ambiguous.

"You naughty little cook!" she said with a coy smile.

Now, I've become a 'cook'; *mama mia*! I don't reject 'naughty,' but 'cook'… Come on! Although, now that I think about it, 'naughty little cook' is not that bad a compliment after all: it prefigures an interesting intimate program… But I am not telling you anything more about it - I don't have to reveal to you all the meanders existing in my twisted brain!

"Now, tell me," Condi said, seizing a fork full of fettucine, "why do you think that our action in Iraq has been unsuccessful?"

"Well, besides the fact that you shouldn't have gone there in the first place, one of the main reasons, I think, is that you were unable to secure a broad alliance that would have given you the kind of unanimity Desert Storm had."

"I think the Europeans - the French, the Germans - betrayed us," Condi said. "Even the others that came on board did so reluctantly and participated in a mildly symbolic manner."

"They didn't believe your Administration was making a wise decision."

"Whatever…"

"I think I know the real reason why the Europeans don't want be part of the war in Iraq," I suggested.

"Because they are weasels," Condi said.

"That perhaps is one reason… and because they resent American's global influence is another reason."

"That is exactly it! No need to look further: my opinion is already made up," Condi said, satisfied by what she just heard.

"I believe there is one more reason," I continued. "Western-European societies have become too sophisticated and too delicate after half a century of global peace. None of them wanted to be drawn into the kind of anti-colonial insurgency type of war that some of them had experienced not so long ago. They knew the human cost would have been too heavy by today's standards. They calculated that even a few casualties would have been perceived as unbearable by their respective public opinions."

"But aren't we richer than all these countries and aren't we more developed than them?" Condi asked rhetorically. "Why do we accept the sacrifice and not them?"

"That's a very good question – as politicians would say - but I am afraid I can't give you a simple answer, as it would certainly require some thorough, wide and in-depth multi-disciplinary studies to come up with a comprehensive response. What I can say though, is that it has to do with many things, including the fact that, by contrast, in this country, the military has been presented as a sacerdotal duty, one of the pillars of the 'patriotic dogma' by which you cannot question the flag, the military or the President in his capacity as Commander in Chief, otherwise you are branded as 'unpatriotic,' 'un-American,' and you are mercilessly pilloried."

"I think that it may also be because we are so huge, and therefore we are much more able to absorb shocks and accept casualties," said Condi, before adding: "Perhaps, too, because we are more used to violence: just look at some of our TV shows!"

"Yes, you are probably right: scale matters," I agreed. "But coming back to my initial postulate, I think we are an overly militarized society when compared to similar nations of the developed world and we indoctrinate our kids from kindergarten upwards to bow to this patriotic dogma..."

"Come on; you are exaggerating here... What's wrong with being patriotic?"

"Absolutely nothing; as long as it doesn't collide with the First Amendment and it's not used as a tool to force censorship or vilipend those who question the soundness of an Administration's policy."

"Are you referring to the war in Iraq?"

"Absolutely; that is the most recent example. But I could also mention Vietnam, Nicaragua, Afghanistan or even what's happened in Guantanamo, Abu-Ghraib, Bagram, etc..."

"You are probably right," Condi said. "In some areas, it seems as though we are acting as a Third-World country."

"That's the nature of American society: a young Nation, still wild in many ways and yet apparently completely tamed when it comes to some issues..."

"You're right: we are all wild! So, why don't you 'take a walk on the wild side,' babe?" Condi said, with a smile and intoning Lou Reed's song to conclude an exchange that had been perhaps overly serious considering the circumstances.

"Would you like some ice-cream? That's all I have for dessert."

"After such a savory dinner, I think it would be a good addition: what do you have?" Her large cheerful mouth seemed to be insatiable for the good things in life.

"I've got an excellent mango ice cream that I buy from a Thai restaurant: it's a real treat, you'll see," I offered enthusiastically.

Condi smiled. "You're really getting everything from gourmet places."

"Not everything; but as far as food is concerned, if I've liked something during my trips, for example, once I return home, I try to get a flavor that is as close as possible to the original."

"You're right. I do the same with French pastries: that's my little weakness; I can't resist them."

"Really...? I thought you guys hated the French over the Iraqi dossier," I reminded her, underlining the irony of what she had just confessed.

"We did resent their attitude," she explained diplomatically, "but that doesn't mean that I should deprive myself from the good things in life - and food being one of them."

"You are so hypocritical," I pointed out, faking outrage.

"Yeah, sure…" she replied with indifference. "Do you know what I was doing at the height of the tension with Paris?"

"No, tell me."

"I was sending a girlfriend of mine to get me some carry out," she said giggling, proud of her stratagem.

"You are awful. While your pit-bulls were calling all day long on Fox to boycott French and German products, you - duplicitous little …sneaky… cute… little thing - you were indulging your sinful weakness for refined food: you ought to be ashamed of yourself!"

She laughed. "Don't remind me; I feel so guilty…"

We had moved from the dining table to the living room, from the living room to my bedroom and we were now back in the living room, not smoking a cigarette – as you would have expected me to say - but drinking a hot cup of green tea to soothe and relax.

"So much energy, Madame Secretary," I said with the last ounce of remaining vigor. I was dead tired. So much fury, so many thousands of calories burnt in so little time: she is indeed an athlete.

The two lustful encounters, compressed in time, had created a true intimacy between Condi and I. At this late hour, we were exhausted; all the toxins from our bodies had been drained out. We were in a calm, positive, agreeable mood, lounging on large comfortable chairs like two dilettantes. And as you well know, this is the kind of situation that leads to the type of confiding one almost certainly regrets later. Since I am no different than any of you – despite my ludicrous claims sometimes - I felt confident enough to evoke the '1492' affair with her:

"Did I tell you that I've recently been hired by Interpol to help them untangle a very strange case?" I threw in.

"Very interesting," she said. "So, what do you do... chase Bin Laden?"

"I leave that to you guys - since you're so good at it," I said, tongue in cheek. "To be serious for a minute, we're not interested in OBL and his kind: there are already battalions of your agents busy tracking them. These guys, at Interpol, have a special section called Erebus that deals with – hold your breath – 'unconventional terrorism'..."

"That's a remarkable formula," mocked Condi.

"I was surprised, too; but we have uncovered that there is a circle of very influential people, here in Washington, who are plotting something directed against the Middle-East."

"What?" Condi asked, stunned. "Are you serious?"

"I can't be more serious than that!"

"Do you know who, how, when, where and why?"

"I can partially respond to that: as I told you, we know it's aimed at the Middle-East; we know very influential people in politics and in business are involved; we think the motivation may be to 'pacify' that region and the motive is probably faith-driven. But we are ignorant as to how and when the plan will be executed."

"I am honestly shocked!" Condi said.

"I thought you may know something about it, since you guys in the Administration – the so called 'Vulcans' – are pretty much into this kind of ideology-driven adventurism."

"I backed the decision to invade Iraq and I stand by my position, but as far as doing something of the kind you described, this would be out of the question, even very dangerous."

"I am glad to see that, after all, there is room for reason in your mind," I commented with sarcasm.

"Get out of here," Condi yelled laughingly and throwing the nearest pillow she could grab at me.

"Seriously, Madame Secretary; could you look into this very discreetly and tip me off if you hear something – anything – that could be relevant to this story?"

"Yes, sure; in fact, I am going to talk about it with my colleagues and see if they have heard of anything like that," she suggested.

"Oh, no, no, don't do that! This could be fatal to you," I cautioned her.

"You are not serious; you're just kidding, right?"

"This is very, very serious. I am not kidding! In a matter of days, there have been at least five deaths of people related directly or indirectly to the case."

"I have a tough time believing you: I haven't seen anything related to this in the media, nor have I heard anything - even distantly close – in Administration chatters."

"You want proof?" I asked her as I approached my computer. "Come here and take a look!"

"What is it: a traffic accident? What does this have to do with what you just said?" Condi asked, expressing doubt.

"Look at the sender and look at the time!"

"The sender is 'fourteen ninety-two'..." she read out loud. "I don't understand..."

"This picture is a photograph of the accident that cost the life to Senator Gareth's wife. It was taken minutes before anybody could reach the location of the 'accident' and e-mailed to me: isn't that odd?"

"For the least..." acknowledged Condi. "If what you are assuming is true..." reasoned Condi, while attempting to understand the logic behind the act, "that the Senator's wife was assassinated and not the victim of a traffic accident, then the question is: how was she or - more likely - how is the Senator involved in this affair?"

"You'll never cease to amaze me, Condi!" I genuinely marveled at her sense of deduction.

"Oh, it's nothing; I used to play Clue a lot when I was a kid," she replied with a demystifying smile. "But still this is a bit thin: the e-mail's time could be the result of a technical problem: you know how these things are never attuned…"

"I disagree with you," I protested. "How many cadavers do we need to understand that something very big is in preparation and that these guys are not joking? Look at this picture! This is Dr. Necromonti: he worked for Interpol on this investigation. He was shot along with another of Interpol's guys, who died on the spot. This picture was taken the day after the shooting in Necromonti's hospital room and sent to me by e-mail as well. By the time we got back to the hospital, he was dead. This was the first such e-mail."

"That's pretty scary! Now, I believe you."

"I am begging you; don't say anything to anyone! Even your shadow should be kept in the dark – so to speak."

"If I can't say anything to anyone, how can I help you? How can I gather information for you?"

"I understand but *dura lex sed lex*: if you want to stay alive, you have to abide by these strict rules," I insisted.

"All right, honey," Condi agreed reluctantly.

"Did you just call me 'honey'?" I asked with amusement and underlying stupor.

"Perhaps, I did. I don't know," she said innocently. "It came inadvertently… Perhaps, because I've been confused, upset by what you've just shared with me and that is so… so tragic."

"The real reason is that you can't resist me!" I said, teasing.

"Get lost, you pretentious thug!" she yelled with laughter before throwing another pillow at me.

Georgetown Twist

Senator Pat Gareth had called Ava telling her that he wanted to meet us ASAP. We offered to meet him in his office, but he suggested some place more 'neutral'; and Ava, for some reason, had proposed for us to meet at the Sea Catch, in Georgetown - whereas I hate seafood: it stinks! It was lunchtime on a rainy day and the restaurant was almost empty.

Senator Gareth was sitting with his back to a large bay window overlooking the C&O canal. The pouring rain, while giving the view outside an appearance of appeasing romanticism, added to the gloomy mask the Senator was sporting inside. He seemed worried. His round, almost jovial face - despite the circumstances – from the last time had disappeared and now looked emaciated, grave, as though he had been seriously sick or deprived of sleep for days.

"Friends," the Senator started to say with much gravitas, as if he were getting ready to drop us over Normandy or Sicily, "I've thought over and over what you told me the other day and it makes sense... it all makes sense," he said, as he played with the fork in his hand.

"What 'makes sense,' Senator?" Ava asked.

"Hush," he whispered, bringing his hand to his mouth in a quick move. "Don't call me Senator! It's Pat; just call me Pat."

"Oops, sorry; I understand," Ava said.

"What 'makes sense,' Pat?" I repeated Ava's question.

"Do you remember? The last thing you told me, when you came to see me in my office the other day, was that you suspected an unknown terrorist group, whose name had something to do with '1492,' to be behind the assassination of my wife?"

"Sure," Ava replied.

"Well, hold your breath because what I am about to tell you is going to be explosive," whispered the Senator as he approached even closer, bending over the table. "This may cost me my life, but the hell with it! If they have done what I think they have done..."

"We are ready, Pat?" I said.

"Listen! Some time back, I got drawn into a secret agreement with... I can't say it..." the Senator suddenly interrupted.

"Pat, you are our only chance. You know you can trust us; you must trust us," I insisted.

"...But then again, why should I spare them, if they didn't care about my wife's life... God damn it!" the outraged Senator wept.

"Who are they?" Ava asked.

"...I called him and I asked if he had anything to do with her death," the Senator continued in what seemed to be more of a soliloquy than a dialogue. "He pledged ignorance but then, in the same breath, he advised me to stay focused on the essential and not let myself become distracted from the larger, higher goal – i.e. the accomplishment of our plan - can you believe it?"

"Pat, could you tell us who you are talking about and what is exactly this 'plan' you are referring to?" I asked.

"Our deal was that I would bring the backing of the Senate for his plan and, in exchange, I would be on the presidential ticket in the next election."

"We still don't get it, Pat: could you be more specific?" I asked with some impatience this time.

The Senator was perceptibly so ill at ease to give us a name that he resorted to write it down instead. He took his pen, asked for a piece of paper and wrote down: 'The Vice President.' I looked at the piece of paper with stupor and passed it on to Ava, who was as flabbergasted as I was. That's another Hiroshima! I thought.

"Are you positively affirmative on this?" Ava asked.

"Trust me!" the Senator said with confidence.

"Now, I understand why you were so reluctant to even mention the name," I commented. "How about the plan: you haven't told us what the 'plan' is?"

"I don't have all the details; I think that only he has the blue print – in his brain. But what I can tell you is that he has designed for something to happen in the Middle-East that would require our military intervention."

"Why?" I asked.

"America would use that as a pretext to occupy the Holy Land and pacify a region that has been a cause of trouble for too long."

"What's the relation with '1492' then?" Ava asked.

"We believe that it was not purely accidental that Christopher Columbus discovered America the same year as the Reconquista was half-achieved…"

"What do you mean by 'half achieved'?" I asked with curiosity, trying to comprehend.

"Well, the job was not done. They should have continued their Reconquista all the way to the Holy Land."

"So, you believe that it lies upon America to finish the job Ferdinand and Isabel had not completed more than five centuries ago…" I deducted.

"That's exactly it," the Senator confirmed with a smile, proud of his participation in the scheme. "And we would force Jews and Arabs to live peacefully together under our leadership."

"Forgive me, Pat, but this is insane! You and 'you know who' are out of your minds. I am not sure you realize what you're doing..."

"Why would it be insane? Only we, Christians, can bring those Semitic nations together and stop the bloodshed in the land of our Savior Jesus, the Apostle of Peace. It's our duty, as Christians, to bring back the Word of our Lord to those misled and erring, to bring those lost sheep back to the herd."

What the Senator was telling us was pretty chilling. It seemed as though he were reading a page from something written by some evangelical fanatic such as Pat Robertson or Jerry Falwell or others cut from the same cloth. Emilio was right: extremist evangelical ideologies had not only a niche in the White House occupied by '43,' but their thoughts are being actively acted upon, even if it is to the detriment of world peace and of the American people.

No matter how imbecile and naïve I thought the Senator appeared now, sitting on his fat ass and weeping in front of us because he believed there had been a breach of trust in his deal with the Vice President, I had to swallow my outrage and spare the man simply because we needed him to catch the bigger fish.

"Why do you think that 'he' may be involved in the assassination of your wife?" Ava asked.

"He is a control-freak with a devilish mind. During one of our encounters, when we were discussing the progress of our plan, when he told me that he envisioned me as his running mate for the next presidential election, I got so enthusiastic that I said I couldn't wait to see my wife's reaction when I'd share the news with her. I immediately understood that it was a grave gaffe on my part. He got angry and threatened that he would not tolerate stupid mistakes. Something had changed: I could sense it."

"Do you suspect him of personally sponsoring your wife's killing based on that exchange alone?" Ava asked. "I think that this would be very difficult to prove in a court of law."

"I know the man: he is a cold-blooded animal. Nothing matters to him other than his goals and ambitions."

"Ah, ambitions, ambitions…" I commented with irony.

"I may be ambitious, too, perhaps even very ambitious - you know how addictive politics can be - but that doesn't mean that I am ready to sacrifice my own wife to appease the sickly suspicious mind of this… this monster."

"I understand your furor, Pat," I said. "But what else can you tell us about the plan itself: do you know how he is planning on creating the conditions that would require a military intervention by the United States?"

"I have no idea; he wouldn't tell me."

"…And I guess that he wouldn't tell in prevision of the present kind of hazards to his plan," I reflected. "I understand his thinking: he has very intelligently compartmentalized all sections of the conspiracy so that, other than himself, nobody knows who else is involved and how much they know about what others are doing."

Ava's cell phone rang.

"Yes, all right; make sure to send me a soft copy, too… yes… yes… all right. And thanks again; I owe you one. Bye!"

"What was it?" I asked.

"The results of Necromonti's second necropsy. In view of what we found out about Emilio's death, I asked that Dr. Necromonti's corpse be reexamined."

"What's the outcome?" I asked anxiously.

229

"The real cause of his death is the same as his brother's."

"For some reason, I am not really surprised," I commented. "I had guessed that his death was too sudden; whereas we had witnessed a dramatic improvement just minutes earlier at the hospital."

"I had the same kind of suspicion," Ava said.

"I don't mean to interrupt your *aparté*," the Senator said, annoyed by an exchange that ignored him for a couple of minutes, "but is there something you would like to share with me?"

"At this point, I guess, we can tell you..." Ava said as she glanced in my direction, looking for my mute approval. "Dr. Benvenisto Necromonti and Hector Shumington were two very fine Interpol inspectors working on the '1492' case and they were both shot by your friends. Necromonti was lucky enough to escape the assassination attempt, but not for long, because they finished him off at the hospital."

"Why do you say 'your friends' as if I had something to do with the criminals who committed the murder? I can assure you that I have nothing to do with it."

"Pat, we are not here to judge you. What Ava was pointing out here was that the people you were involved with are no saints," I interpreted in an effort to avoid any friction at this time.

"Do you think that I don't know that? Why the fuck do you think that I am sitting here with you in this stinky fish restaurant? They killed my wife, and if they learn that I have talked to you, tomorrow you could very well find my corpse drowned in the canal behind us."

The Senator was enraged. I had to intervene to cool things down; otherwise, our encounter was going to turn sour and that was the last thing I wanted to happen at this early stage – maybe later...? So, I gently kicked Ava underneath the table to make her understand that she needed to drop it.

"Pat, we know how much courage it takes to do what you're doing and we appreciate it immensely," I said to flatter the Senator and put him back to a more agreeable mood. "It's not easy to put your career and your life at risk because of your belief in justice and the rule of law. Your wife, wherever she is, can see you; and she is very proud of you. You are a man of honor and integrity. Pat, believe me; when the time comes, you won't need to be on anybody's ticket: you'll head the ticket."

Maybe I have exaggerated a little bit and put the old fat Senator on a pedestal, but flattery always works and especially with politicians. My desperately phony and hypocritical sweet talk put the Senator in a beaming mood - so much so that if he could, he would put me on his ticket right away.

"You, Mr. Haftemizan, you are true to your reputation: a man of intelligence and a gentleman," the Senator said, evidently in a more positive mood now. "And you, young lady, I don't know what they've taught you at Interpol, but you should learn from this man."

"Yes, Sir," Ava said, keeping her emotions in check while giving me a harsh kick under the table.

"Pat, be very careful," I advised him. "And if I may make a suggestion, write down what you just told us, seal it and mail it to your lawyer and another copy to a trusted friend – if you have one."

"Sure; can I mail one to you?"

"You're welcome to do so. And one more thing: at this time, the safest thing to do for you is to continue to play their game as if nothing has happened."

"Sure; you can count on me."

Azuelos Residence, Washington DC

"We came as soon as we could," Ava said, as we were led in by Jim Azuelos.

"I knew you could do it, Jim. I am very proud of you," I said enthusiastically, as we were walking past the corridors of their residence.

"It was not easy, believe me. It started with drama and could have ended up in tragedy," Jim said with a smile.

"That bad...?" I commented, understanding that he was probably exaggerating a tad bit.

"I'll tell you the story another day," Jim said, before stopping in front of a door: "Dad, here they are!"

"Come on in, please! I am Joachim Azuelos, Jim's pitiably imbecile father."

The sight of Jim's father, leaning on a walking stick, and introducing himself in a self-deprecating way was indeed touching. The man, as powerful and accomplished as he was, had not been able to withstand a blitzkrieg launched on him by his proper son - a battle he lost for his own good.

Joachim Azuelos received us in a small but roomy and beautifully arranged library. From side to side, the walls were covered by wood paneling and book shelves made of the same walnut wood that had gently darkened with time. The style seems to indicate that the room had probably been so arranged in the late nineteenth century.

"Mr. Azuelos, thank you for receiving us and thank you for sharing with us what you know," I said in introduction. "We realize how hard it must have been and I would like to seize this opportunity to thank Jim, too, without whom none of this would have been possible."

I know I sounded like one of those guests at some dopey awards ceremony, but I was taken away by the moment…

"Indeed, Mr. Azuelos, we are very appreciative," Ava added.

"You're welcome. I am now trying to amend for my mistake. I'll do whatever I can to help you," Joachim Azuelos said.

"What can you tell us about the plan dubbed '1492'?" Ava asked without wasting a second more.

"I don't know how much of it you already know, but this was a plan designed with the greatest secrecy at the highest level of the Administration. I'll spare you the details at this time, but the idea was to provoke a conflict that would involve Israel and some of its Arab and/or Islamic neighbors, which would require America's intervention to put out the fire. The Administration would then use that opportunity to occupy the Holy Land and its surroundings as 'peace-keepers' - preferably with a UN mandate."

"How would have the conflict started?" I asked.

"I have no idea!"

"Did you know that those thought to be linked to '1492' have more than likely acquired deadly viruses from some former Soviet Republic? Do you know how they intend to use them?"

"I have no idea. It's the first time I'm hearing this."

"Dad," Jim interjected with sorrow, shaking his head, "they used your money to buy it."

"What was your role in the conspiracy then?" Ava asked.

"My role was to participate in the financing of the plan and my reward would have been to head a water management consortium for the entire Middle-East."

"You pointed to the highest level of this Administration, could you name names?" Ava asked.

"My take is that this has been the Vice President's baby."

"That confirms it… And how about the President: do you think he is in?" I asked.

"Based on what Dick told me, he is involved; although he asserted that the President is unaware of all the 'technicalities' associated with '1492.'"

"Wow! This is an explosive revelation," I reflected out loud.

"What my father failed to tell you," Jim said, "is that these guys have ideological motives: they want to bring back the Holly Land under the rule of Christianity."

"So what? Christians, Jews, Muslims… we are all the same," Joachim said.

"But, Dad, this was to the exclusion of the others. Once my father told me what it was about, I convinced him of the preposterous aspect of the scheme. I reminded him that our family was among the Jews expelled from Spain in 1492 and that it would be a shame for us to participate in such an infamy today. I warned him that, should he let himself be misled by unfounded theories and professed good intentions, he would lose his son forever – and I can assure you that I was not kidding."

"Reluctantly, I finally succumbed to my son's plea," Joachim Azuelos said.

"Why you, Mr. Azuelos?" Ava asked, continuing to pose one pertinent question after another.

"And if I may add," I said, "didn't the Vice President know that you were of the Israelite confession to confide in you the way he did?"

"Dick and I go a long way... We've known each other since we were college kids and I don't think he has ever suspected that I am Jewish."

"That's pretty amazing," I commented.

"I guess he never did, because I was raised in a very laic family environment. In addition, to be very frank, I have never paid much attention to my religious identity."

"So, when he told you about the one-sided symbolism of 1492, you did not protest or show any reaction?" I asked.

"No, I did not. I did show some reserve to the messianic part of it but I did not protest vehemently, I must confess. As I told you, I am mostly and foremostly an American and laic by tradition; besides, at first, the perspective seemed positive to me: what are a few hundreds or a few thousands of deaths if the result is to put an end to decades of war and bloodshed?"

"There you go again, Dad. I thought you understood that this is a scheme for Evangelicals and oil-thirsty vultures to feed on our dead bodies: for them a good Jew is a converted one and a good Muslim, is a dead one!"

"I think you are over-blowing this, Jim," Joachim said. "But I agree with you that this is not the best way to bring peace in the Middle-East and improve the dialogue between religions. This is why I am here, on your side, and I have dropped the idea."

"You did very well, Sir; otherwise you could have become another Alfred Rosenberg or Erhard Milch, referred to in history books with an asterisk beside your name and a footnote, at the bottom of the page, to elucidate the mystery of your participation in an inhumane enterprise in spite of reason and humanity."

"My intentions were good though..."

"The road to hell is paved with good intentions, Mr. Azuelos," I retorted with a piece of obvious – though trivial – aphorism.

"Absolutely," Jim agreed, raising his eyebrows while looking towards his father as if to say 'I told you so!'

"Mr. Azuelos, your son told us that you gave money to finance '1492': have you kept any trace of it?" Ava asked.

"All in all, I have contributed close to twenty-five million dollars. It's all in cash and I have no proof other than Dick's word."

"Are you saying that you were giving the cash to the Vice President *mano a mano*?" Ava said, excited.

"No, I would give the cash to a courier and sometimes later, I would get a nod from Dick, making me understand that they got it."

"Can you tell us at least who the courier was?" Ava persisted.

"I have no name to give you, but I could recognize the guy if you'd show me a picture. You've got to understand one thing. In the type of relationship Dick and I have had, a simple word is enough because everything is based on trust."

"It must be difficult for you to breach that trust," I remarked.

"Oh, it's a real torture! Dick and I have known each other for almost four decades. But the truth of the matter is that I had to make a choice between my old buddy and my only son. Besides, Dick has not been entirely truthful either: I was very disappointed in him when Jim told me of the murders that had been perpetrated because of '1492.' I had naively agreed to what I viewed as a generous idea – with some exciting business opportunities on the side, perhaps – but I've never wanted to be associated in a criminal enterprise."

"There is a fine line you're tracing that I can't see, Dad," Jim said.

"You are right; I was blinded. Reflecting back on my commitment, I think I was taken by the excitement of the moment, the secretive aspect of it and the exhilaration and sense of empowerment it was giving me... I am sorry," Joachim said in a voice that was emotional, sincere and with visible tears in his eyes.

This was a moment full of pathos. Father and son embraced each other, and taken by the emotion, they gave Ava and I accolades too. I don't think the emotion was faked. I really believe that Azuelos senior was just starting to realize in how big a blunder he has gotten himself into and how grateful he should be to the clairvoyance of his son for having – painfully – awakened him to reality. Otherwise, his name would have been synonymous with infamy for generations to come. He could have ended up in some kind of national, even international, criminal court of justice: not an enviable perspective for a man visibly tucked away from the hassles of everyday life in his historic villa at the heart of Georgetown. Azuelos was used to getting things done the easy way, generously hosing with money some Washington corrupt politicians always open to the highest bidder.

"Joachim, I meant to ask you - I hope you won't get offended - are the Miro, the Klimt and the Turner that are hanging on the walls of your library originals or reproductions?" I asked as we were exiting the room.

"All pure originals, a hundred percent certified," he replied with humor. "These and a few antique books that I have are my real treasures, Mr. Haftemizan."

"They are absolutely splendid pieces! I could sit here for hours and contemplate them."

"You're welcome to do so anytime. I am flattered that my taste has won your appreciation; come on by and we'll have a cup of coffee and even play chess, if you'd like," Joachim Azuelos offered in a very sincere and amicable way.

"Do not tempt me," I replied with a smile. "The outcome could be tragic for you and for your collection."

237

Dr. Zhivago

Thanks to the providential help of Senator Gareth and the enormous work of persuasion led by Jim Azuelos with his father, we had certainly moved forward on several fronts. But on one major issue – i.e. that of knowing what would trigger the conflict - we were more or less clueless.

We sat in Ava's apartment listing action items that would significantly move us forward to check the '1492' threat and checkmate its mastermind.

It was a sunny early afternoon. We had ordered some Chinese: not very original. The food was barely edible. The problem with Chinese restaurants is that you never know what you are getting unless you've tested it. If you expect that your Szechwan chicken is going to taste the same, no matter where you are ordering it from, you are gravely mistaken!

My phone rang to the tune of 'The Pink Panther,' which I had downloaded to add some humor to an otherwise 'unenjoyable' overall environment.

"Hey, Your Badness, this is Condi," she said in a naughty voice.

"Good afternoon, how are you doing?" I replied in a more formal tone, signaling that I was not alone.

"Am I calling at a bad time... you can't talk?"

"Yes, you are absolutely right on this one," I said, trying to talk in the most neutral and casual way possible in order not to arouse Ava's suspicion.

"That's too bad, because I am able to free up some time for you to meet 'Madame Secretary,' if you know what I mean..." Condi said with sensual longing in her voice to tease me.

"I really wish I could join you for that unscheduled meeting, but I am afraid I can't right now. Maybe some other time..." I said with real regret.

"Can't you just drop whatever you're doing and get over here? I am at a day long seminar at the Washington Plaza; you could come, get a room and I would surreptitiously join you: what do you say?"

"Let me see how I can rearrange my schedule... I'll do my best and I'll get back to you."

"Call me when you get here."

"Sure, bye!"

Condi was apparently in the mood for a 'nooner,' which by tradition is said to be more the result of males' biological clock than that of women – although, I have discovered that it's not rare for a woman's clock to tick at that time of the day, too. Condi is a very smart woman. She knew she would catch me at a time of weakness with her very alluring offer. But I couldn't leave Ava right away like that; because, for one, we still had some work to do; and second, although all we had thus far – I believe – was some kind of flirtatious connection, I felt as if I'd be cheating on her.

Somehow, and especially since the plane episode, I had the impression that if I made my move, Ava would not reject me – which is a euphemism to say that I think she would reciprocate - moderato - my fondness for her. But based on past experiences, I decided that I would avoid sentimental adventures with a colleague. This rule is even more relevant in this case where we are chasing after something out of the ordinary with consequences that would affect the entire planet. Therefore any romantic liaison could be a distraction and an impediment with grave consequences. I should say that it is even more difficult to show restraint in this case where there is a larger degree of emotional and physical proximity, which usually promotes romantic and sensual involvement.

Despite my initial commitment not to respond to Condi's invitation, I could not resist the temptation. Just a few minutes following the conclusion of our review of the day's event, I left Ava and hopped in a cab heading for the Washington Plaza, booked a room and called Condi. She was happily surprised and told me that she would try to sneak out as soon as possible.

Ten minutes had not passed when she called me on my cell phone telling me that she was on her way up and asked me to leave the door open. She entered swiftly with a large smile on her face. She said we had less than fifteen minutes to do it, because, if she disappears for more than that, the Secret Service people would start looking for her and her escapade could become a nightmare.

Condi swiftly removed a pink fuchsia ensemble to reveal a set of lingerie of the same color - only one shade lighter - and jumped on the bed and from the bed to the large round table and… I can't tell or describe – even in an edulcorated fashion - the rest of what happened during the next thirteen minutes or so, because it would be unveiling too much of my personal life while pleasuring your voyeuristic tendencies; but what I can say is that it was intense, erotic, and... Oh, gosh, so much pleasure in so little time!

"What do you think of our relationship?" Condi asked, as she was putting her clothes back on and powdering her nose in a rush.

"I don't know; Gosh.... what do you think?" I returned the question to her in a very smart move.

"Can we say 'wittily lustful'?" she giggled.

I smiled. "I guess that's a very good assessment."

"I've got to rush now," Condi said, as she put herself together and stood for a second in front of a tall mirror beside the door, as if she were getting ready to make a grand entrance on stage, before adding: "You bad, bad, naughty boy!"

"Not as bad as you, Madame Secretary," I replied with a large appreciative smile. "Oh, and before you go, call me whenever you have a chance; I have got some staggering news about what I told you the other day. I think you're going to like it... or not."

"Sure," she said as she rushed out and ran towards the door leading to the staircase.

The White House, Private Quarters

"George, honey, you know that tonight we are watching a movie," Laura reminded her husband.

"Sure, honey; I haven't forgotten. What have you got?" '43' asked.

"I have chosen 'Dr. Zhivago': I think you are going to love it."

"Honey, you know I don't like hospital movies," whined '43.' "I've spent half of my life watching General Hospital with mom..."

"But honey, this is no hospital movie; this is an extraordinary epic film that takes place in the USSR."

"I don't give a damn crack! Get me something more – I don't know – huh... philosophical. Something that talks to the soul and that shows what great leadership can do in times of adversity."

"All right, honey; give me a title and I'll have them bring it up for you," Laura said, always trying to be accommodating.

"I don't know, gee... How about a Jackie Chan flick?" suggested '43.'

"Sure, honey, anything for you," Laura said. "I'll watch Dr. Zhivago in the other room."

"Hey, Laura, make sure I've got some pretzels to munch: you know how I like that when I watch movies."

"It's already taken care of, honey," the First Lady said with a smile.

'43' had just seated himself comfortably in the projection room, a bowl of pretzels on his lap and a Russian Czar-Pushka cold beer – courtesy of his good friend Vladimir Putin – in his hand, ready to enjoy a flick with a 'philosophical message' – as he put it - when an usher knocked at the door:

"Mr. President, Mr. Floss is here and is requesting the permission to see you," the usher said.

"The hell with him! Tell him that I am sleeping."

"Sir, he insists. He says that it's a very important matter."

"All right, bring him here," the President said with nonchalance. "How many times a day do I need to see the DCI?

I'll have to talk to Dick about it: every time I see this guy, he gives me a headache."

"Good night, Mr. President," Porter Floss said as he entered the room.

"Come on in, Porter. So, what brings you here so late and so - shall I say - unexpectedly?"

"I am really sorry to show up like this, but there is an issue of importance that requires your attention," Porter Floss said with gravity to underline the priority of the matter.

"Couldn't this issue wait until tomorrow morning's briefing?"

"I had to, Mr. President… I think this is a matter of National Security that I needed to share with you at the earliest possible…"

"All right, go ahead! I am listening," '43' said, as he paused the movie that had just started.

"Mr. President, I think we may have uncovered something very bad – I mean very, very bad - going on!"

"That's your job, Porter; I have hired you to do that."

"This is something that went below the radar and, had it not been for Molinero's perspicacity, it could have gone unnoticed until it exploded in our faces!"

"Your name is 'Floss' and it's Molinero who is finding crumbs between the CIA's teeth…" '43'joked.

"You know, Mr. President, when I accepted this job, I didn't know what I was going to be up against: I have no family life, no rest… I am overwhelmed," the DCI said, in an attempt to preemptively justify why he had missed the piece of information he was about to transmit to the President.

"Stop whining, Porter; we're all overwhelmed! Do you think that I have time for any leisure? We are all on the same boat… That's what makes us strong men, men of value."

"Sure, Sir," Floss said tamely.

"All right; so, what have you got?" The President wanted the matter to be out of the way so he could watch his Jackie Chan movie.

"We have received intelligence reports indicating that the Syrians and the Iranians are under the impression that we are about to launch strikes against them from the neighboring countries we occupy – namely Iraq and Afghanistan."

"I am not aware of such a plan," '43' said.

"I didn't know either," Floss said. "So, I went straight to Rumsfeld and asked him if it was one of his under the belt coups to undermine my Agency – i.e. if the outcome is good, the DOD would take the credit and if it's a shameful debacle, the blame would be put on the CIA once again - and he assured me that there were no such secret operation led by his guys on the ground."

"Then what is it?"

"Satellite photos show that there have been movements in two specific locations very close to the borders of these two countries."

"Movements of what?"

"Missile launchers, Sir," Floss said.

"You are not serious! So, if we didn't do it... then it's probably some Al-Qaeda terrorists who are doing this to compromise us and create more trouble for us."

"Well, that's an option we explored, but at this time we are suspicious of a rogue operation led by former or current US military and/or intelligence guys..."

"That can't be..."

"That's not it, Sir. We have investigated through the NSA and it appears that there had been communication between those two locations and here."

At hearing the "here" from Porter Floss, the President choked on the piece of pretzel he had just put in his mouth. His face turned red as he was attempting to cough it out. Floss understood immediately what was happening to '43' - since this was not the first time – and he immediately seized the President from the back and executed a Heimlich maneuver on him. Fortunately, the piece of pretzel came out quickly and the President hydrated his throat with some cold beer he had on hand.

"Thank you, Porter; you just saved my life!" '43' said, regaining his composure after a couple of minutes of deep breathing.

"Don't mention it, Mr. President; but I would suggest, if I may, that you stop eating pretzels, because I think you may be suffering from an anomaly in the way your esophagus is built, which causes larger pieces of aliment to easily get caught in its meanders."

"What the heck did you just say?"

"I am saying that you should be careful, Mr. President, when you eat things like pretzels," Floss rephrased it in layman's terms.

"Thanks, that's what Laura keeps telling me," the President said. "It's a good thing she is not here; otherwise she would ban me from eating pretzels. Imagine watching movies or sports without pretzels!"

"I understand," Floss said, trying to be sympathetic.

"To come back to what you said earlier, when you said 'from here,' did you mean from here, the White House?"

"We are unable to provide that degree of precision. But from this city... yes, assuredly," Porter Floss said with conviction.

"Oh, good...! But who would want to do that and why? It could as well be another intelligence failure - if you see what I mean."

"I don't know that, Sir; but I can assure you that we are on it and we'll find out. I am going to send teams ASAP over there."

The President winked. "In the meanwhile, I think that we should keep this quiet, Porter. We don't want to alarm people unduly until we know exactly what we are talking about... See, I've learned my lesson!"

"Very well, Mr. President."

"Hey, Porter, do you want to watch Jackie Chan with me?"

"Thank you, Mr. President; but it's getting late and I've got to go home before my wife gives me the boot," Floss replied politely.

"Are you sure? Because I've got some good Russian beer that my friend Vladimir has sent me and we've got these pretzels too..." '43' insisted, to be hospitable but also to soften his DCI, who was on the verge of discovering something the President suspected could mean trouble for him.

"Good night, Mr. President."

"Nighty night!"

Porter Floss's 'revelations' had made '43' nervous. As soon as the DCI left the room, he called the Vice President to alert him:

"Dick? It's '43.'"

"Good evening, Mr. President," Dick said, a bit surprised to receive a call at this late hour. Dick wondered what the hell was going on.

"Dick, I have some bad news for you."

"What is it, Mr. President?"

The President laughed. "You're busted. The DCI just visited me."

247

Assem Akram

"Really, and what did he want: resign because he's got too much work and therefore he doesn't have enough time to chase the bimbos of Daytona Beach...?" Dick suggested with sarcasm.

"You are being tough on him; he is a good guy. Besides, you are going to have to be nicer to him because he is onto something..."

"Really?"

"I am afraid he is," '43' said. "He knows that there is something fishy going on with some missile launchers in Iraq and Afghanistan and they have traced calls from those locations to Washington. He told me that he is going to send investigative teams over there: I could not refuse."

"That's not good at all!" Dick said. "But I am not too worried: our guys in Iraq have a first-rate alibi: they are doing it under the auspices of the arms collection and destruction program."

"It's all 'legit' then... You're my man, Dick!"

"They can go there and dig as much as they want, but they won't find anything. Nada." Dick said with assurance. "What worries me a little bit is Afghanistan..."

"What about it?"

"The situation is quite different over there..."

"What do you mean?"

"We have a huge SS-25 and its launcher over there that we've 'imported' and reassembled. So, it's not really 'local,'" Dick said, already trying to figure out a scheme to save the situation.

"Can't you figure out something?" '43' asked.

"We'll figure out something, Mr. President. Don't worry; we have ample time to think about a stratagem."

"If nothing else works – although, you don't like the guy, perhaps you can try to recruit him to join our little plan. This

248

way, you won't have to worry about him breathing behind your neck."

"This is a very good idea, Mr. President; but, as you know, I don't trust him: he is just a gigolo..."

"All right; it's your call. But I'd suggest you think about it, in case your other options fail. Remember what's at stake."

"Sure, Mr. President."

"Nighty night, Dick."

"Good night, Mr. President."

"Oh... and don't forget to replace the batteries before you go to sleep," '43' giggled, enjoying his joke as much now as the first time he uttered it.

"I won't forget," Dick said, with a forced laugh, wondering what grave sin he has committed to have to endure this...

"Hey, Dick, I forgot to ask you: do you want to come over and watch a Jackie Chan flick with me? Laura has left me all by myself; she is watching some kind of medical movie called...hum... oh, yes: 'Dr. Chicago'..."

"It's probably 'Dr. Zhivago,' Mr. President. Thank you for the offer, but I am afraid I can't: I have some work to do but most importantly I have to take care of this issue before it gets out of hand."

"Well, too bad because I've got here some pretzels and some amazing Russian beer my friend Vladimir has sent me."

"Very thoughtful of you; perhaps another time..." Dick ended the conversation, before muttering "moron" once he had hung up the phone.

As soon as he ended his conversation with the President, Dick picked up his satellite phone to call Colonel Bernardino in Iraq but he stopped short of finishing dialing the number. He thought that it would be unwise now that they suspect something. The call, even encrypted, could be traced and deciphered. So, he reflected for a moment on alternative ways to alert Bernardino and the others – i.e. Chewbacca and El Ladron – in Afghanistan. It was out of the question for him to send an e-mail, and the matter was too urgent to think about any other means of communication.

After a few minutes of reflection and analyzing the pros and cons of each solution, he thought that perhaps his first instinct was a good one: he's been having regular exchanges with Colonel Bernardino and if he suddenly cuts off the channel or delocalizes the call's origination, it would alert the investigators. So, he called up Bernardino and alerted him, in a coded way, to be on the look out for 'unexpected visitors' coming soon to inspect their 'weapon collection.' Bernardino got the message 10-4 and didn't seem otherwise alarmed by the perspective, confident in the infallibility of his cover.

"Honey, aren't you coming back to sleep?" Lynne asked, standing at the door.
"I am coming, honey; I still have some work to do," Dick said.
"You always have some work to do… Come on, sweetheart; If you come to bed now, I'll treat you with my specialty," Lynne said, with a naughty intonation. "You know how you like it, you big bad boy!"
"I can't right now, honey; the President called me earlier and tasked me with an important matter."
"That's unfair! Pretzel Boy is unloading all his work on you…"
"I know, honey; but remember what you always remind me of…"
"…That you need him for your plan. I know, I know…"
"Exactly; so let me finish this and I'll come over ASAP," Dick said with some enthusiasm.

"No need to hurry, honey: I am not in the mood anymore!" Lynne snapped.

"Come on, sweetheart; don't be that unforgiving. Remember, I am your little 'chili pepper,' your cute 'pickle in the sky'…"

"Forget you! *Ciao*, Mr. Vice President," Lynne said, before closing the study door and returning to the bedroom.

"How about giving me some baklava instead?" Dick yelled, but she had already left and could barely hear him.

The solution Dick had found for the part of the operation in Iraq was not so complicated. Inversely, in the case of Afghanistan, Dick needed to show more caution: 'Chewbacca' and 'El Ladron' were working free-lance for him and their action did not enter under any recognized program validated by the DOD, the CIA or any other US agency.

For this call, Dick, who has always more than one trick up his sleeve, decided to use one of those pre-paid cell phones, which are completely anonymous and highly difficult to trace. He always kept several in stock along with pre-paid phone cards – the kind sold at ethnic marts that give the customer hundreds of minutes of long distance calling at unbeatable rates.

"Chewbacca is that you?" Dick asked, talking loud.

"Yes, Sir. Good morning, Sir," Chewbacca said. He had jumped out of his bed to respond to the early call on his satellite phone.

"It's night time here, but good morning to you."

"Is everything all right, Sir?"

"Yes, everything is absolutely fine here but I wanted to alert you guys that you may soon receive unexpected visitors."

"I understand, but I thought we were covered locally here," Chewbacca said.

"Yes, you are… Unfortunately, this comes from higher ups in Washington …and in space."

"I understand that we've been spotted," Chewbacca said, quick to get to the point. "Don't worry, Sir; we'll take care of this issue."

"Protect your mission but don't do anything irresponsible."

"Sir, this is Fred," El Ladron said. He had joined Chewbacca and wanted to enter the conversation.

"Good morning. Nice to hear you, Fred."

"Don't worry, Sir. I know exactly how to divert this kind of attention," El Ladron stated with assurance. "I know it's the night where you are; so, please, go back to sleep and let us take care of it. We'll keep you updated."

"You guys are the best," Dick said, feeling tremendously relieved.

'Chewbacca' and 'El Ladron' didn't provide him any details on what they planned to do because the format of their communication did not allow it, but Dick trusted them to come up with the appropriate response.

The apparent resolution of what appeared, at first, as a possibly lethal blow to the accomplishment of '1492' was seamless beyond his expectations. At this moment Dick felt very proud of the choices he had made in picking these men. He definitely repelled the doubts he has had at times about Bernardino, Chewbacca, El Ladron and their select group of A-grade teammates. Dick went to his room for a quiet night of sleep, confident that he had taken the necessary precautions to fend off an unbearable neutralization of '1492.'

Haftemizan's Apartment

"I'm coming," I yelled as I woke up to respond to the knocking at my door. It was past midnight. Who the hell could it be? When I looked through the Judas hole, it was Condi, dressed in jogging pants and a sweater with the hood pulled over her hair to conceal her identity.

"Finally, you're opening," she said. "Don't tell me you were sleeping." She smiled as she made her way inside.

"Some of us need to sleep from time to time... We are not all nocturnal creatures."

"You told me to get back to you, so I decided that I might as well drop by," Condi said, with a smile that meant something for which I was too tired and too sleepy to consider.

"That's an excellent idea," I said, remembering that I had indeed told her that. "But, before I start, I need to drink something that will wake me up a little bit; otherwise, I'll be stringing one inane sentence after another without making sense."

I turned the coffee machine on and went to wash my face with cold water. Meanwhile, Condi was going through my collection of books and CDs.

"Nice books," she commented as she began flipping through the pages of one of them.

"Thanks; this is typically the kind of frustrating enterprise..."

"What do you mean?"

"Well, you can never have all the books you'd like to, either because you can't find them or because they are antique and they cost an arm and a leg."

"I see what you mean, although I don't have a collector's mind set. So, I guess I don't suffer as much as you do."

"Would you like some coffee?"

"No, thanks; I just exercised for an hour; I am all right. I'll have some water instead," Condi replied. "So what was that explosive news that you wanted to tell me about?"

"Oh, yes… But I shall warn you that I want your complete, ultimate discretion on this matter because it's no laughing matter," I insisted.

"You have my promise."

"Do you give me your word that you won't tell anyone, even your closest friends and fellow politicos?"

"Come on, spit it out, Haftemizan!" Condi said with impatience. "I've been second-guessing what it could be the entire afternoon and evening, so I am not going to wait one more second."

"Fasten your seat belt, because you are going to enter a zone of turbulence, once I reveal this to you," I said with a bit of dramatic effect. "Do you remember what I told you the other day about a plot?"

"Yes, I do."

"Well, it appears that the Vice-President and - to a slightly lesser degree - '43' himself are involved in this extraordinary conspiracy named '1492,' mixing extremist evangelical beliefs, the kindling of a war in the Middle-East requiring our intervention and occupation of the Holy Land and, last but not least, all of the above would pave the way for the election of the Vice President into the White House."

"Are you fucking kidding me?" yelled Condi in total disbelief and cursing in a way that was not habitually hers. "You can't be serious!"

Condi was so shocked that she didn't know what to do: she walked nervously to the window and back, then sat on the edge of the table, finally returning to her seat.

"I am dead serious. On top of that, I can almost definitely tell you now that people belonging to the '1492' plot have conspired to kill Senator Gareth's wife."

"How can you be so certain?"

"Senator Gareth talked to us," I replied with a measure of pride. "He took the initiative to confide in us and helped us to have a better understanding of this rather unattractive conspiracy."

"What was his involvement?"

"He was promised to be on the presidential ticket in exchange for rallying Congress behind a decision to intervene in the Holy Land."

"Those SOB's," Condi said, as she hit the table with her fist.

"Come on, Madame Secretary, mind your language, please," I said sarcastically.

"I should have listened to him," she said.

"To whom?" I asked.

"Collin... He warned me not to trust these guys. I can't believe I was that naïve! Just days ago, Dick - the weaseling stinky bastard - sat one on one with me at his residence and told me that he was planning on running for the Presidency and offered me to be on the ticket... not Gareth - that fat, ignorant, lardy bigot," yelled Condi with disgust and anger: obviously, she didn't like the old Senator.

"One can legitimately wonder how many other people he has been able to dupe like this," I commented with a smile.

"This is no laughing matter! I trusted this President; I sacrificed for them; Dick was my mentor, my 'master Jedi'... You can't imagine how disappointed I am! The world, my political potting soil, is vanishing under my feet... I think I am going to faint," Condi said, as her voice became veiled and thinner.

The shock was like a gigantic tsunami for Condi. She was so overwhelmed that she could barely breathe. She had been betrayed by the people she had trusted the most, with whom she had worked from father to son, despite the criticism of her friends and other well-wishers. She realized that the Vice-President's offer was a way to ensure that she would stick with the team and back the Administration no matter what... And that 'what' was '1492,' of which she had been carefully kept in the dark – reminding her of what they had done to her predecessor and of which she was a part.

She was angry at herself for having bought into Dick's sweet-talk and she was repulsed because she realized that, if it were not for these developments and her fortuitous relationship with Haftemizan, she would have backed the Administration's scheme to intervene and invade the Holy Land for the benefit of a group of voraciously ambitious and religiously extremist people: a dark alliance she would have been a part of just because she was promised to become the first African-American VP.

"Come on, Condi; don't beat yourself up!" I said, in an attempt to boost her morale. "You've been duped: it happens all the time - in politics as in life. Take comfort in that they are the bad guys, not you."
"I need to lie down somewhere," she said, as she stood up to walk straight to my bedroom where she took off her exercise outfit and slipped under the blanket, retracting her body into the fetal position and allowing only her head to be seen. I was standing there, looking with commiseration at the feline - almost frighteningly full of self-confidence - creature melting down,

shivering and showing a kind of fragility that was as frightening and disarming as her self-assurance.

"Could you do me a favor?" she asked in a very frail voice.

"Sure; what? Would you like some Tylenol or some Alka-Seltzer?" I offered. "Or, perhaps, some ice-cream and a box of tissues?"

"I am not in the mood for your sarcasm," she replied. "Could you rather put on some music and leave the room for a moment? I need to rest."

"Sure; but are you certain that you're all right? You seem so pale."

"Yes, I am fine. Just do that for me, would you?" she begged.

"Not a problem. Any music in particular?" I asked.

"Chopin, if you have..."

"How about his Nocturnes interpreted by Rubinstein?" I asked as I pulled the CD from the rack.

"That's one of my all time favorites," she said, smiling. "Thank you so much, honey. You're the best."

"You're welcome," I replied as I placed the album's two CDs on the player's carousel before quietly leaving the room. "And if 'Madame Secretary' wants to see me, I'll be sleeping on the couch in the living-room," I said with a tad of innuendo before shutting the door.

"Don't count on it," she replied with a comforting sparkle of awareness, reassuring me that, while she may be down and visibly depressed, she has not totally lost her ability to gauge humor.

Assem Akram

Conversions

Condi was still sleeping when I left home to go and get something fresh for breakfast. I had a bad night: recurrent nightmares, uncomfortable sofa and everything associated with them. And just as I was about to get some sleep earlier in the morning, the combined incessant rings of Condi's cell phone and Blackberry awakened me mercilessly.

When I returned home just half an hour later, Condi had left a note saying that she had early meetings to attend and that she would get back to me whenever she had an opportunity. The note ended with a 'kiss' and a post scriptum thanking me for everything and in particular for the Chopin CD with a smiley sign.

I had not yet dropped the shopping bag on the kitchen counter when my phone rang:

"Sorry to wake you up so early in the morning" but I have got a bit of bad news," Ava said without prelude.

"What is it? What happened?"

"Joachim Azuelos was transported to the hospital a couple of hours ago," she said.

"Oh, shit! Did they try to kill him?" I asked supposing that the '1492' plotters had learned of his 'betrayal' and had consequently attempted to assassinate him.

"No, he attempted to commit suicide."

"Why in the hell would he do that?" I asked.

"Jim told me that his father had written a note in which he was expressing his regrets to have been part of a shameful conspiracy and that, after weighing what it could mean if it were brought to completion, he could no longer be able to look at himself in the mirror."

"It's too early for him to end his life: we still need him," I said, showing more disappointment than sympathy. "By the way, did he happen to include something in his note to the effect of leaving some of his paintings or antique books to me?"

"You are a horrid person!"

Naval Observatory, Washington

"Dick, thanks for receiving me this early in the morning," Condi said, as she sat in the dining room where the Vice President was taking his breakfast.

"Is everything all right?"

"Yes, absolutely all right. I learned something the other day and, since you have been a father figure - a mentor - to me, I thought you deserved to be given a chance to clear what is perhaps just a misunderstanding…"

"What are you talking about?"

"I know about '1492' and I know about you picking Gareth over me for the ticket."

"I don't know what exactly you may have heard… Did the President tell you about it?" Dick said, realizing that he had just made a grave faux pas.

"No, but thanks for letting me know."

"I don't know who told you what, but it's not what you think..." Dick attempted to explain.

"All I know is that you have mounted a scheme, willing to sacrifice the lives of thousands of innocent people – Jews and Arabs maliciously brought into a war by your plan – just to make the ground favorable for your own election here..."

"Come on, Condi! We all know that a good Jew is a converted Jew and a good Muslim is a dead one," Dick said, as if he was stating some truism while lowering his voice to make it appear as a confidence.

"Allow me to strongly disagree with you on this one. I never thought that you would have this kind of preachy and dangerously intolerant mind."

"You know what I mean," Dick said, as if to tell Condi that she should look beyond the expression he had just uttered.

"Yes, I do; and now I understand how much of a bigot you are. And I believed you when you told me that I would be on your ticket: how naïve and stupid I was!" Condi was outraged.

"Believe me; I did not lie to you. I promised it to Gareth only as an incentive – a bribe - to get his full cooperation... You know how these politicians are with their big egos and their insatiable ambition..."

"I know; that's exactly how you got me."

"Trust me, Condi; you are part of this plan and the promise I made to you in this house, in that sunroom, was sincere."

"I don't know," Condi said, overwhelmed by doubt now.

"Have I ever let you down?" Dick looked straight in her eyes. "Have I not always been behind you, despite the bigots of our own party?"

"Yes, you have, Dick. But how could you and George not let me know and marginalize me like this?"

"To protect you... We didn't want you to suffer the consequences if all fails."

"Thanks, but then how could you come up with a plan that involves so many deaths and harbors such an outrageously intolerant religious bias?"

"If you think about it, it's not outrageous. We want to bring peace and stability to a part of the world that has suffered beyond what is acceptable. Think of it as a philanthropic enterprise. This is the Holy Land where our lord Jesus was born and we can't lie back and see this ignominious confrontation continue till the end of times... Because then we will be doomed for having been able to do something and not having done anything."

"Still, we can't just go there and impose our rule: we would be viewed as the worst of the imperialist powers. Haven't we been criticized enough on the Iraqi case? Our allies are leaving us one after the other."

"You are right, but we have to... It's in our destiny as a Nation: Columbus discovered this Promised Land the same year Spain finished re-conquering its Christian territory, chasing the Muslim Arabs - by the same token, Ferdinand and Isabel invited the Jews to convert or to leave - that's why I say that the scepter was passed on to us. We, Americans, have a mission to finish the work started five hundred years ago and establish the Pax Christiana - Pax Universalis over the Holy Land," Dick said, in a pitch that he had practiced more than once and in which he knew how to put the right intonations in the right places to be convincing.

"Gosh, Dick, I don't know... This is so huge..." Condi said, overwhelmed by Dick's seemingly convincing argument.

Condi was taken over by doubt. It's always difficult not to believe somebody she had trusted for more than two decades: What if Dick was right? What if this was the right solution? What if he was not lying about her being on his ticket in the coming Presidential election?"

"Think about it, Condi. Think about the difference you can make: being the first African-American VP – and probably soon the first such President - bringing peace to a land where no one has succeeded since the inception of the problem; and you'll be doing all that, Condi, while spreading the Gospel: wouldn't that be extraordinary? What do you say?"

"Dick, you know how to talk to a woman."

"I am just stating the plain truth. You know how much the President and I appreciate what you do. We have the greatest expectations for you."

"All right, Dick; you've convinced me," Condi said, with a large smile and looking Dick straight in the eyes while squeezing his forearm as a gesture of reassurance. "I've got to rush now; I have a meeting at the Department in ten minutes. But I'll get back to you later today or tomorrow so you can apprise me of the details – if you still want me to be part of it."

"Sure; not a problem at all. And, of course, not a single word to anyone."

"You know me," Condi said.

Dick was so relieved to have been able to return Condi's mind a hundred and eighty degrees that he completely forgot to ask her who had tipped her off about '1492.' So, he picked up his phone right away and called her on her cell phone.

"I meant to ask you something while you were here, but then I completely forgot about it…"

"Yes, go ahead… what is it?"

"Who told you about it if not the President?"

"I can't tell you right now; we'll talk about it when I see you… I've got to finish reading this summary before the meeting. Bye now!" Condi said, before turning her cell phone off.

"Damn it!" Dick said, as he hung up.

Department of State, Washington

"Hi, Maureen," Condi said, in a girlish voice as if she were seventeen years old.

"Who is this?" Maureen said.

"This is your shopping girlfriend, Condi."

Although the two women were not friends per se, they had developed some type of complicity through their shopping habits, despite being on opposite sides of the political spectrum.

"Oh, hi! How are you doing?" Maureen said, with her soft but nasally and perhaps a bit monotonous voice – in sharp contrast with the verve and vivacity of her columns.

"I'm doing great. How about you? I saw you the other day at Saks, but I was in a hurry, so I didn't catch you."

"I found a fantastic yellowish silk tweed jacket from Dolce & Gabbana: I fell in love with it right away! I think I am going to wear it tomorrow; I have a nomination to introduce to the press – we're sending Gingrich off as Ambassador to China," Condi said.

"Great! As for me, all I did was window-shopping. I tried on some of those floral print dresses that are in vogue this season, but I was not sure if they'd go with my pale complexion," Maureen said.

"I am sure you'd look just sensational, dear," Condi said. "Girlfriend, I need to see you to talk about something," she added in a mysterious way.

"Sure, why not. Where? People will gossip about it if they see us at a restaurant or a coffee shop."

"You're right; tell me about it...!" Condi laughed to go along. "We'll be meeting at one of my very good friend's place in Washington: can you make it tonight?"

"Sure; I'll catch a flight. It's just a jump from here," Maureen said. "Remember that I am a DC girl! Just give me the address..."

As an op-ed columnist at the New York Times - in the limelight and always hunting for some juicy stories, Maureen couldn't say no to the Secretary of State who used the shopping affinity connection to call her up and seemed to be pretty anxious to see her. Her instinct was signaling to her that it was unlikely that Condi wanted to meet with her to talk about sales at Bloomingdale's...

"All right, then; I've got to go now. I'll text-message the address to you as soon as I can - probably around noon," Condi said, before turning off her cell phone and rushing into another meeting.

Haftemizan's Apartment

My flat had turned into London during WWII. Everybody was meeting here – even scheduling meetings without my prior knowledge – to dodge indiscreet eyes. In addition, I am required to entertain them. Tonight's improvised guest was Maureen from the NYT, invited by Condi. Humorization apart – as someone I know would put it - tonight's gathering is a very promising one because it may mean that the Secretary of State is probably planning on using the press to attack those she believes have betrayed her - namely, '43' and the Vice President.

Maureen and Condi both showed up at around nine o'clock, as expected. Since Condi did not want anybody else to be there, I didn't say anything to Ava. Although, I would have liked her to participate because she sees things from Interpol's perspective, which of course I don't, since I am just a novice with a temporary mission.

Both women, despite their political differences, enjoyed some kind of inexplicable complicity, as if they had been classmates since the age of five. While I was acting *es-qualité* of host – which in fact pretty much meant attending to the comfort of my guests, pouring drinks, passing peanuts and cashews, preparing dinner (or rather catering), etc. - Condi was drawing the picture of what she presented as a plot directed against her personally, a cabal led from within the White House to discredit her by trying to implicate her in the shadowy conspiracy that includes the occupation of the Holy Land.

While Condi was pressing her agenda – completely absolving herself from any wrongdoing and therefore rejecting any involuntary association with the plotters – Maureen was surreptitiously looking at me. But I would not pay too much attention and concentrated instead on Condi's pitch.

"Haven't I seen you somewhere," Maureen asked with a smile, looking at me straight in the eyes, despite her natural shyness.
"Perhaps, I can't remember."

I am not good at remembering faces in a crowd, unless I have personally interacted with them. In this case, I obviously knew who Maureen was but I couldn't remember having personally met her somewhere. It was nevertheless kind of her to try to indicate that she may have seen me somewhere and that she remembered me.

"Now, I know," Maureen said. "Your publisher had sent me a copy of your book... I recall the picture on the back: interesting ideas; although, I must confess I didn't read it in its entirety."

"That's all right; nobody does," I replied. "You have a pretty good memory though," I added, admiring her ability to remember a bad picture on the back of a cover from among the hundreds of books she probably receives each year.

"I've got what they call a 'photographic memory.' But now that I've met you personally, I am going to dig it out and read it through," she said with a serious face.

"That's what publishers should do: send the author to deliver the book personally to get the maximum impact..."

"I agree: If I had met you then, I would have probably read it from cover to cover overnight," she said with a smile.

"Come on, honey; we don't have time for flirting at this time," Condi said, annoyed. "We have got something bigger to take care of."

"You're right; we'll do that after," I joked, winking exaggeratedly.

"I think this story is so huge that, of course, I have no reason not to believe you," Maureen said. "And you probably do not ignore that I haven't lost a single opportunity to denounce this Administration's failed policies, focusing on the role played by your pals..."

"Don't tell me about it. You have hammered us in every single column you've written: I know that for a fact," Condi said.

"This is why I think that I should not be the one to break the news: it would be instantly branded as a 'liberal conspiracy' and would get drowned quickly," Maureen said.

"I think she has a very good point, here," I said.

"We could instead have an AP release and then I would put out a column with the juicy story citing as source a 'top ranking Administration official': what do you think?" Maureen suggested, skillful in the art of agitprop.

"Wow, I am impressed: hats off!" I exclaimed.

"Believe me; this White House has had its share of agitprop operations – I'll spare you the details," Condi said with disenchantment. "Are you sure that it's going to work?"

"I am no Karl Rove, but I can guarantee you that it's going to be pretty devastating."

"Now, we have to figure out a way to leak it to the agencies," Condi said.

"I can take care of that," I volunteered cheerfully. "All I need is an anonymous phone call to AP and that is it... boom!"

"I don't think it will work like this," Maureen said. "This is too big a story; the guys at AP are not going to release it before calling fifty different places - including the White House directly - to see if there is any truth to it."

"How to do it then?" Condi asked.

"Let me handle it; this is my sphere," Maureen said. "I have some good buddies over there."

"You're the best..." Condi said.

"It's the least I can do; after all, you're probably giving me the biggest story a journalist can dream of."

"Don't mention it. You are the one helping me out, here."

"How soon can you do it?" I asked.

"It will probably be too late tonight when I return to New York, but first thing tomorrow morning," Maureen said.

"Wait! I have got a very good idea," Condi suddenly said, her eyes glowing. "Can you make them release the news at a particular time?"

"Yes, sure; that's customary: each type of news has a preferred slot for release based on a number of criteria - you know that, Condi..."

"I was asking this because here is what I have in mind: tomorrow, as you may perhaps know, the President is receiving at the White House - the controversial – Mugabe and, at 1 PM, there is a media appearance scheduled in the Rose Garden. If you could arrange for the wire to be released at 12:55 PM – just five minutes before the photo-op, there is 99% chance that the reporters would have had a chance to get it, whereas the President would not..."

"Very clever," Maureen said.

"I think this is more than clever; this is sadistic: It's going to be like Mogadishu," I added, rejoicing at the idea that '43' was going to be mercilessly ambushed in front of national and international audiences, live!

White House, Rose Garden

"Mr. President, Mr. President," called up one journalist.

"Yes, David, go ahead."

"Is it true that the Vice President has said that 'a good Jew is a converted Jew and a good Muslim is a dead one'?"

"I have never heard that... Nonsense," '43' said, moving his shoulders up and down and snorting.

"Mr. President!" called another reporter from among the pack standing at a distance in the Rose Garden.

"Yes... go head, Nora."

"Thank you, Mr. President," the NBC journalist said. "Is it true that the White House has plans to invade and occupy the Holy Land?"

"Gee, I have no idea where you guys are getting your information from, but I can assure you that there is no such a plan on my desk or anyone else's in this Administration."

'43' chewed his lower lip and retracted it at an angle, a clear sign of stress. He was made very uncomfortable by the turn this press briefing was taking.

"Can we please focus on the reason we have gathered here?" '43' suggested in an attempt to dodge the unpleasant questions of the White House press corps. "My good friend, President Robert Mugabe of Zimbabwe is here today to talk about his country's contribution of troops to help our effort in Iraq and in Afghanistan to fight terrorism. So, please, ask questions in relation."

"Mr. President" called another reporter while raising his hand, waiting to be acknowledged by '43.'

"Yes, you… go ahead."

"Hafez Al-Mirazi, Al Jazeera…" the tall reporter said, representing a network cordially hated by the Administration.

"Go ahead, shoot," the President joked, inviting the journalist to ask his question.

"Sir, could you tell us if Arab allies of the United States were consulted on this plan? And also: will you be occupying just the Palestinian side or both Israeli and Palestinian territories?"

"There is no plan; therefore there is no consultation; therefore there is no occupation: am I clear?" '43' said, annoyed by the questioner as much as by the question.

"John King, CNN. Mr. President, could you tell us if Israel was consulted and agreed to the plan?"

"God, damn it! I've already told you that there is no such a plan: not here, nor anywhere! Read my lips: NO PLAN! Is this clear enough for you?"

"Katty Kay, BBC. Mr. President, could you elaborate on the plan and tell us if London - considering the special relationship - was consulted?"

"I am not going to respond. Thank you all for coming and I thank my guest, President Mugabe, who is a steadfast leader, a great leader and...I am humbled by his friendship. Thank you all and good-bye."

The President did not expect to be assaulted the way he was on the subject he expected the least to pop up during a press briefing dedicated to his guest's visit to Washington. Conversely, Robert Mugabe was very pleased by the way the press forgot about him and his problems with regard to the non-respect of Human Rights and focused on the hot topic "du jour" that had just miraculously emerged. The Zimbabwean dictator was so happily surprised that he kept a quiet smile throughout the entire time journalists were insistently grilling his host.

"You know, Robert," '43' said, as they were walking back inside, "sometimes, I envy you..."

"What do you mean, George?"

"At least, you have control over your media. Here, they have too much freedom and show no respect for their leader."

"I see what you mean."

"We do everything we can to put some control on it though: we filter to the maximum the info we allow to be made public; we don't allow our staff to have any contact with the press without prior approval; and we've pushed some journalists, who are real patriots and understand today's challenges, to enter the media arena and aggressively fight the liberal monopoly... And still, you saw what happened: they are like a pack of enraged dogs out to get me."

"You should do what I do," suggested Mugabe trying to be helpful. "On the one hand, I use censorship to muzzle the press; and, on the other hand, I keep some of these journalists on my payroll."

"Straightforward censorship is difficult to impose here - though we had some good success in inciting self-censorship for a couple of years after 9/11. We've also tried the payroll thing… But, as you can see, we have not been very successful… Damned dogs!"

The President accompanied his guest to the Grand Foyer to attend the luncheon given in his honor at the White House. There, '43' took Dick in *aparté*:

"Did you see what happened at the press conference? Did you see how I was ambushed out there?"

"Yes, Sir; I saw that…" Dick said.

"Who is the SOB who has leaked it to the media?" '43' asked, with his head leaning to the side and as close as possible to that of the Vice-President doing the same.

"I am not sure, Mr. President, but Condi came to see me yesterday. She was pretty upset about having been left in the dark. I thought that, maybe, you had deemed necessary to let her know…"

"I didn't tell her anything. Do you think she may be the whistle-blower?"

"I am not sure, but based on the kind of questions you were bombarded with, I would bet my neck it's her."

"I am very disappointed," the President continued to whisper. "You can never trust these people. See what Powell did to us? And this Mugabe guy - chatting with Laura and Lynne over there - he had the audacity to give me advice on how to handle the media. Can you believe that?"

"I know, Mr. President."

"All I am saying is that you'd better figure out who leaked it and launch a quick damage control operation. Otherwise we are going down."

"Yes, Sir," Dick said.

"Let me correct what I just said: you are going down alone; I know nothing... nada: capisce?"

"Sure, Sir; I understand," Dick said, before turning his attention to see the Secretary of State enter: "Here she is, Sir; but please act as if you didn't suspect anything."

"Don't you worry: that's my specialty," '43' said with a complicit grin and a complimentary wink.

Assem Akram

Lifting The Veil

"Did you see the news earlier today?" Ava asked with excitement.

"No, what was it?" I replied, faking ignorance.

"It seems that something has transpired in the press: the President was asked by reporters today about allegations that this Administration has prepared a plan to take over the Holy Land..."

"You are not being serious," I reacted, pledging ignorance.

"Oh, boy! You should have seen him struggling under fire, while Mugabe was smiling angelically: it was a real treat."

"Too bad I missed it."

"I wonder who could have leaked it. From what I know, there are only two people who could have done it: Joachim Azuelos or Senator Gareth."

"Ava, did I ever tell you that I knew the Secretary of State?" I said with a mysterious air.

"What does this have to do with the story?"

"Well, she is an old acquaintance of mine... and I thought it would be useful to use her as a fifth column and inflict as much damage as we could to stall the '1492' conspirators' evil plan."

Having said that, I went on to update Ava on where we stood and how we had used some friendly accomplices to set up the stage for today's uncomfortable episode '43' had to undergo.

"That was the initial salvo. We have to continue with a nourished fire if we want to bring them down. We have to convince Jim's dad and the Senator to either issue press releases or – even better – to hold a press conference," I suggested.

"I agree with you for the dramatic effect, but aren't we putting the lives of these people at risk?"

"This crossed my mind, too, but I think in this kind of situation, exposure is the best way to save them. Once their faces and stories are all over the media, should anything happen to them, everybody would know where to look," I replied.

"That's a good argument. Now, let's see if we can convince them," Ava said, thinking that it would be a hard sell.

"To save time, I think what we need to do is to split up: you go visit Jim and his father and I am going to drop by the old Senator's office," I proposed.

"Why not the other way around?"

"It's very simple: the old Senator didn't seem to like you too much after the exchange you had with him at the restaurant, whereas Jim seems so bedazzled by your beauty that he can't even look at you, let alone dare to say 'no'…" I explained with a zest of humor while stating the obvious. "Why do women have to have so much power over us, poor little male creatures?"

"All right, I got the picture," Ava cut me off with her hand held up high signaling me to shut up.

I was on my way to the Hill when my cell phone rang – I really love it: every time it plays the theme of the Pink Panther, it reminds me of some hilarious scenes from the movie series with Peter Sellers playing the goofy inspector Clouseau...

"Your Badness, it's Condi!"

"Hi, Madame Secretary."

"No time for that kind of innuendo," she replied with a depressed voice. "I think they may know: the President was distant with me at the lunch for Mugabe…"

"How would they know?" I asked.

"I have no idea," she replied.

"There is no way they would," I assured her. "But even if they did, don't you worry, because we have much more in the works for them."

"Good," she said with a sigh. "Because they are not yet down on their knees; they are going to refute everything as being 'nonsense,' 'machination,' 'left-wing cabal,' etc; you know, the usual rhetoric. Believe me, it works," she added with some anguish. "If we don't finish up the beast now, we are the ones who are going to perish."

"I understand your apprehension and I agree a hundred per cent with your view – after all, you know exactly what you are talking about - and, as I said, we have got much more in the pipe for them."

"All right, then; Your Badness, you have boosted my morale. I really needed this," Condi said, her spirit high again, ready to take on her own clan.

"Condi, it's essential that you act totally normal until this story unwinds one way or the other. Otherwise, your odds of being on the losing side might be too high for comfort."

"It goes without saying," Condi said, true to her political self.

Naval Observatory

"Can you believe this, honey? The plan that I had spent years and months concocting is in jeopardy because of some rascal... some traitor who has apparently released bits and tads of it to the media," Dick said with rage.

"I know, honey; but it's not a big deal at this time: all they have is 'gossip.' This Administration has been accused of the most devilish and Machiavellian plans ever since its entry in function... It's not going to take a lot of effort to brand this one too as baseless rumor maliciously spread by the liberal media to discredit the President."

"I guess, you are right, honey... You always see these things with circumspection whereas I tend to get too emotional."

"Always give credit to the word of the Ancients who said that it's always wiser to let the dust settle to be able to see clearer: wait a couple of days – perhaps a week or two – and the issue will be forgotten and stocked on a pile with tens if not hundreds of other 'baseless' rumors."

"I was about to call my guys in Afghanistan and Iraq and ask them to suspend indefinitely – or at least until further notice – the plan, but after what you just said, I am going to wait and let the dust settle," Dick said, with a devilishly optimistic smile. "Honey, I love you. You have boosted my morale. I feel like a roaring lion again... I am hungry for success; I have regained my appetite for the Grand Destiny I deserve - by the way, could you get me some baklavas?"

Ava's Apartment

"It's me, Haftemizan; may I come in?" I asked standing in front of her door, unannounced.

"Sure; come on in. What a surprise!"

"I have got this," I said, as I showed her a DVD case.

"What is it?"

"Do you remember when we were in Italy, I told you about a movie starring Vittorio Gassman, but I couldn't recall the name?"

"Oh, yes…" Ava said, vaguely recalling it.

"Well, here it is. A promise is a promise! It's called 'Anima Persia' and was directed by Dino Risi: it's really a fascinating movie."

"Thanks a lot. I'll watch it. Perhaps you wanted to watch it, too?"

"It was more or less our deal," I remarked. "Do you remember: dinner and a movie…?"

"Oh, yes; but you're catching me a little unprepared here. Perhaps, we can do this some other time."

"Don't you worry; I have thought it all up and made a reservation: all you need to do is get dressed and we are dining out," I replied enthusiastically.

"How nice of you," Ava said, visibly surprised. "Give me a minute to put something suitable on and I'll be ready."

"All right; I'll be standing right here… I am not moving."

I was standing by the window, keeping a wary eye on my convertible double-parked just in front of her building, when someone knocked at her door. I looked through the Judas and saw a tall and rather large pizza deliveryman smiling widely. I naturally opened the door, thinking that Ava had certainly ordered pizza for herself, unaware of my plans.

"Who is it?" asked Ava as she emerged from the hallway.

"It's the pizza you had ordered," I replied, turning my head towards her.

At this precise instant, the delivery guy, who had taken advantage of my exchange with Ava to surreptitiously step inside the apartment and close the door behind him, knocked me so violently on the back of my neck that I fell on the floor. In much less time that it takes to describe it than to do it, like a quarterback, the pizza delivery bull ran straight towards Ava, tackling her on the ground and immediately proceeding to strangle her. Ava was battling as hard as she could to untangle her aggressor's lock, but the man was overwhelmingly too large and too powerful for her, so much so that she could die from suffocation before the strangulation could achieve its effect.

It took me a few seconds to regain total consciousness. I was obviously no match to take on the 'pizza ogre' in a one on one confrontation. I looked around in search of an object I could use as a weapon. The first thing that came to my mind was to use a dining chair to break over his head, then I thought that, for one, it would not be lethal and, two - like I've seen it in some movies – the monster will get even more enraged and attack me with renewed fury. So, I decided to look for a different solution all the while Ava was being literally flattened under him. As the 'pizza ogre' sat on her chest and attempted to strangle her with his two fat hands, he began yelling: "Why are you trying to go against God's will? Why do you care about some fucking Jews and Arabs?"

As I browsed the room in search of the ideal weapon to take down the ogre, my eyes fell upon the sword the Emir of Bukhara had given to Ava's grandfather. I gathered all my energy, jumped up and rushed as fast as I could to seize the sword from atop the cabinet and approached the 'pizza ogre,' hoping to slice open his throat. But, alas, my lack of experience made me hit him with the back of the blade... At that point, the 'pizza ogre' released Ava's throat and turned towards me in rage, moving a hand towards the inside of his jacket – probably to seize a gun. I had to act very quickly. This time, I aimed straight at his large chest and, because I had not been able to gauge the distance properly to adjust my strike, the tip of the sword went upwards instead and ripped through his jugular. As a reflex, the man seized his throat with both hands to stop the heavy bleeding but to no avail: he fell to the side.

Despite his heavy weight, I was able to pull the 'pizza ogre' a few inches away to free Ava. I immediately used what I had learned in CPR classes to insufflate air into her lungs and reactivate her breathing. Ava's skin had tuned light pink, almost colorless. But after about a minute of my efforts, she started to breathe easier and it was visible from her changing complexion that she was doing better.

"Are you all right now?" I asked while sitting on the floor to her side. Her clothes were blood soaked and so were mine.
"Yes, I believe I am. What the hell was that?" she asked in dismay.
"I guess you had ordered a pizza with everything on it," I joked. "Or... you are a bad tipper and the delivery guy – the 'pizza ogre' - had enough of your fifty-cents tips and wanted to avenge the affront."
"I wish I could laugh; but if I did, my lungs would collapse."
"Don't beat yourself up. Did you hear what he said while he was trying to choke you?"

"No, I was too busy trying to wrestle off this freaky sack of flesh and fat sitting on my chest."

"Well, he yelled with furor why we acted against God's will and why did we care about what could happen to some Jews and Arabs?" I echoed, trying to be as faithful as possible to the original version.

"With that at least there is no room for doubt left as to who has sent this killer after us - I mean after me," Ava said.

"What do you mean?" I asked.

"Did you see how he brushed you aside with just one hit and focused all his murderous rage on me?" Ava said, caricaturing on purpose how easily I had been taken off guard and knocked off.

"Should I remind you, tough lady, that if it weren't for me, you'd be flatter than your carpet?"

"Do I feel some sensitivity here? Did I hurt the macho male in you?" Ava joked, laughing.

"No, that's not it... but since you seem to imply that the 'pizza ogre' was able to 'brush me aside,' I just wanted to remind you that, first off, I was caught by surprise and then, as soon as I came back to my senses, I fought back."

"I was just teasing you... You saved my life! What you did was very courageous and I'll be obliged to you for the rest of my life," Ava said, shedding a tear.

"Don't mention it, please. I thought maybe we had something going on – me, you, the movie, the dinner and *tutti quanti* - so I didn't want to see my chance burnt out before I had an opportunity to seize it."

"You are such a horrible person," Ava said, as she inched closer to plant a kiss on my mouth, "but I like you just like this," she added with a flirtatious smile.

If it weren't for all the blood surrounding us - and above all the rather unbearable smell of it – and the unsavory view of the 'pizza ogre' lying lifeless on the ground at our feet, I would have probably pursued this 'kissy-kissy' moment further - since there is some real chemistry between the two of us - but it was not an opportune moment. So, I decided to keep the credit earned intact to use at a more auspicious and enjoyable time.

"Do you have a digital camera?" I asked.

"Yes, I do; but what do you need it for?"

"It's time to turn the table on the '1492' villains who've been sending me pictures of their murderous acts before anyone else knows about them: now I am going to respond to their e-mail with a picture of the lifeless 'pizza ogre' before anyone else knows about it," I said with a vengeful and frankly sadistic feeling filling my guts.

The Next Day

Maureen's op-ed column had set the nation's political and media scene ablaze. The White House was besieged by phone calls and requests for interviews with - or at least clarifications or comments by - '43' and his Vice-President.

The Administration issued a statement in which it categorized Maureen's allegations as 'baseless rumors and gossip colported by the liberal media eager to mask the Administration's successes and defame the President.'

At noon, the Press Secretary, McCullan, was assaulted by questions from reporters, who asked him to comment on the article and the allegations comprised in it. Poor McCullan had a tough time to respond adequately since he was not a part of the

'1492' conspiracy, which, at the same time, played to his advantage as he appeared sincere in his denegation.

"Scott," started one reporter, "where do you think the NYT has found its source for this story?"

"I don't know. They should have contacted us and cross-checked with us and we would have told them that it was undoubtedly a hoax."

"Scott," asked a second reporter, "could you confirm or infirm whether the Vice-President actually made that comment about Jews and Muslims? And if so, could he be forced to resign?"

"I can assure you that the Vice President would never make such comments. These are baseless accusations and the White House reserves the right to pursue legal action for defamation."

"What about the plan?" a third journalist asked. "Could you tell us how the White House intended to take control of the Holy Land?"

"And could you define 'Holy Land' for us, please?" added a fourth reporter.

"This is insane… I have the impression that you are not paying attention to what I just said and what the President stated very clearly yesterday. So, for the record and to make it very clear to you once more, I'll repeat it: THERE IS NO PLAN!"

"Scott, the *Yomiuri Shimbun* here; in the New York Times, the article was referring to potential ideological motives behind the plan: could you tell us something about it? And could you also elaborate on the relations between this White House and the so-called Evangelicals?"

"Unfortunately, I can't speak Japanese, Toshiro; otherwise I would have told you the same thing that I just said in your language."

"At the risk of sounding insistent," intervened another journalist from a German newspaper, "could you elaborate on the role of this President's faith in determining his policies?"

"This would be the subject for a book and we obviously don't have time for that," McCullan said. "But all I can tell you is that this President has always said that religion plays an important role in his life, including his public life... All right, ladies and gentlemen, this concludes our session today. I have more copies of the statement for you on the desk, here, if you need them."

"Scott, Scott," David Gregory of NBC yelled. "In the hypothesis that there is some truth to the revelations made by the New York Times, do you think that the President and the Vice-President could face Impeachment?"

"Pointless speculation, Dave," the Press Secretary responded as he was swiftly exiting the tiny pressroom to avoid being assaulted with more questions for which he did not have answers.

"Fucking dumb journalists... I have had enough of this job; I am going to quit... I swear to God, I am going to leave this hell..." McCullan mumbled in the hallway outside the pressroom.

"He reminds me of McCurry during the Monica-Gate," a veteran White House correspondent said.

"You're damn right," another one replied, standing by his side and staring at the deserted stage. "Let the grill party begin..." he added with a laugh.

1 PM, Georgetown University Hospital

Despite his poor health and the recommendations of his doctors, Joachim Azuelos had agreed to make a public appearance to reveal what he knew about the '1492' conspiracy. His son Jim had invited the media for an impromptu press conference in the hospital room where he was recovering, adding drama to the event.

I had not been unable to convince Senator Gareth to hold something similar on the Hill. Gareth said that he needed more time to decide what to do and, frankly, I did not insist because I could easily understand that he was trying to salvage his political career.

The hospital, to which Joachim Azuelos had contributed large amounts of charitable donations throughout the years, had been very helpful in providing a large suite and some security personnel for the event. Whereas Ava and I found it preferable to be part of the media melee – incognito - Jim was proudly standing beside his father's bed acting as moderator.

Talking painfully and slowly, Joachim Azuelos told the crowd of overly excited reporters about his longstanding friendship with the Vice-President, about the plan, about the fact that it included kindling a conflict between Arabs and Israelis. He further told the stunned reporters why the plan was dubbed '1492,' its missionary aspect as well as its business part, in which he was involved.

"Mr. Azuelos, could you tell us if you were the source for today's New York Times article?"

"No, I was not."

"Could you tell us if the President is involved in the '1492' conspiracy?"

"All I can tell you is that when I posed the question to the Vice President he told me that he was, even though he said he didn't know about all the 'technicalities' of it."

"Could you give us names of other people involved?" another journalist asked.

"I can't."

"Why don't you want to give us names? Are you protecting someone?"

"I can't simply because I don't know. My only contact was with the Vice President and a courier he would send to pick up the cash."

The reporters mumbled.

"Mr. Azuelos, are you saying that you contributed cash to the '1492' conspiracy and that the money was going to the Vice-President?"

"I was giving the money to the courier who was introduced to me by the VP, but I don't know where exactly he was taking it to."

"Folks," Jim said. "My father is recovering; he needs rest and I think that he has told you more than you need to know. So, please, be kind enough to leave now and let him get some rest... Oh, so that I don't forget, on your way out, we have put on the table, by the door, copies of my father's bio and a picture for those of you who would need one."

"Why is he hospitalized? What is he recovering from?" one journalist yelled before leaving.

At that moment, Jim looked at his father for approval before giving an answer:

"My father attempted to end his life."

"Why?" the journalist asked, befuddled.

"Because I was ashamed of myself, ashamed of taking part in such a terrible conspiracy..." Joachim Azuelos said, with tears in his eyes.

"All right, now, ladies and gentlemen," a security guard yelled. "Please, leave the room; the press conference is over."

Once the pack of reporters left the room, Ava and I approached Joachim's bed.

"I have only one word to say: *bravissimo*!" I exclaimed with enthusiasm. "Maureen's article this morning was like Hiroshima and your press conference was like Nagasaki."

"Do you think that these bastards are going to capitulate?" Jim said.

"No matter what they do now, their evil plan has been checkmated and hopefully we have avoided a cataclysmic tragedy," I remarked happily.

Paloma Picasso Vs The Japanese Emperor

Joachim Azuelos' revelations gave credit and full backing to Maureen's article in the public eye. The news spread like bushfire throughout the world. Israel, Egypt, Syria, Iran and other countries in the Middle East announced that their armies have been placed on high alert and that they are ready to face any potential threat with adequate means.

In an emergency meeting, the UN Security Council, despite the denegation and nagging of the US ambassador, voted on a resolution calling all powers and countries in the region to condemn the use of force and seek the resolution of all conflicts by peaceful means and in obedience of International Law. The UN Secretary General published a statement in which he condemned as a question of principle the meddling of all kind of religious proselytism and religious extremism in world affairs.

"Your Badness, this is Condi."
"Hi," I replied.
"I just read the wires and saw the cuts on MSNBC, CNN - and even Fox: we did it!" she said.
"It was like Nagasaki…"
"Guess what," she giggled. "There is more to come…"
"What? Have you got something new?"

"I'm resigning," Condi revealed with giggles of satisfaction. "I'm jumping before the ship sinks."

"But why?" I asked with stupor. "There already are talks of impeaching the President and the Vice-President… You know that you could be next sitting in the Oval Office."

"Yes, I would if it weren't for the Presidential Succession Act of 1947," she said with regret.

"What's that?" I asked. "My constitutional studies classes are a bit behind me now…"

"Based on that Act, I am only fourth in the line of succession."

"Damn it! This kind of golden opportunity doesn't present itself every day: why did these stupid people have to change it?"

Haftemizan's Apartment

In the evening, we had all decided to gather in my apartment to celebrate our achievement. The last forty-eight hours had been pretty hectic and the day saw a line up of events, each more unfavorable and devastating for '43' and his Vice-President than the other. Like those clustered fireworks that explode one after the other - when you think it's finished, there is another one exploding into a bouquet of a thousand colors - the succession of events had been extraordinary.

Ava, Condi, Jim and Maureen had come over and I was in charge of feeding everyone – once again! Joachim was still in the hospital and Senator Gareth had excused himself for more or less obvious reasons. Ava had brought along large pictures of Shumington and Necromonti and asked that we place them around the dining table because they deserved to share the joy of our victory. By unanimous consent – as they say – we decided to make room in the seating arrangement for Father Emilio Ungari, too - Necromonti's brother - but since we didn't have a picture of him, I wrote his name on a piece of paper and placed it before a seat reserved in his memory.

This may look ridiculous, but we all felt that our little celebration would not be the same without paying homage to our fallen friends.

"What is it?" I asked with some surprise as Jim Azuelos handed me a large, rather heavy, gift box.

Jim smiled. "It's nothing much… Dad thought you'd like it."

"But why…?" I asked as I began opening the box and could see with incredulity a framed drawing by none lesser than Picasso.

My enthusiasm was quickly replaced by exhilaration when Jim told me that it was not a lithograph or a reproduction, but an original drawing made in 1965 representing the genius's daughter, Paloma.

"It's my father's way of thanking you for what you've done. He knows that you are an art lover and that you'll appreciate it."

"This is really too much; I can't accept this. I don't want to deprive him of a piece from his collection."

"He's got five of them; it's part of a series."

"All the more reason for me not to accept this."

"Well, perhaps, in his own way, my father wants to indicate that after this episode there is a different type of link that connects him to you."

"I am honored. Now, I cannot refuse anymore..." I said, touched by the sentiment accompanying the gift. "Please, tell him how much I appreciate it; tell him that I said *'muy obligado'* and that I'll come to visit him some time next week to see how he's recovering."

"Sure; you are welcome: any time!"

Later, while we were savoring our victory, we were shocked to learn that Senator Gareth had committed suicide, lodging a bullet in his frontal lobe. In the posthumous note he had left, he apologized for any wrongdoing and denounced the qui-pro-quo deal he had made with the Vice-President. The senior Senator from the South added that he could not forgive himself for having been the cause of his wife's death, because he had made the fatal mistake of selling his soul to the devil to satisfy his political ambitions and eagerness.

As heartbreaking as the news of his suicide was, the Senator's final note was a compelling testimony against the '1492' conspirators, and primarily against its mastermind.

Naval Observatory, Washington

"That was a close call," Dick said, moving his eyebrows up and down frantically.

"What is it, honey?" Lynne asked.

"Do you remember that you told me yesterday to hold on calling off the missile launch operation altogether?"

"Yes, honey, I recall like it was yesterday... and perhaps it was actually yesterday," she added with a smile.

"And I thought that I was becoming senile..." Dick commented, not without humor despite the circumstances. "Well, in light of what's happened today, I wanted to call my guys in Iraq and in and Afghanistan and tell them to cancel the plan and get rid of the evidence ASAP..."

"How are they going to get rid of huge missiles just like that? Forgive me, honey, but these are not exactly of the suppository dimension, despite their shape: it's not going to be easy to conceal them."

"That's not what concerned me: depending on the case, we have some good alibis to justify their presence. My apprehension was rather that the bio-weapons – you know; the Congo-Crimean Hemorrhagic Fever thing and the Anthrax we were planning on using – would be discovered..."

"What? You intended to use bio-weapons with your missiles?"

"Didn't I tell you that...?" Dick said, acting innocently dismissive.

"No, and if you had, I would have prevented you from even considering it," she said, rather upset.

"Come on, honey; all we wanted was to make a psychological impact."

"I am very disappointed in you. This is criminal: how could you?" she reprimanded him, crossing her arms on her chest and sitting back in her chair.

"All right; I have had it," Dick yelled.

"Had it what...?" she yelled back at him.

"I have had it with your hypocrisy: launching swarms of missiles over the heads of Arabs and Israelis to start a war and conspiring to rise to power is okay by your standards; but adding some few 'ingredients' to make our plot... let's say... more efficient and more credible for the sake of the success of '1492' – so that Madame can become the First Lady and stop nagging about having to sit behind Laura during each and every ceremony

- that is not acceptable to you… that disappoints you: give me a break!"

"There is a difference. There is the same kind of difference that exists between killing somebody with a bullet from a distance and trying to do the same by butchering the victim with a kitchen knife."

"The result is the same."

"Yes, but the methods are different and the psychological impact is very dissimilar."

"Exactly my point; thank you honey: we wanted to make a psychological impact… that's it!"

"Honey, our discussion isn't going anywhere: my mind is made up."

"Suit yourself, honey," Dick said. "Anyway, to come back to my story, I wanted to call them and, thank God, before I'd done it, I got a phone call from Floss – the DCI - who told me that, based on an investigation launched a few days earlier – which Pretzel Boy had told me about and of which I had immediately warned my guys - they have taken over our two bases in Iraq and Afghanistan, put seals on them and have commenced their investigation."

"Gosh, that was a close call! Do you think they will talk when pressed?"

"I don't believe they will… I trust them more than I trust that weaseling Pretzel Boy. Speaking of whom, you'll never guess what he told me yesterday at the reception for Mugabe?"

"No, honey; what did he tell you?"

"He told me that I was on my own if this turns out to be a fiasco and that he would plead ignorance and put all the blame on me."

"That gutless chicken! I knew he was not a stand up guy: his father had warned you," Lynne said, outraged. "Honey, you've got to promise me one thing."

"What, honey?"

"If you go down, you make sure that you take Pretzel Boy with you."

"How about my promise to '41'…? It's because of my promise to the old man to look after his stupid son that I have endured so many things, silently, all these years. If I drag '43' in the mud with me now, the old man is not going to like it."

"Don't you worry, honey! I'm more than certain that he would not be upset all that much… After all, Pretzel Boy has erected himself and his Administration's profile as anti-'41,' hasn't he?"

"I guess you're right. But first, I am going to fight and when I am cornered against the ropes and there is no more hope left to find an exit, I'll drop the ball."

"Well said, honey; I am with you," Lynne said, demonstrating martial determination.

Haftemizan's Apartment, 1 AM

"Hey, this is Ava…"

"Hi, is everything all right?" I asked a bit worried, because she had just left my apartment a minute ago with the other guests.

"I'm fine… Are you already asleep? Because I was thinking we could watch that 'Anima Persia' movie tonight," she offered with a longing voice, making her intentions clear - in case there was any doubt.

This was it! Our part in uncovering the '1492' conspiracy was more or less finished now - which means that we no longer were tied professionally - and the timing – i.e. a victorious night – couldn't be better. Somebody once said something like 'good things come to those who demonstrate patience': I think that, in this particular case, I have shown a lot of restraint – believe me, it was not easy - and now is the time for my reward.

While I was talking to Ava, my cell phone rang – tirelessly playing the Pink Panther's theme for my enjoyment and for those who appreciate it, too:

"Hold on a second, somebody's calling me on my cell phone...yes, hello, this is Haftemizan."

"Your Badness, this is Condi!"

"Hi, are you okay... did you forget something?" I asked.

"I am more than okay: I am in a bombastic mood! I don't feel like going home right away...I am on my way back to your place: Madame Secretary is yearning to see Your Badness. "

This is not good at all. Why am I so luckless? It's all or nothing. 'All' is impossible to manage as a harmonious heterogeneous entity and it is more exclusive than the 'nothing': on one side, I have this gorgeous girl – Ava – with whom I've been flirting since the beginning of our encounter in this Interpol misadventure, and now, finally, the right moment has come; on the other side, I have Condi, with whom I have more of a lustful relationship, doubled with an intellectual connection, and who has behaved extraordinarily throughout this ordeal up to this minute: you can't say that I am not facing a heart-scrapping, brain-bugging dilemma here!

While putting both ladies on hold - and in less time that it takes to say it than to do it - I decided that I would not make this decision tonight, no matter what my carnal temptations or my sentimental desires may be. So, I told them, one after the other, in the most diplomatic and gentle way possible, that we were all very tired, that it had been an exceptionally hectic day and, therefore, that I preferred to have a restful night of sleep – at least, what remained of it – with… Paloma.

I had just hung up when my phone rang again. Who could it be this time? It was Maureen:

"Hi, are you all right? Did you forget something?" I asked very casually.

"I am feeling great… Actually I haven't felt like this in years," she said.

"Oh, great…" I said, trying not to guess where she was trying to go with that.

"I don't feel like sleeping; I want to go clubbing. I was thinking that, if you are not in bed already, maybe we could go and have some fun."

"Thanks a lot; it's so nice of you, but I am in bed right now and…"

Why is this happening to me? Why wasn't she calling me three weeks ago, when I was alone? Why won't she be calling me in two weeks, when I'll probably be alone again, God damn it!?

"So, let's go to a nice bar instead: what do you think?" she insisted. "Come on; don't let me down!"

"You know that I'd really love to, but tonight I am beat," I apologized. "How about we have lunch tomorrow or on any day that you'd like?"

"That's a date. I hope I didn't disturb you… And say hi to whoever is on the other side of the bed," she added in her shy, self-effacing but inquisitive way.

"Sure, thanks. I'll say hi to Paloma on your behalf."

"Paloma…? Oh, yes… Paloma," she laughed, as she understood to whom I was referring. "You are something! For a second, I thought you were with someone… I'll see you tomorrow then: pick me up at noon at the paper."

In my bedroom, I temporarily removed a Dali lithograph that I had on the wall facing my bed to hang the Picasso instead - and be true to my word. I guess I needed to disconnect for a moment from the violence and the outrageously bigoted and cynically ambitious views that had driven '43,' the Vice President and a number of other people to be part of the '1492' conspiracy, which could have killed hundreds of thousands of people and annihilated the Middle East as we know it to reshape it to fit their ideologically-driven insane agenda.

No doubt, the irresponsible actions of a few 'Dr. Strangeloves' in Washington would have upset the order of the world we inhabit and thrown havoc and chaos and, in the end, to engender the revival of an all out religious confrontation we all thought had disappeared centuries ago.

While I was reflecting on this nightmarish plot and on what we've been through – always remembering the outburst of Emilio and Benvenisto's father and haunted by the perspective of visiting him one day soon in his bereavement - I looked at the drawing Pablo Picasso had made of his daughter Paloma: the lines, the tracing… are so vibrant that one could think the artist has just finished executing it and that the ink is still wet.

One thought leading to another, I came to reflect on the life of the Spaniard genius, who loved life, women and friends and whose existence was nothing less than a celebration of creation in all its forms. From procreation to prolific artistic creativity, he's left a legacy to Life, to Culture and to Humanity.

On the other side of the spectrum of life and creativeness, of respect and tolerance, there are the Sorcerer's Apprentices, the Over-Zealous, the Over-Ambitious, the Born Again... Whether they are plotting from the dark caves of Tora Bora or from the gilded rooms of the White House, they equally aspire at erasing from the surface of this fragile Earth the 'other' – always viewed as the enemy – at dominating without compromising, and at imposing Hell on Earth to gain their ticket to Paradise.

White House – Private Quarters

"Honey, George, come back to sleep. It's three o'clock in the morning."

"I can't," replied a nervous '43,' circling the room. "Do you realize how this failure is detrimental to my Presidency? I might very well be impeached. And if that happens, honey, we'll be the laugh of the family. I can already imagine dad's face."

"And Jeb..." Laura added.

"Don't tell me about him...I wish I were the Emperor of Japan in the old days, and be able to order one of my subjects to commit suicide by hara-kiri because he failed to fulfill the mission assigned to him."

"What do you mean?"

"I mean that I would have asked Dick to perform hara-kiri on himself and spare us all the embarrassment of this mess."

"But weren't you involved with him?"

"Yeah...but now it's everyone on his own, honey; and – officially – I know nothing, nada: capisce?"

"I got it, honey; but you don't have to yell at me... You and Dick screwed it up, not me. I am going back to sleep."

15 Minutes Later

"Mr. President, Mr. President..." the Secret Service officer knocked on the door.

"Yes, what is it? What's happening?"

"Sir, Officer Johnson, here, has just come from the Old Executive Building where something terrible has happened..."

"What is it?" '43' asked, as he stepped out of the suite in his pajamas and cautiously shut the door behind him.

"Johnson has found the Vice President dead in his office," the man revealed.

"I was routinely checking on the Vice President, who was working late - like he often does - when I found him unanimated," Johnson said.

"When did you notice that?"

"Just five or six minutes ago, Sir. As soon as I understood what had happened, I rushed here to inform you."

"Excellent reflex. Were you able to determine if it was a natural cause or suicide?"

"Suicide, Mr. President. The Vice President was lying back in his chair, arms and legs wide open."

"That's not enough to determine whether it was a suicide or a heart-attack," '43' said.

"You are absolutely right, Sir. I believe what made me instantly think that it was a suicide was the fact that there were two envelopes on his desk: one labeled 'Police' and the other destined for 'Lynne'..."

"Did he shoot himself?" '43' asked, mimicking the gesture of somebody shooting oneself in the head.

"No, Sir. I was in the next room and if he had used a pistol, I would have heard it. Besides, there was no blood spill anywhere."

"How about an empty bottle of medicine or a syringe?"

"No, Sir. There wasn't anything like that. The only other things that I saw were an unfinished cup of coffee and a plate of some Middle Eastern pastries the Vice President always eats – rather, he used to eat - I think they're called baklavas."

"Johnson, it is a matter of national security that you go and get me the letters the Vice President has left on his desk," '43' said in a solemn voice.

"Here they are, Mr. President. I kind of anticipated that you would say something like that," Johnson said.

"You are a man destined for a great career!"

"Thank you, Mr. President. I am just trying to do what's best in the interest of our great nation."

"You are a true patriot and you'll be rewarded for that. Now, you can go back to the Eisenhower Building and call the Police. I'll take care of these letters."

"Yes, Sir."

"And remember: you never came here..." '43' warned before going back inside, revitalized and already enjoying the idea that he was going to be able to sleep with peace of mind.

"Honey, what is it?" Laura asked half-asleep. "What's going on? Who knocked at the door?"

"It's nothing, honey; all is well. Go back to sleep," '43' replied, as he slid under the blanket with a large smile on his face. "Maybe I am a Japanese Emperor after all..."

Next Day, 8:30 AM

"Ava, it's Haftemizan. Did you watch the news?"

"Yes, I did: it's a real hecatomb! But I am not going to shed too many tears for this one."

"Guess what?" I said, upset and, frankly, even quite scared.

"What...?"

"I've received another e-mail from 'fourteen ninety-two,' this time showing the Vice-President dead in his office..."

Three-Horned Lion, Inc.

www.threehornedlion.com
Contact: 1492@threehornedlion.com